GRIM PRAYERS

Grim Series Book 2

Wiktor Miesok with Felix 'Krest' Charin

WHITE MATTER AS

Book Cover by Kristiina Vihervuori

First edition 2026

ISBN 978-82-694132-5-0

TABLE OF CONTENTS

The *GRIM Series* is more than a story, it's a growing world, and a community built around it.

Visit **grimcircles.com** to connect with fellow readers, discover powerful books, and grow alongside people who share your hunger for meaning, grit, and transformation.

With Honor,

Wiktor, Andrej, and Krest

Part 1

1985

CHAPTER 1

To Survive The Darkness, One Must Become Its Shadow

Sidoy gave me his own knife for the mission. It was a good piece, not your typical camp shank made from a long nail or an old spoon sharpened on concrete. Sidoy's was a proper knife, with a thin blade, maybe ten centimeters long, and razor-sharp. He kept it hidden inside a drainpipe below one of the barrack sinks, and it only came out when things turned serious.

I kept the blade clenched between my teeth as I crawled through the dugout passage underneath Barrack 6. I had to pull back my lips so they wouldn't get grazed by the edge. The cold, metallic taste spread through my mouth, while my nostrils filled with the smell of mold, soil, and decaying organic matter. Slowly, but deliberately, I moved toward the hatch leading out into the Zone.

I reached forward with my left hand and pulled myself along, pushing with my right leg; just like in bootcamp, where we practiced crawling through mud under barbed wire. I stretched out my right hand and felt something brush against my forearm. A squeak came from the darkness, and tiny claws pinched my skin as a rat ran along my arm and up my back. I shook it off and continued.

Down beneath the barrack floor, in dirt and darkness, I wriggled forward, with rats, spiders, and bugs as my companions. The space was tight. In some places, I had to squeeze myself between the ground and the floorboards. The wet, moldy beam beside me was slick and stank of rot. I kept the knife tight in my jaw. Losing it down there would be a big problem as I could easily cut myself reaching for it blindly.

The dim light at the end of the tunnel got closer with every motion. Finally, I reached the entrance: a set of wooden boards with cracks between them forming vague slits of barely perceptible light in the otherwise pitch-black space. I probed the boards and gently pushed them forward.

Altogether, it took no more than a couple of minutes to reach the exit, but it felt like an eternity spent in the underbelly of the prison camp.

Now, the lamplights and open space outside were welcoming me. It was time to hunt. Time to do my job for the *Bratva*, so they would take me in and save me from a fate worse than death.

Before crawling out, I thought about the deeds that had brought me to the penal colony. I thought about how I had denied being a crook at first. How I had wanted to carve my own path as a lone wolf.

It had all come crashing down, and I realized I was about to confirm myself as a solid criminal, one willing to spill the blood of another human being for the sake of survival.

The memory of my last conversation with Aslan returned, still fresh, and weirdly uplifting.

It was the day before, during our shift in the forest, when I shared with him my predicament. The thought made me hesitate, and for a moment, the vision of the pine trees and the blue sky above filled my mind. Perhaps I wanted to escape reality, to get away from what I was about to do, even if only for a moment.

The future was bloody and uncertain. And as I was about to cross a new threshold, the events of the past days seemed to come as if from a different lifetime.

The look on Aslan's face, when I told him what I had planned to do, was not what I expected. He arched one thick, black eyebrow and pursed his lips in a mockery of a grave expression. Despite the gravity of the situation, he chuckled and patted me on the shoulder.

"You do what you have to do, *bratan* – brother," he said lightheartedly as if he were discussing the weather. "All of us will meet God eventually. It is just when and how that makes a difference."

We shared a laugh, and I felt a surge of confidence. Aslan's carefree reaction made me smile despite a burning coal of anxiety in my stomach. My Chechen friend was not feeling sorry for me, nor was he trying to change my mind. He understood. In the Siberian penal colony, there was no room for needless pity or pretense. The debt to Pilot had to be repaid. How I got into it, what my motives were, even who I had been until this moment – it didn't matter.

The choice laid out before me was simplified to the extreme: there was death and there was life. In Soviet prisons unpaid debt was one of those serious breaches of unwritten inmate law that could see a man cast down into the bottom of the hierarchy. I'd rather die. So, to continue living under the protection of the *vory*, I had to make Ivan Rostovkin bleed.

I gazed up at the watchtower where Ivan was stationed that day. His large frame filled the platform as he scanned the area below with his hands resting on the railing. After the incident with Tsikhiy, the corporal in charge of the convoy guards kept him away from the prisoners. It was a relief, but even at a distance he was looking for an opportunity to find a victim.

I spat and turned back to sharpening my axe, while casting glances towards Ivan's post. Everyone in IK-22 hated the bastard, even other guards cringed at his sadistic tendencies. He had been already on thin ice, but the day he tried to brutalize Tsikhiy in the work area, he brought about his own ruin. Tsikhiy was a *vor v zakonye* – thief in the law, member of the criminal elite in the Soviet underworld.

When Ivan raised his hand on Tsikhiy in front of everyone, he crossed a line of an unspoken agreement. It was a provocation meant to incite a reaction, an attack that would justify a killing. But Tsikhiy didn't react, instead he decided to make a point. Rather than fighting the guard and giving Ivan pretext to unload the bullets from the AK, Tsikhiy mutilated himself with the help of an exposed drive-belt of a diesel engine. His bloody, mangled hand was a testimony of his implacable defiance, that was a trait of the *blatnye* – career criminals, who followed the Thieves' Code.

I wasn't aware of it when it happened, but the fact that Tsikhiy had to make that point, put a sentence on Ivan. The *vory* had to punish him.

Just as they had been making their plans for retribution, I got tricked in a card game by a gang leader called Pilot. Using unwritten prison rules to his advantage he'd trapped me into a substantial debt.

Feeling pressed against the wall, I had asked Evgeny, a kind-hearted killer, to help me out. I first met him in SIZO – a pre-trial detention center, and I quickly became fond of him. We shared a cell there, and later we were transported in the same train car to Siberia and the gulag IK-22, to which we were sentenced.

In IK-22, I helped him write love letters to his wife, Matryona, while he shared the contents of his food packages with me and gave me advice. We were as close as a *vor* can be with a *muzhyk* – an everyday man, and I think Evgeny had a soft spot for me for those reasons.

I looked in his direction. He stood out in the work area with a group of other *vory*. He was wiry and broad shouldered, with the broken nose of a street-fighter and a voice burned with vodka and rolled-up cigarettes. Despite his sharp, unwelcoming features, he was one of the calmest men I've ever met. He often broke up fights and served as a mediator among the prisoners.

He had taken the case of my debt to the *blatnye,* and I went to plead for assistance in front of their seniors: Dima Sidoy, Kamen, and Evgeny himself. Sidoy said that they could protect me, but only if I joined them.

At first, I refused, as the remnants of my old, idealistic self were pulling me away from career criminals and their ways.

But when one of Pilot's guys, Klerk, tried to make me his bitch, and I narrowly escaped a beating and rape, I realized that I could not survive on my own in these circumstances.

The recollection made me cringe, as the bell rang calling us to work. Another day of felling trees in the Western Siberian taiga, part of our Soviet-style reeducation.

"What's your plan then, Andrycha?" Aslan asked as we walked towards the tree line, with freshly sharpened axes in our hands.

He was my closest friend, and the one who had jumped in to help when Klerk and his lackeys were beating the shit out of me in between the barracks. That's why I shared with him, perhaps foolishly, what the *blatnye* had demanded of me: Ivan Rostovkin was to be removed from the colony. It was supposed to be bloody, an example for others. But there was also a catch: he should survive to keep the peace between the guards and the *Bratva.*

"I will move to Barrack 6 today. The *blatnye* arranged it already," I said, looking around and making sure no one else was in earshot. "I'll get him at night."

"How?"

"The thieves have their ways."

"Risky," Aslan hissed.

"Better odds than me against Pilot's gang." I shrugged.

"I'll pray you walk back in one piece," he said, placing one hand on the pine tree he was about to cut down.

"You watch your own back, bratan," I whispered, feeling a pang of guilt for leaving him in Barrack 11 with the regulars. "Klerk won't forget you stood with me."

"I can take care of myself," Aslan replied, turning to me. "You focus on your task."

"I'll do my best."

I was ready to leave, but Aslan made a step forward with his hand raised. I clasped it and we shared a moment of camaraderie, when our eyes said more than the words could tell. He was squinting with an encouraging smile, but also with hardness and determination on his bearded face. I returned the smile and nodded to show that I was not afraid.

All of a sudden, a loud yell reverberated among the pines.

"Get to work, you maggots!" Ivan's loud, rumbling voice came from the watchtower. "I swear I'll shoot if you keep talking romance down there!"

"*Mudak*!" I cursed.

A glance towards the tower was enough. Ivan held the rifle aimed at us. Even at a distance I could see his caveman-like features twisted in a mad grin. He was eager for prisoner blood, but the time was coming to spill his instead.

Aslan grimaced at this and raised his axe.

"Remember Andrej, you're doing all the *zeki* a favor," he said, swinging his axe in a smooth arc and making the first notch in the tree trunk. "Each day this rabid dog of a guard stays in the colony there is a greater chance he will finally kill one of us. Do it right and survive, so we can stand together again."

"Your words to God's ears," I replied before walking away to work.

After coming back from the work area, I went to Barrack 11 where I shared a double bunk with Aslan, and I packed my meager *zek* belongings. I folded up the bed sheets and placed the aluminum utensils on top.

The *kozel* from my group looked at me sideways and seeing I was about to leave, he came over and blocked my way. He was a short guy, with a pair of wire-framed glasses and stubble on his face that grew in patches, like the fur of a mangy dog.

Kozly – the goats, were the collaborators, performing duties like counting the prisoners at roll-calls and making sure camp rules were followed. For being good servants to the authorities, they were rewarded with better jobs and privileges, but were despised by most of the inmates. Pilot's gang gave them protection, and in turn benefited from their access to food storage and the outside world.

"Where are you going with this stuff?" the *kozel* asked, trying to feign authority. "Barrack 6," I replied, and stood up with my fists clenched. The *kozel* slid away like a snake and left the building in haste.

Not thinking much about the nosy collaborator, I finished packing and walked outside with my bundle. As I walked through the prison yard with the golden rays of August evening sun in my eyes, I saw a bunch of guys gathered in front of Barrack 2 to my left. It was the lair of Pilot's gang and the man himself stood there, in sunglasses and a blue, Soviet aviator cap. His hairy arms folded, he seemed unmoved, but I was sure the word got to him that I was moving in with the *blatnye*. That meant I was under their protection now.

At that time, our penal colony, IK-22, was a Black Prison, meaning that what was going on inside was controlled by the inmates. The guards kept us locked in, but the criminal hierarchy determined and enforced the laws inside. It stood in stark contrast with the pre-trial detention center, SIZO, in Saratov where I had spent a few weeks after my trial. I met Evgeny there, and I began learning the harsh realities of prison life. That SIZO was a Red

Prison, where guards ruled inside with impunity, and the prisoners had to obey or face torture and sometimes death.

In the camp, however, deep in the woods near the town of Iskitim in Western Siberia, it was the *Bratva* who enforced their own code. But they were not the only organized group inside. The two main criminal factions balanced each other and kept the guards minding their own business.

There was Pilot and his gang: a loose rabble of crooks and collaborators. Despised by the 'honest' thieves who called them *suki* – bitches, Pilot and his men kept their position in the Zone through a mix of subservience to the guards and black-market commerce. They had access to food and contraband channels, giving them a monopoly in many goods craved by the *zeki*.

The *Bratva* – Brotherhood, on the other hand, with their code and their quiet influence over smaller criminals, were a different breed. It was composed of the *vory – thieves*, also called *blatnye – career criminals*. Led by Dima Sidoy, a seasoned thief, who still remembered Stalin's time, it was a tight-knit group following strict rules. To the regular *zeki* – prisoners, they were like kings, to be watched from a distance and obeyed without question. The guards respected them and their autonomy within the Zone, knowing that the *Bratva* could both keep other inmates in check, but also start a war if pressed too hard.

I crossed the yard under Pilot's angry stare, hidden behind dark sunglasses. Ziya and Klerk flanked him. Both had sour looks on their faces, but at some point Ziya smirked, and I felt a chill running down my spine. Whatever idea came to his head, I was sure it was something wicked.

Then, as I was approaching Barrack 6, Kamen emerged from its main entrance and welcomed me in front of everyone. His gaunt face with a prominent nose looked as if carved from granite, and his posture was solid like a mountain. He was *smotritel* for the *Bratva*, the envoy between them and the officials. A diplomat of sorts. We clasped hands out in the open and it was settled. *Zeki* witnessed me embraced by the *Bratva*, the word would spread. But to make it last and have my debt paid, I still had to perform my little task. At least I had Klerk off my back for now.

I entered Barrack 6 and passed by the doorman, a big guy with thick arms and a thicker, bald skull. He made sure no one entered the space of the *vory* uninvited. His *klichka* – nickname was Byk which meant bull. A rather simple fellow, he was good at guarding the entrance and took his job very seriously.

Inside, I was greeted by Evgeny who showed me to my new bunk. He told me to not worry about the *kozly* or the guards. Everything was arranged, and the books would be amended. It was part of the plan which I had previously discussed with Dima Sidoy and Kamen after I agreed to their terms. Barrack 6 was almost like a sovereign territory inside of IK-22, and the *Bratva* ruled it as they wished.

I settled myself in my new living space and waited for the curfew to begin. I remember the sweat on my palms when I sharpened the blade, and the sick feeling as I imagined using it on another human being. I later asked Sidoy why he would give me such a good knife for my mission. In the penal colony, a weapon like that had a great value. He said I was dealing payback for one of the *vory* and that their reputation was on the line. He simply wanted to make sure I had the best tool for the job.

Kamen came to sit with me, and we hunched together over a hand drawn map of the camp with all the buildings and patrol routes marked. The shadowy areas where spotlights didn't reach and other good hiding spots were marked on it as well. The plan was to sneak out of the barrack after lockdown, and to hope that Ivan will be the one patrolling the Zone. Then all I had to do was to make a surprise attack from the shadows.

"Nothing complicated," Kamen said with a sly grin, as we finished rehearsing the plan.

Evgeny came over with a steaming cup of *chifir* and handed it to me with a nod. The over-saturated tea was strong, even for prison standards. It was hot, its sticky bitterness burned on my lips and tongue as I took a small sip and tried to cool it down in my mouth.

"Drink up. It will keep you sharp out there." Kamen tried to encourage me. "Keep your eyes and ears open and stick to the shadows. The guards are lazy and predictable. We've done it many times before, and they had no clue."

I swallowed, feeling an immediate rush, but I was not really reassured by his words. If I had time, perhaps I could come up with a better idea, but the clock was ticking and Pilot was not going to extend my debt payment deadline. Night was my best shot as during the day there were simply too many guards and *zeki* around. After curfew, only a few guards remained on the watchtowers or patrolling the Zone, while the dogs were released into the 'dead strip' between the fences. All the barracks were locked from the outside at ten in the evening and opened again before the morning roll call.

Theoretically, it meant the *zeki* were all confined to their living spaces after dark, but Barrack 6 had a hidden trapdoor in the floor. It was carefully concealed, and required a special hook to reach between the boards and loosen a wooden handle, which locked the trapdoor in place. The *blatnye* put a lot of work and ingenuity into having this unofficial entryway in and out of their living quarters. When they showed it to me, I understood that I was being allowed to share in their secrets and considering what I was supposed to do, it made sense. However, Kamen made it clear that if I were to spill anything about their operations, they would get me, even if I were to change prisons, or land in the isolator. I had no doubt about it.

I finished drinking the *chifir* and time began to flow faster. Soon, the shouts of the guards outside announced the curfew, and the lights went out in the barrack. A heavy metal bar was dropped into place with a clanking of iron, locking the outside door. Then silence announced the arrival of the night.

We waited half an hour longer for sleep to fall over the prison camp. When the time came, Kamen nudged me and we walked silently to the corner where the trapdoor was hidden. Kamen lifted it up while I put on a face mask made of an old sweater. I was dressed lightly and in dark colors to better blend with the shadows. Like the knife to do the job, the *vory* provided the clothes too. So many things one could get in the Zone, it was just a matter of price.

"Good luck, *droog* – friend," Kamen said.

Evgeny was there too, and he patted me on the back as I lowered myself into the dark passage with Sidoy's knife clenched between my teeth.

The trapdoor led to a tight space underneath the barrack floor. It was dark, moist and it smelled of mold. There was barely enough room to crawl, and I could both hear the squeaks of rats around me, and feel their furry bodies brush on my skin. The exit was situated on the side of the building that was facing away from the fence and the watchtower floodlights.

Thinking about it now, that hidden passage was the way to my salvation, or damnation perhaps. But back then, I had other things on my mind. I was stuck on the threshold between worlds, clinging to those memories of the forest and my goodbye with Aslan, while the necessity of the moment pulled me towards action.

It was time to face the future, and my destiny.

I went out, entering the Zone like the living dead emerging from the grave. I had five days before the deadline that Pilot gave me to settle the debt.

I remember vividly each of the nights when I went outside and stalked the Zone. They were like a living nightmare, where I was the monster in the dark. The night itself became my reality, my refuge, something more personal perhaps – a silent companion.

The memories are etched deeply. Even now, if I were to close my eyes, I could feel it all once more. Recollections come almost like a song in my mind – the lyrics of the thieves...

Hello, Night. Cold. Dark. You're the friend of lovers and criminals.

I am here with you, looking for someone.

Ivan. I must get him. We want him out, but not dead. That would be too much. Dima Sidoy was clear about that.

So, I move under your cover. I wait and I observe from the shadows. I see, without being seen. Guards on the watchtowers, lamp posts on the perimeter. Bright lights cutting through the blackness. I stay away from them as I search for my prey.

I freeze hearing footsteps.

A guard is walking close by; he mustn't see me.

Blending in with the shadows, I watch him. He has an *ushanka* hat on and his jacket is buttoned up. The nights are getting cold with approaching autumn. He's a young guy, possibly my age. I think about my service in the Border Guard. Was it much different? Is that guy a volunteer, or maybe some circumstance forced him into service?

I disregard the thought, and I sneak behind him, from shadow to shadow. I memorize his route. Every turn, every step. It is as the *vory* had told me. They had done their homework, watching the guards and their habits for many years.

The only thing they didn't know was when exactly Ivan would have his night patrol in the Zone.

Tonight, it is someone else, but the patrol route should be the same. So, I stalk the young guard. I want to be ready when I get the chance with Ivan. I practice. At first, I keep my distance, but slowly I become bolder. Wrapped in darkness and silent on my feet, I get closer – nearly at arm's length.

The guard walks into the light beside the fence, and yells at his comrade on the watchtower nearby, "Don't shoot, it's me!"

A curse and a laugh come from the watchtower. The young guard resumes his patrol, unaware that I am just a few meters away. I wait for him to move past the light and continue my stalking game.

Three nights I spent like that. Getting out after curfew and shadowing the patrolling guards. Scouting, learning their routes. Nights became my only reality as I merged with the shadows – wide awake, my senses heightened, and my eyes wide open with a strong dose of *chifir*.

The days I barely remember. I was just getting through them, lethargic, allowing the camp schedule to carry my sleep-deprived body.

Then came the fourth night, as clear and sharp in my memory as the blade I carried.

I finally see him. The tall, brawny man, his square jaw outlined clearly as he passes through a spotlight beam.

My heart beats faster, like a war drum. It is happening, it must happen. I don't have much time left. I do not think about the consequences. I have no past nor future. I am just there, just to do that one thing.

I sprint quietly between the barracks, on bare feet wrapped in cloth. I stick to the shadows finding my way through the darkness until I reach the spot. I calm down my breathing and I wait.

I feel a pang of anxiety in my stomach. What if he takes a different route? I wait, listening. I close my eyes and focus only on the sound. I am crouching between some barrels behind the mess hall. I smell rot in the air as there are dumpsters nearby. I listen further. Time slows down painfully, and doubts begin to gnaw at my mind.

I then hear the crunch of footsteps. They are getting closer. I squeeze the knife handle. I had sharpened the blade myself, killing time before the hunt.

A silhouette appears in front of me, the dark outline of a bulky person in a guard's uniform, and an AKM on his back.

I wait as he passes by me, and I slide out of my hiding place. With a few quiet steps, I am behind him and in a flash, I wrap my left arm around his throat, and as I choke him, I drive the knife into his glute. I don't want to hit any vital organs.

He is strong, but he had been taken totally by surprise. I stab him in the back of his thigh, the blade piercing the muscle, and he falls to his knees with me hanging on his back.

I think about Evgeny whom he had beaten for no reason on our arrival day. I think about Tsikhiy and about Ivan's AKM pointed at me, his finger twitching. I know he would have pulled the trigger if I had given him the slightest reason.

I stab a few times more. The flesh is soft and the blade sinks into it with little resistance, but it twists and bounces off when I hit his hip bone.

Ivan keeps struggling. His hands are powerful, and he manages to free himself from my chokehold. His scream breaks through the silence and so I back off, hitting him in the head with the round metal butt of the knife. He falls to the ground, moaning like a wounded animal.

I escape through the shadows, like a fox running back to its burrow, while more shouts emanate from the guard towers and spotlights are sweeping frantically throughout the Zone. I reach Barrack 6, squeeze myself into the hole, and crawl back to the trapdoor.

Evgeny, Kamen, and Sidoy are waiting for me. They help me up and lead me to the water basin. My right hand is sticky with blood. I see eyes gleaming in the darkness. Some men are not asleep, and they are watching me from their beds. Soon, I lay on my own bunk as the Zone becomes engulfed in the ringing sound of the alarm bell and shouting of the guards.

CHAPTER 2

In Solitude And Silence The True Self Is Revealed

The next day at the penal colony was hectic to say the least. The camp commander – Major Koralov and the guards were furious. What an outrage! One of them attacked in the Zone. Koralov screamed at us from the platform at the assembly ground.

"Was I not good to you, *mudaki*? Is that how you repay me for all the privileges you have in this place?" The old Major's voice cracked across the yard with surprising strength. Then, his tone turned icy as he announced, "No food parcels for three months unless the bastard is found."

The morning roll call stretched on for hours as we were made to stand at attention while the guards searched the barracks. The exhaustion I felt from four sleepless nights was hitting me hard. I barely kept myself standing, and the visions of what I did just a few hours earlier seemed to be burning into my memory. With that came pain and a certain disgust I felt for myself, but also a feeling of relief. It was done.

I looked among the ranks to see the group from Barrack 2. I spotted Pilot there, his face set in a bitter expression. Beside him, whispering with each other were Klerk and Ziya – my former partner in crime.

We started together in Berlin. He helped me slip out from under the iron hand of the Stasi – East German secret police, and we made a circuit through the Eastern Bloc in a beat-up Barkas van. For a while, things were looking up.

Then Ziya's hidden agenda surfaced. We were caught with drugs in the car; heroin, smuggled without my knowledge. Everything went downhill from there. The SIZO. Interrogations. Torture. Prison. And finally the verdict: twelve years in a penal colony.

We ended up in the same camp. At first, we stuck together. But soon enough, he wanted to pull me into his heroin business. I cut ties with him. Not long after, I found myself trapped in debt to Pilot. I've always suspected Ziya had a hand in it.

"Keep yourself straight, *droog*," Evgeny's words reached me through my stupor. "You don't want the guards to notice."

I realized I was leaning heavily to the side, both from tiredness, and to peek at Ziya. I straightened up, feeling dizzy.

The game was not over, I thought. I might have done the job for the *vory*, but I was entering new and uncharted territory. Now it was time for the guards and Pilot to make their moves. I sighed, numb with resignation, and focused on keeping myself from collapsing on the ground.

Hours passed, and search squads returned from the barracks with their reports. Some contraband was found, but no evidence related to my crime. The *vory* knew how to cover their tracks, and Barrack 6 was full of secret hiding places.

The work brigades were then sent off to do their labor, and we were expected to fulfill our regular quotas, even though we spent the entire morning on the assembly grounds. I walked through the forest like a robot, my entire focus on taking step after step towards the work area.

The guards were jumpy, and they yelled harsh commands. They kept their submachine guns and rifles pointed at the ground beneath our feet, as if they were expecting a sudden bloody riot. I couldn't blame them. One of their kind was driven out of the Zone in the camp ambulance, an old UAZ truck. For many, especially young ones, it must have been a shock.

We came back from work after dinner. There was no food waiting for us, no chance to wash. Instead, we were marched straight to the assembly ground and made to stand there until curfew.

The late August evening was mild and damp. Mosquitoes swarmed over our unwashed bodies, eating us alive. I was used to long standing punishments from my time in the GDR military. I bent my knees slightly and loosened my hips, keeping them from locking up.

Time dragged on. As the sun sank, some of the *zeki* couldn't take it anymore. One by one, they sagged and squatted, their legs trembling. The guards were quick with their batons, snapping them back upright.

When the night air finally cooled, the mosquitoes thinned out. Or maybe they'd already had their fill.

All of that was meant to break our spirit, and to weaken the zeki before the coming investigation. Major Koralov wanted someone's head, and he was hoping one of us would rat me out.

Before locking us in for the night, the guards pulled a few inmates from each barrack. They mostly went after the ones who could barely stay on their feet. We watched them being marched toward the guardhouse.

Interrogations followed. Over the next few days, more men were called in for questioning. Most of it was perfunctory though. The camp couldn't afford to slow its work for long, and breaking a thousand prisoners takes time.

A handful of men from Barrack 6 were taken at random and beaten hard. One ended up in the infirmary. The others came back marked, with swollen faces, broken ribs, their eyes dulled by pain. They paid the price for my crime, but they knew it was part of the game.

No one complained, and more importantly, no one snitched. Not even when food packages were suspended for three months, a punishment that hurt everyone. And I knew the *blatnye* in my new barrack were already aware of my part in Ivan's downfall.

We didn't hear about his fate until a few days later, when news came back from Novosibirsk that despite deep lacerations, and severe injuries, he would live. The guards cooled down at that news, and soon the interrogations stopped.

In a way, everyone saw that tragedy had been closing in on Ivan Rostovkin. Most just assumed it would end with him snapping and gunning down a few *zeki* with his AK. Perhaps my actions prevented those deaths, and at the time, I wondered whether it may have taught the sadist a lesson. As we were to find out in due time, the lesson had only made the madman madder, and I came to regret that I didn't finish him off that night.

As for me, my debt with Pilot was settled and I began on my path to become a *blatnoy*. It took me some time to regain my senses. I barely slept during those four days and nights, when I was stalking the Zone under the cover of darkness.

Something changed in me back then. It was as if I had descended to a lower level of hell. It felt like touching the abyss and having it stick to me. I could feel its taint on my soul and my mind, just like Ivan's blood tainted my hands. Whatever was left of the young Andrej was lost in that abyss, and a new man came back, truly ready to join the *vory* and embrace their code.

As I emerged from my earlier nightmare and into my new position in the camp life, I felt I was becoming a part of something bigger. With my prospect task complete, the attitude of *blatnye* towards me shifted from cold indifference to respectful and embracing. Suddenly, hardened criminals, who before barely noticed my existence, came to talk and ask how I was doing.

Those who came back from interrogations not only kept their mouths shut in front of the guards but also harbored no hard feelings for the fact that it was my crime that made them run the gauntlet. It was just like any other day for them, and at the time, I was astonished by their indifferent attitude towards the pain and suffering they had to endure.

But that was part of their way, as I found out day by day while being introduced to my new life by Evgeny and Sidoy. I spent my evenings with them, learning *fenya* – the thieves' language, being instructed on how the *vory* operated, and the code they followed. I was still sort of an apprentice, and I was told that I would go through a baptism come first snow.

The more I learned, the more I understood how detached the *vory* were from the rest of society. It was not just a separate tribe; their very existence was an act of rebellion against the system in all its aspects.

At the time, it felt as if I had found the brotherhood that I always yearned for. After escaping the clutches of mediocre existence and persecution in the GDR, after seeing the rot of other Eastern Bloc countries, and after experiencing firsthand the Soviet system's inadequacy and brutality, this felt like something real, and uncorrupted. So, I welcomed the fraternity with open arms and I drank from the cup of wisdom that Sidoy offered me with almost paternal sentiment.

He was my first mentor, old Dima, and I wouldn't be the man I became without his introduction and guidance. He taught me about honor, about loyalty, and about the heroic resilience of the thieves. And his words were not empty.

The actions of the *vory*, their attitude, outwardly and inwardly, reflected their code. They were the embodiment of an idea, and I began to see it in their tattoos as well. There was something mystical about the way they both reflected the *vor's* inner world and inspired each of them to take action, and I was waiting impatiently for the time I would receive my first ink. As I was becoming one of them, embracing their attitude, I found myself eager to prove myself, and wanted to show my devotion to the community.

The opportunity came a week after I had dealt with Ivan Rostovkin.

It was the middle of the night and despite the curfew, I was sitting on Evgeny's bunk, holding a candle, and watching him getting a new tattoo on his shoulder. This time it was a werewolf with bared teeth, an indication that he was a killer. Sasun, the Armenian tattoo artist was not a *vor*, but he lived in Barrack 6 and was respected and treated well thanks to his talent. Sidoy sat beside me, explaining different parts of the already existing story written on Evgeny's body. My curiosity was stirred by an image of two cats surrounded by flowers tattooed on his stomach, but I didn't want to interrupt Dima in his tale telling.

Suddenly, the doors slammed open, and the lights went up. Guards came storming in, shouting and with *dubinkas* – rubber batons in their hands. There was at least a dozen of them, and they quickly swept between the rows of bunks, ordering the men out of their slumber and into the living space.

It was yet another *shmony* – a random search of our living space.

Sasun managed to hide the ink, and his tools under the bed, before a guard came over, ordering us to stand at attention. Only Sasun stood up. The smell of the freshly extinguished candle hung in the air, and the guard yelled at us asking what we were up to.

"Just sleepwalking chief," I said standing up and leaning on the bunk – already taking on the half-serious, half-mocking attitude the thieves had towards the authorities.

The guard pushed me aside with his baton and ordered us to line up in the living area of the barrack. Sasun scurried there in haste, while I followed Sidoy and Evgeny who took their time standing up, stretching, and walking at a leisurely pace.

We lined up with the others in the living space, and soon a guard came over with the handmade needle, and the ink that Sasun was using on Evgeny. The guard ordered Sidoy, Evgeny, Sasun, and me to step forward.

"Which one of you, dirtbags...?" the guard growled, his eyes sweeping over us as he held up the contraband.

No one spoke. We all just stared back, trying to look surprised, innocent – anything but guilty.

I finally broke the silence. "If you're giving out gifts," I said, "I'll take it."

Someone had to take a fall and I felt it might as well be me. It was partly because of the fondness I felt for both Sidoy and Evgeny that I would not want them to suffer the guards' wrath. But in a large part, I just wanted to prove myself to both of them. Making a public display of my defiance in front of everyone in Barrack 6 felt like the right thing to do.

I was young and eager, you must understand, and as my new identity was growing on me, I wanted to show to myself, and others, that I was really cut out for it. I didn't know then that the guards would not have put a finger on either Dmitri or Evgeny. Not at that time anyway.

Another guard came over and cuffed my hands behind my back. I was led out of the building while the search continued inside. More baton-wielding guards waited outside and some of them joined my escort.

As they walked me towards the isolation cell, one of them pushed me, kicking my feet from under me at the same time.

I fell hard, barely managing to turn my head to the side to avoid hitting the ground face first.

One of the guards held my legs together, while another used a piece of rope to tie them tightly. I was lying on my belly in the Zone's dirt, helpless and unable to move.

The guards proceeded to work on me with their long, rubber batons with a regular cadence, like farmers threshing grain. Blows fell on the full length of my body, while one of the guards kept a boot on my neck, pressing my face down into the ground.

I moaned and grasped for air as the batons slammed into my legs, my glutes, and all over my back. When they finished, I was delirious with pain and in shock.

They lifted me up like a sack of potatoes and carried me to one of the isolation cells near the dog kennels and separated from the rest of the Zone by an additional fence. I was thrown into the small, dark room, headfirst and left there on the ground with my hands still cuffed, and legs tied together.

I spent the rest of the night that way, and as morning came, I heard the bell ringing, announcing the time to wake up and the ensuing roll call. I thought about the men lining up in the assembly ground, and a thought crossed my mind, that it wasn't so bad to wake up early, and go off to do forced labor.

As the optimists say: things can always get worse, and I was now longing for the morning gruel, mosquitoes, and the feel of an axe in my hands. But I had to pay to join the *vory*, and it seemed the price was pain and suffering. I wasn't even really one of them, just a young blood on his way to be initiated, but I understood the process, at least I thought so.

The camp quieted down as the men walked off to work, and no one even came to look at me. I wriggled on the floor, covered in dirt and straw, changing from one uncomfortable position to another.

The back of my body was unbelievably tender and I felt like a schnitzel, flattened out and stored in the fridge to be fried later. I tried to pull my hands from behind my back and around my feet, but the pain in my back was so sharp that I gave up after a few attempts.

The day went on and still no one came. Hunger was nothing new to me at that point, but I was getting really thirsty. My mouth was dry, and I fantasized about wetting my lips with fresh water.

It was the first time since the beatings in SIZO that I felt so helpless and scared. Weak thoughts invaded my mind, telling me that I had been forgotten. That I was going to rot there, and die of thirst, without anyone caring about my fate.

I felt regret for hurting Ivan Rostovkin, and I felt I was getting my just deserved punishment for my crimes. That fear only grew as I heard brigades returning from work, along with the sound of evening and nighttime roll calls. The final yells of the guards confirmed that the barracks were locked and everyone sealed in.

I gave up being hard, and I wanted to scream for someone to come, but my throat was so dry that I could only manage a pathetic whimper. I wanted to cry, but tears were too precious to spare.

The terrible pain I felt for my mother's death, returned. I had pushed it down these past three months, but it stabbed at me in the darkness like the knife I had used on Ivan. I began to repeat the Jesus Prayer, she had taught me, whispering it like a mantra:

"Lord Jesus Christ, Son of God, have mercy on me, a sinner."

The words looped in my mind and hung quietly on my cracked lips. It hurt so much, my entire body, inside and out. But it didn't matter, the unbearable pain would end one way or another. I kept repeating the prayer, and it calmed my breathing and most importantly, my soul. A spark, hiding within me, now kindled into a small flame. I felt its power giving me warmth and strength.

I rolled on my side, and once more began pulling my arms down to free my hands. It didn't work, so I just lay on my back, invoking pain in all the bruised muscles. I couldn't ignore it, but I pushed through it anyway. I clenched my teeth and strained my muscles to stretch my hands, while pulling my legs inwards.

I still couldn't do it. But I tried again. This was my fight, this was one thing that I could do, and I put all my resolve into it. I got angry.

The small flame grew into an inner conflagration. I tried again, crying out feebly, as each further stretch invoked a sharp stab of pain, and eventually I succeeded. I laughed through clenched teeth and tears that wouldn't flow. It was a small victory, but it gave me confidence and fired me up.

The piece of rope used to tie my feet was cheap and made of coarse threads. I began working on them with my fingernails, separating, and cutting through them individually.

When the guards finally showed up the next morning, I stood up to face them. One waited outside with a *dubinka*, while the other looked at me, at the piece of rope on the floor, and told me to turn away and face the wall. I was expecting another beating, but he just put a small loaf of bread wrapped in grey paper and a cup with water on the floor then told me to turn back to him.

He uncuffed my hands and looked me in the eye. It was the young guard I had stalked on my first night out while preparing to ambush Ivan.

"You've got a month in isolation for the possession of illegal items," he said with a hint of apprehension, and we stood there for a moment.

It surprised me. The guard was waiting for something. I realized he was treating me as if I was one of the *vory*. I nodded an acknowledgement and curved my lips in a fake smile. He looked at me with a mix of pity, disdain, and a little fear. Then he walked out, and the door closed with a thud, followed by the metallic sound of the lock.

And so, I began my first longer stretch of solitary confinement. It was tough and it took me time to adjust, but I already had some mental tools that I used to keep myself sane. Over the years I have had to endure periods of isolation on many occasions, and some people have asked me how I did it, always coming out untouched.

I thought about it, and I told them there were simple rules to keep yourself together in circumstances of loneliness and isolation.

Number 1: Move your body! I tell that to all my young associates, and it is the simplest rule to follow. In isolation, it is easy to fall into despair and just sit or lay down all day. This drains your energy, makes you weaker. Your body is made for action, so give it some.

With four walls and a floor, you have an entire gym at your disposal. You can do body weight exercises, like push-ups, sit-ups, and squats. You can go for isometric exercises like planks, wall-sits, or pushing against the wall. You can condition your fists and shins and get your neck stronger for fighting.

Figure out a routine that works for you, and stick to it, every fucking day. Your body and your mind will thank you for that, and you will build a first pillar to support your existence through the dark times of isolation.

Number 2: Calm your mind. Isolation means you must be alone with yourself, a terrifying prospect for most modern people. We do everything in our power to be distracted, entertained, and amused, and not to be alone.

When you are locked up in a small cell without any gadgets or other people to distract you, the silence will be like an ice bath. At first, very uncomfortable, but eventually bearable, and then empowering. The silence is like the cold, it is your friend, if you are brave enough to hold its hand.

Number 3: Use your mind. Now that your body is active, and your mind is calm, focus it, and think. Contemplate on your mission, *droog*, on what you will do after you get out. Play chess in your head or pretend to write stories and letters.

During my first long stretch in isolation, I began composing letters in my head. Not the soft, affectionate ones I used to write for other *zeki*, but letters filled with anger and hate. I poured out my disgust: at my Stasi father, at the GDR, at the whole Soviet machine rotting with corruption and lies. In my mind, I filled page after page with contempt for the camp, its guards and most of all, for Pilot, for my old partner Ziya, and for every *suka* in their gang.

Sometimes to know who you are, you must know who you are not, and by defining your enemies, you come to understand your values. This was an important lesson for me, and I learned it by using my mind productively in isolation.

Number 4: Rein in your emotions. Despair, anguish, loneliness, anger, envy, pain, and other negative feelings will come to haunt you. Don't fight them. They can all be painful, but pain is just pain, it won't kill you.

Look at the feelings, observe them, learn from them. As you turn your inner eye to see them, you will find them vanishing, like a morning mist, chased away by the rising sun. When you master your emotions, you won't be afraid of solitude ever again.

Breathwork can be helpful. Used boxed breathing: inhale, hold, exhale, hold again, each at a count of four. This should help with reducing your heart rate, and calming your nerves down, if the emotions get out of hand.

Number 5: Keep faith. It is a well-established phenomenon that people with faith often survive, heal faster, and overcome more than those who believe in nothing. Scientists call it the 'placebo effect', but I call it the power of belief – and it applies in all areas of life. That power is most needed when you are beaten down and alone, so when in isolation, take my advice and don't be a nihilist, believe in something.

Find a meaning and hold on to it. Be it God, family, or brotherhood. Connect with that meaning through daily prayer and contemplation. Consider your own mortality, and make it fuel your willpower.

Even in prison, you have that choice, the choice between fighting or surrender – the *vory* taught me that well.

In isolation, apply these rules, and you will know peace. In life, apply them, and you will know power. Silence will no longer be your enemy but the most loyal ally at your side.

CHAPTER 3

When The System Offers Mercy, It Demands Your Soul

I waited for the guards' footsteps to die down in the corridor, before squatting and lifting the cup with water to my mouth. I wet my lips first before taking a small sip. Not knowing how often I would get fed, I left half of the cup for later. I took my time, chewing on the bread slowly, and thinking about my punishment.

The isolation cell was a concrete box, three by two meters, and three meters high. The tiny window opposite the door allowed a smudge of light in, and the room was murky otherwise. Besides the simple wooden palette to sleep on, there was no furniture. A dirty bucket stood beside the door, into which I relieved myself. It was replaced by the guards when they brought me meals.

The place was damp and moldy, the air inside was stiff, smelled of urine, disinfectant, and old sweat. The concrete walls had only patches of the formerly white paint remaining, and the floor was covered in dark stains.

One month of isolation that didn't sound so bad at first. I was serving twelve years after all, so thirty days was but a mere fraction. I was to learn the hard way just how difficult isolation really is for a human being.

As the first days dragged on mercilessly, I memorized the schedule of the guards and was awaiting each short visitation by my oppressors with great anticipation. They brought me water and bread in the morning. Then another serving of water and a bowl of *kasha* in the evening. It was usually the same young fellow handling my food, an Estonian named Tamm. He was a tall, lanky guy, with wire-framed glasses, and the sad eyes of an intellectual. I had no idea what brought him to serve in IK-22. Perhaps he failed to get into university.

Each time he came in with a meal, I would stand up and greet him with a broad smile. You might think I was crazy or trying to ingratiate myself with the guards. But the fact is, that after days in solitude, I was genuinely happy to see another person, even if briefly, and even though he was a guard, and I was a prisoner.

Somehow, he was excluded from all the hatred I felt for the system of oppression in the camp. And he seemed decent for a guard, nothing like Ivan Rostovkin.

These visits were brief and driven by prison efficiency. I would move back to the wall, while Tamm placed the food and water on the floor and picked up the tray from my previous meal before leaving. Sometimes we would exchange a few words.

"How are things in the Zone?" I would ask.

"*Vsio normalno* – Everything in order," he would respond.

Or, pointing to the small window, close to the ceiling, I would say: "The weather looks good today, are the mosquitoes out?"

"Eating us alive," would come back the answer, then we would laugh like two school friends, sharing a common joke.

Our fragile sociality lasted for no more than a week.

"Why do you bother with this one, Tamm?" the other guard said one day, holding the door to my cell. "He's in for drugs and assault on a *militsiya* man."

Tamm looked at me differently after that, and he stopped responding to my lighthearted questions. It took away a bit of enjoyment I had in those days, but I still waited for their visits, even if all I got from the guards were scornful looks and stale bread.

The rest of the time – the long, empty stretches between the two brief breaks in an otherwise solitary day – I spent clinging to my sanity. Solitude warps time: every minute stretches into a score of oppressive seconds. Each second falls like a heavy drop of water on the forehead of a tortured prisoner, pushing him to the edge of madness.

I began longing for the long marches to the forest, for the physical labor with the axe in my hand, and other men around me. Out there we suffered together, and there was even some camaraderie to be found. There was fresh air, and the smell of pine sap, the rustle of birch leaves on the wind, and there was space. Even the Zone itself was not surrounded by walls, but by two fences of barbed wire, which gave our souls more room to breathe. We could always see the trees from the inside.

There was no room to walk normally in my cell but as my body craved movement, I established a routine of various exercises that I kept following religiously.

I would take a 'stroll' after meals: five short steps towards the door, turn on my heel, and five steps towards the window. I would count the steps, aiming at five thousand. Sometimes I would lose focus and forget the count, so I would start over. After this breakfast walking session, I tried to emulate my workday in the forest. Doing pushups, squats, and sit-ups in sets of thirty. When I was too exhausted to continue, I lay on my cot and tried to take a nap. In the evenings, after the dinner 'walk', I prayed and asked God for mercy.

At first, I was angry at the guard who told Tamm about my charges. It ruined my only human interaction in the isolator. I felt resentment and a sense of injustice in it all, but the more I contemplated it, the more I realized that I couldn't really argue with what the guard had said.

It was true – I was arrested together with Ziya for possession of a couple of kilograms of heroin. My former partner had it stashed in the car, beside smuggled carpets we bought on a black market in Saratov.

When we were stopped by *militsiya* – the Soviet police – on the road to Moscow, Ziya told me these could be gangsters in disguise. I fought as hard as I could, but there were also criminal investigation unit officers following us, and we were arrested and tried in a swift execution of Soviet justice.

To make the matters worse for me, I had now proven to be a criminal, by assaulting Ivan and sending him off to the hospital. Of course, neither Tamm nor the other guard knew about it. But I did, and it was eating me alive.

Sometimes the guilt kept me awake at night. In those darkest hours of isolation, when the concrete walls of my little prison seemed to close in around me, I hated myself for what I'd done. But eventually, sleep would come. And after the long night, a new day would rise, bringing me one step closer to the end of that solitary struggle.

On the fourteenth day of the isolation, I got a message from Dima Sidoy that lifted my spirits and reminded me that I was not alone. The little piece of paper was rolled into a ball and stuck into a tiny incision in the bread that I was given by the guards in the morning.

I found it when I broke the loaf in half to eat, and I unfolded the rolled-up paper with reverence and excitement.

"You are strong, Andrycha. Your *Bratva* is waiting, and we will take care of you. Whatever comes, remember that you're soon to become one of us. We do not fear death, pain, or isolation. We live by our own rules, and the rest of the world can go to hell." – Dima

The two guards came with the regular visit that evening. Tamm left the bowl of kasha on the floor, without looking at me, but the other guard lingered before closing the door. He took out something wrapped in paper out of his pocket and threw it on the floor. It was a piece of sausage, and a pickled cucumber. The *vory* found a way to deliver more than a message.

I got more of those extra rations, and they kept me going. It was not just the food that brought relish and fuel for my body. The fact that I was not forgotten, and there was a brotherhood waiting for me outside, gave me hope and mental fortitude.

I continued with my routines, and I learned more about myself, as the days dragged slowly. I haven't even noticed when the painstaking solitude transformed into a merely bearable discomfort.

In time, I came to see that the real punishment for our sins isn't what happens to us, but what we become. I accepted that truth – and with it, myself: a criminal.

A week before the prescribed end of my isolation came the day when I had the only opportunity to leave my cell. It was midday, and instead of Tamm and his grumpy-faced partner, two other guards came in, telling me to face the wall. Each held a *dubinka* in his hands, and they seemed eager to cause damage, so I followed them without question.

I was cuffed and led outside. The sunlight hurt my eyes, and I felt like an underworld creature emerging into the open plains. The guards nudged me with their rubber batons towards the small guardhouse, located close to the isolator building. There I was pushed into a room, where a familiar officer sat with a bunch of papers on his desk, and an inviting look on his face.

It was Captain Svietlov, the second in command of IK-22.

The camp commander, Major Koralov, was an old-timer of the Soviet penitentiary system who still remembered the Gulag.

GULAG was originally an abbreviation for *Glavnoe Upravlenie Lagerei* – the Main Camp Administration – and it was born shortly after the Soviet Union. It oversaw a vast network of forced labor camps scattered across the most remote, wild, and inhospitable corners of the Soviet empire.

Under its supervision, millions of men, women, and sometimes children suffered terrible fates, often never to return.

The organization was disbanded after Stalin's death in the 1950s. And when I was first imprisoned in 1985, the GULAG no longer officially existed. However, the forced labor camps hadn't changed much. They were still colloquially referred to as Gulags, especially by the political prisoners.

Being at the end of his career, a witness to countless atrocities, and a veteran of many Siberian winters, Major Koralov had a cynical, and resigned attitude towards running the IK-22. His mouth was full of Soviet slogans about reeducation, and building socialism, but he was rather happy with keeping the status quo and avoiding problems within the camp.

But where old Major Koralov lacked energy and resolve, Captain Svietlov showed up with vigor, and a fierce sense of Soviet justice. I had met him on my first day in the Zone, when I stood in front of the commission that determined my allocation in the camp. After seeing my charges, and deciding I was not a *blatnoy*, he sent me off to the grinder of the general labor.

Later, that same day he'd stopped Ivan Rostovkin and other guards from beating Evgeny and me to a pulp, so I wasn't sure what to expect of him now.

I stood straight and looked at him. Not with confrontation, but with curiosity about what I was into now.

Svietlov was a tall man, slender and fit, with a neatly shaven, long face, well-arched eyebrows, and a straight line of a nose, over equally straight, thin lips.

"Sit down," he said, and offered me a cigarette.

I took it and while sitting down, I turned my head briefly to look behind. The two guards who brought me in were standing there with eyes fixed on the wall behind Svietlov. They acted disinterested, but I knew they would quickly beat me down if I caused any trouble.

This was not my first rodeo, so to speak. I had been through Stasi interrogations in the Magdeburg prison, and the torture sessions in the Saratov SIZO still haunted my nightmares. So, I picked up the cigarette and put it in my mouth, bracing myself mentally for another round of pain.

"You are a student of literature, Lenkov," the Captain stated flatly, folding his hands together on the desk.

Lenkov. The fake name from the passport of a student from Kaliningrad. Ziya got those fake papers for me back in the GDR. So far away, I thought. But I mostly wondered about what Svietlov was getting at.

I didn't speak. After a moment, Svietlov held up his lighter. I leaned down and lit my cigarette on its flame, still quiet.

"What are your favorite authors?" he asked, putting his lighter back in his pocket.

It wasn't entirely unexpected. I learned already that interrogators often began with seemingly unrelated questions. Asking for personal details to befriend their victims and open their mouths. I gave it some thought before answering.

"I like Tolstoy," I replied, "but in this place Dostoevsky feels more appropriate."

"Why so?" The Captain leaned in on his desk.

"Tolstoy dreamed of redeeming men through love. Dostoevsky showed that suffering is the only teacher some will ever listen to."

Svietlov pursed his lips, and scoffed, but his eyes narrowed with amusement.

"You are quite the *umnik* – a smart guy, aren't you?"

I shrugged, wondering when the beating would start.

Svietlov picked up a piece of paper from the desk and tapped it with a finger.

"You're an educated man, with no prior record. What the fuck are you doing in Barrack 6? I thought I assigned you to Barrack 11."

So that's what this was about. He figured out I moved in with the *blatnye*. Was he suspecting my part in Ivan's demise?

"I got a better bunk in Barrack 6."

"Is that so? Do you know what you're getting yourself into?" Svietlov put down the paper. His voice turned cold. "I don't know what kind of use the thieves will have for you, but staying with them is the shortest way to extend your sentence. I've seen it before. Rub shoulders with crooks long enough, you become one of them, and you'll be punished for it. Should be obvious for someone who admires Dostoevsky."

Again, I shrugged. He was obviously trying to make a point, and I wanted him to finish.

"But... There are other ways here. Better ways." He leaned in, rested one elbow on the desk, finger pointing upward. "Instead of becoming a prison dweller and spending the rest of your life going from one sentence to another, you could redeem yourself. Not through love, but through service. We have plenty of work for *umniki*. Imagine: no more marching into the forest every morning. You'd help us run this place. Stay out of trouble and I'd personally vouch for your good behavior. Your sentence could be reduced. Maybe even by half. You could resume your studies. You're still young. You'd have a future ahead of you."

I sat in silence, pretending to think it over. Then I said, "Not interested, comrade Captain."

"You're not?" He jabbed a finger at me. "You want to spend your life in here?"

"We are all in this together," I said, taking a slow drag from my dying cigarette. "Each of us is serving time in this hell. But I like clear boundaries. I'm the prisoner, you're the guard. Let it stay that way. Otherwise, it gets... confusing."

"This is the only time this offer is on the table," he said, leaning back in his chair, eyes narrowing. "If you're afraid of the *vory*, we can give you protection."

"Right," I chuckled, knowing all too well that if the *vory* could get one of the guards, they would get a prisoner as well if they wanted to. "We are all afraid of something, and we all have some prison guards making sure we follow the line. For me, the reality is clear. Is it for you?"

I locked eyes with him, tired of the waiting. I then pinched out the cigarette, set the butt on the table, and braced for the rubber batons, so I could have it over with.

"You made your bed. Time to sleep in it." He waved his hand dismissively, and the two guards shifted behind me. I stood up, ready to be dragged to the cellar for a beating, but they just nudged me out of the room and led me back to the isolator.

Later that evening, I replayed the dialogue with Svietlov in my head, and I wondered why he let me pass. Perhaps he thought I was going to suffer enough under the *blatnye* rule. He didn't know yet that I was becoming one of them, but he was right about something. I made my choices, and now I was getting accustomed to suffering the consequences.

CHAPTER 4

Choose Your Reasons, When You Can't Choose The Circumstances

After the thirty days of my sentence had passed, I came out of the isolator. I was lighter, not only in body weight, but also when it came to my heart. It felt as if some parts of me had been left back there. The source of weakness and despair, which I felt on my first day when I was beaten up and laying on the floor, seemed gone, replaced by a steely determination.

I came back to Barrack 6, and was welcomed by the *vory* with hot *chifir*, and *tushonka* – a Soviet canned delicacy of ground meat and fat.

To help me recover, Evgeny spiked the *chifir* with a mushroom remedy he received in one of the food packages from his wife. I was surprised how much it reinvigorated me, and I asked him about the recipe, but he shrugged and said it was his woman's business.

As I sat, eating and drinking, Evgeny and Kamen brought me up to speed on the developments in the camp.

They told me the sad news, that poor Seryozha from my work brigade was found dead in the *banya* – the prison's bathhouse. He hanged himself and rumor was he did it because he couldn't repay his drug debt. I cursed Ziya, and Pilot's gang, for preying on the weakness of men like Seryozha, and selling them dope. But there was nothing I could do about it. I was glad that I cut ties with my former partner, and that the people I was now with seemed to be honorable and aligned with my values.

Kamen explained also that the investigation into Ivan's 'accident' was officially closed. The guards eased up with the *shmony* – the searches, and their abuse and violence against the *zeki* fell to 'normal' camp levels.

Unfortunately, Koralov decided that there would be no more packages at least until New Year. Perhaps he still wanted to pressure the *zeki* and make someone rat on the assailant – that was on me. This left me with a sense of distrust towards the regular prisoners and solidified my commitment to the *vory*. For one of them to rat, would be worse than a death sentence.

Other than that, life in the Zone continued at a steady, tedious pace.

Sidoy observed me from a distance, thoughtful as always, as I got to fill my belly and my soul. It felt good to be back among these men whom I began to see as my brothers, even though I was not yet officially one of them. It was mid-September, and I was waiting eagerly for the first snow so I could be baptized into the fold.

Being out of isolation meant a return to general labor. I walked to the assembly ground the next morning and was happy to see Aslan again.

He embraced me when we met, and told me that I looked like shit, which was true. Despite my exercise routine, I had lost a lot of weight, and my body was pale. I had dark circles around my eyes, and my hair and beard were ungroomed. But being back in the Zone, I had access to more food so I knew that whatever vitality I lost in the past month would come back soon.

I told Aslan that on Sunday I'd go to Barrack 4 where a *zek* named *Britva* – Razor, provided barber services, and until then, he had to suffer my disheveled look while we worked together.

We caught up during breaks, and we had a moment of silence for Seryozha. He was not a close friend, but he had worked with us and shared the same bread and same burdens in the past months. To me, his fate was also a reminder of how close I was to being destroyed by the card debt to the same people.

That reminder, on top of the month in the isolator, made me appreciate being in the forest again. As I walked with the others toward the work area, my senses – long confined to a small, dark cell, that reeked of mold – drank in the richness of life around me.

The colors seemed brighter, the smells sharper, the touch of the breeze on my skin more tender. The fragrance of pine sap mixed with the earthy, moist odor of the undergrowth. The sage-green of pine needles contrasted with the light green of birch leaves. Some had already begun to turn yellow, trembling faintly in the wind.

I ponder sometimes on how our moods change, and how little it takes to enjoy life if one has the right attitude. I know that some people struggle with it, but for me it became easier along the way. The more I suffered and the more I went through, the more I appreciated the small things in life. And even though work was hard, it was a welcome change from the stuffy, grey, and monotone life in the camp, or the grim solitude of the isolation cell.

It was for that reason that some of the *blatnye* participated in the outside work. I learned more about that from Sidoy, on one of our walks, during which he used to explain to me the Code, and mindset of a *vor*.

The next day was Sunday, the day off from general labor.

Right after our morning meal, I went to the barber, who performed his services in Barrack 4. After waiting for a turn in a short queue, I sat on a chair in the wash area of the barrack. Simple washing basins, buckets, and a couple of sinks were located there, to be used by dozens of zeki from the building to wash themselves.

Looking at my reflection in the small round mirror, I told the barber to make me handsome again. Britva, the old killer, gave his usual grin and ran a thumb across his throat. "One cut could end it all," he said, the same joke as always.

I laughed and told him to save it for next time.

After getting a good, clean shave, and a haircut, I gave him almost all my remaining cigarettes. They were the main currency of the prison, besides the balance each of us had in the commissary store. With people like Britva, performing all kinds of black-market services, the camp had a vibrant although undersupplied economy.

After getting myself groomed, I went to meet Aslan.

"You still look like shit, but I guess nothing can be done about it," he said, smiling.

"Yeah, you're right. You're pretty, but sadly too old to grow any taller," I replied, sharing his grin.

He was almost a head shorter than me, but with his barrel chest and thick neck, he carried the posture of a charging bull.

Together, we went to the makeshift exercise area and had a workout. We sparred on the beaten ground beside the pullup bars, and despite my having lost weight during isolation, I was able to take him down a couple of times. He was surprised and told me that the time in solitude made me tougher.

After washing myself in the *banya*, I came back to Barrack 6 and navigated the labyrinth of bunk beds to lay down in my own private space. I wanted to rest before dinner, but Sidoy called my name. He pointed to the curtain-draped exit, indicating he wanted me to accompany him during a walk.

I quickly put on a jacket and hurried behind my mentor who was already stepping outside. I fell by his side wondering what he wanted to talk about, but he just walked slowly towards the double fence line. He took steady steps, with his hands behind his back, head held high, and eyes slowly scanning the Zone.

I glanced at his profile. A strong nose and jaw, cut by a scar that ran from his chin up his cheek. A long white moustache framed his mouth. Even from the side, his eyes drew focus, they were deep green, alert, weighing everything they passed.

We reached the fence, and continued along its length, with the barbed wire to our right. The ground beneath the fences was freshly raked, and I could smell the wet soil.

Sidoy remained silent and I followed without speaking, waiting for him to start. I learned about silence with the old Sidoy, and I had learned to listen.

"Why do you work, Andrycha?" he asked, finally, looking up at the watch-tower we passed.

The guard manning a machine gun up there was smoking a cigarette, and watching us, squinting because of the low-hanging sun.

"Because I am forced to," I replied.

"Is that right? How can you be a *vor* if the state can turn you into a slave?" There was no reprimand in his tone, it felt more like he was explaining something to a child. I was glad we were out of the earshot of the other *blatnye* though.

"I am locked up here, in a forced labor penal colony, and if I don't work, they will make me."

"The state cannot 'make' a *vor* do anything."

"What do you mean?" I asked, confused. "There are *blatnye* in my brigade, even Evgeny is working with us."

"They enjoy their time in the forest. They like the exercise they get from cutting down trees. Ask them, and you will learn their motivation. No *vor* will tell you that the state forced him." He walked along in silence for a moment, then continued. "The reasons why you do things are almost as important as what you do, they define your identity. If you tell yourself that you can be forced to do labor, then you will tell yourself that you can be forced to do other things. Maybe one day they will force you to rat on your brothers or become a *suka*?"

He spat the last word in his usual manner.

I realized at that moment that I never saw Sidoy, or any other senior *vory* working. They just returned to the barracks after the morning roll call. Previously, I assumed that they had some easy work to do in the camp, but then it dawned on me that it must have been part of their unspoken agreement with the camp commander.

I wanted to argue. What he said about choosing the reason for doing something sounded like an excuse, a self-justification. But I remained silent. Already in SIZO I learned that not every fight needs a voice. Sometimes, when a person with authority speaks, it's wiser to hold your tongue and listen. Words can draw blood, but silence keeps you breathing.

I thought about this for a long time later to finally see the point in his words. We do shape ourselves through our thoughts and actions, and it is crucial to keep our identity pure. It might sound far-fetched coming from a criminal, but even in a lawless life there can be honor, and defiance of tyranny. There was a difference between Pilot's gang, and the *blatnye* group led by Sidoy, just like there are many shades of grey between black and white.

When it came to labor, there was a time when no *blatnoy* would lift a finger in the camp, but times had changed, and they adapted. Work was no longer seen as sacrilege, and with the right frame of mind, even participation in outside labor became an act of silent, and sometimes not so silent, rebellion.

I recalled Tsikhiy and his boldness when Ivan Rostovkin tried to bully him. I understood that the mindset which Sidoy described, even if it was an excuse, still defined the lines that should not be crossed.

"Soon you will be baptized, Andrycha," Sidoy continued after a pause.

"We will put ink on your skin. It will become a declaration of who you are, and as you progress through the life of a *vor*, your story, and your identity will be carved into your body. It will tell others who you are, but more importantly it will tell you who you must be. It will guide your thoughts and influence your actions. Either you are what your tattoos say you are, or they will be removed, and you will be cast down. Better make sure in your heart that you're ready for this, otherwise there is still a way for you to back off. Perhaps, we could use another *smotritel.*"

We walked along for a while in silence, as I considered what Sidoy had offered.

In IK-22 each barrack had a *smotritel* – a watcher – appointed by the *vory v zakonye.* The role of these watchers was to keep the other *zeki* in check, and to see if the rules defined by the Thieves' Code were followed. *Smotritel* would also act as an envoy between the men of the Code and the authorities. They were mostly chosen from the regular prisoners, to shield the *vory* from defilement that came from contact with the state and its officials.

The fact that Evgeny, a *vor,* was a *smotritel* in our cell in SIZO was because his predecessor in that place was found out to be a snitch, and the inmates voted in someone they could trust. Evgeny agreed for a short term, but it was a rather exceptional circumstance.

Over the years, I learned that some of the rules of the Code could be circumvented or bent, depending on necessity. The final word always rested on the shoulders of the seniors, the *vory v zakonye.*

Later, I found this flexibility with the rules to be a weakness that was exploited by people who claimed to be *blatnye,* when in reality they knew little of the Code. Without following the laws, they would pretend to be *vory.* It was a way to gain unfounded respect among other criminals.

It became clear later, in the late nineties, when gangsters began buying their crowns and the title *vor v zakonye* – thief-in-law – started to lose its meaning. But back then, in IK-22, the *blatnye* still had integrity. The old ways were mostly upheld, and I was young, eager to belong to that brotherhood.

"No." I suddenly replied, stopping in my tracks. "I want to be a *vor.*"

Sidoy took a step and stopped as well. He turned and faced me for the first time during our conversation.

"So be it," he said, baring his teeth in a wolfish grin as he put a hand on my shoulder, squeezing it in a strong, fatherly gesture.

It was the last day of September when the first snow hit. The temperature had been falling for a week and finally fell below zero. The barracks had to be heated with stoves, which in Barrack 6 was the duty of the *muzhyki* who did most of the work in the building in exchange for protection. Among the *zeki* – prisoners, *muzhyki* – men, were the mass of regular convicts, without any ties to organized crime. Despite being the majority, they were just isolated individuals, and holding no power, remained low in the hierarchy.

Those working for the *vory* had a slightly higher status among the prisoners from other barracks. Some, like the tattoo artist, Sasun, had an even higher standing, and were not delegated to more mundane work like cleaning.

As for me, even though I was not a baptized *vor* yet, I fell somewhere in between. Not a *muzhyk* anymore, but also not a *vor*. That was about to change, and I welcomed the intricate frost designs on the small barrack windows, and the delicate, thin cover of the first snow on the yard and the buildings in the Zone.

The day of the baptism was set, and on that evening, I was ordered to haul water from the *banya* to fill an old barrel, standing outside of the barrack. I was joined by the young *urka* who arrived at IK-22 with me and moved to Barrack 6 on the first night.

His nickname was Lop – Forehead, which he got for headbutting an undercover militsiya man, and dropping him out cold. He was one year older than me and had lost his father in the early stages of the Afghanistan war, when he was still a teenager. His mother tried to keep him out of trouble, but he joined one of Saratov's youth gangs and dealt in petty crime until his incarceration for robbery. He had a rough life, and it turned him into a ruthless and tough man.

Already inculcated into the criminal world at a young age, he felt joining the *vory* was a natural step on the ladder for him, and he treated me with a mix of distrust and disdain, as an outsider, claiming the same status that he craved.

We walked to the *banya*, each of us carrying two buckets. We filled them at the water trough, and began our trip back when Lop sped up, leaving me behind.

I accepted the challenge and with two heavy buckets in my hands I increased my pace, to the point where I was able to avoid spilling any water and still keep just behind him.

Evgeny and Sidoy were sitting outside, leisurely smoking. They had their prison-issue winter jackets on, and *ushankas* – Russian fur hats with earflaps hanging to the sides – on their heads.

Seeing them watching our struggle, I picked up speed and managed to get to the barrel just after Lop finished emptying his buckets into it.

We were both heaving, and despite the cold I could feel sweat running down my forehead. I emptied my buckets and stripped down to my shirt but Lop was already sprinting back to the banya. I ran after him and managed to get ahead. I was faster on my feet, but he was stronger and walked quicker when we carried the water-filled buckets.

We repeated this race five times, before the barrel was filled to the brink. Panting with exertion, we looked at each other with animosity.

"Good job, *patsany*." Sidoy, referred to us affectionately as boys. He came over with a five-kilogram sack of salt and emptied its contents into the barrel. "So, it doesn't freeze overnight," he said. "And the two of you can have a pleasant bath."

I knew what was coming, and I knew it was not necessarily pleasant. The rest of the evening I spent with Evgeny, getting my final instructions, and preparing mentally for the initiation.

The next day, all *blatnye* from Barrack 6 gathered outside around the barrel. There were also a few onlookers from the other barracks, but they stayed at a distance, not wanting to interfere with the *vory* ritual. Even the guards patrolling the Zone that day took a detour, pretending there was something more interesting on the other side of the camp.

Stripped down to our underwear, Lop and I stood in the cold while Sidoy spoke. His voice carried like a judge delivering a sentence. "Lop and Andrycha stand before us, ready to cast off their old lives and take up the Code. But are they worthy of it? Who will speak in their name?"

"I speak for Lop, he is a *vor* at heart, and he completed his prospect task," one of the *blatnye* said out loud.

"I speak for Andrycha, he was of service many times. To me, to Tsikhiy, to the *Bratva*," Evgeny said with a face as solemn as if it was a funeral.

"You will soon say the oath, but first you must show us you can take the pain," Sidoy pronounced.

Before he could give us instructions, I turned around and jumped into the barrel.

The extreme cold shocked my body, and it felt as if my chest was being crushed while at the same time a hundred daggers stabbed at my skin.

I was prepared and I knew what to do. Evgeny told me how to handle the cold, and pain had become a well-known adversary over the previous few months.

I fought the urge to breathe quickly and focused all my willpower on each inhale and exhale. I slowed them down to the point where the initial shock dissipated and it was only me, my breath, and the chill reaching for my bones.

Sidoy was not amused by my hastiness. He walked slowly to the barrel, and put a hand on my head, pushing me down under the water.

I took a quick breath before my head became submerged, and the cold assaulted it like a heavyweight boxer.

Sidoy held me down, and I felt an impulse to stand up. I knew it would be taken as a sign of weakness, so with closed eyes, I suffered in the cold, dark void of my mind, to the sound of my increasing heartbeat.

Finally, the hand was removed from my head, and I rose, gasping for air. I got out of the barrel and stood again in front of the *blatnye*. My body was cloaked in steam from the water that clung to my skin, while my breath turned into a white mist.

"Repeat after me," Sidoy said.

I straightened up and took control of my shaking body.

"I am a *vor*." Sidoy's deep voice boomed among the assembly.

I repeated, feeling the new identity growing roots in my mind.

"I reject the state and the society which would chain me like a slave. I swear loyalty to the *vory*, and to the Code. I will accept no authority, except that of a senior *vor v zakonye*. I do not fear pain, I do not fear death. I will never cooperate with the state and I will always help a *vor* in need."

When I spoke the last words of the oath, Sidoy stepped forward and pulled me into a rough embrace. His voice was low. "Welcome to the *Bratva*. You're one of us now, Andrycha. Follow the Code and never falter."

A strange sense of heat rose inside of me, and I felt my body warming up. Perhaps it was Sidoy's embrace, but there was also something deeper, a new fire stoked in me on that day.

Sidoy released his embrace, and I was allowed to put on my clothes.

The same process was repeated for Lop, although Sidoy didn't hold his head down for so long. I later learned that it was Lop who was supposed to plunge in the barrel first, and I stepped out of line by seizing the initiative and submerging myself.

For that Sidoy tested me with additional harshness.

After the oath was finished, we went inside, and Sasun applied the first prison ink to my body. I got stars tattooed on my knees as a sign that I would never kneel for the fake authorities of the state. The monastery wall on my right hand, with a stretch of barbed wire, and a single small tower with an Orthodox cross told the story of my incarceration in IK-22.

As the years passed, Sasun would add towers with cupolas to the monastery, and spikes to the barbed wire, marking the full years of my term that I spent locked up.

On my left hand, the Grim Reaper, with words "I am here, and I am waiting," symbolized my willingness to spill blood. It was also a reminder that I didn't take Ivan's life, and that the two of us would still face the final verdict of the Grim Reaper one day.

Young, and immersed in the *vory* culture, I was eager to get tattoos on my hands, including various rings. These became a telltale sign of a *blatnoy* wherever I went and brought both respect and hatred in the Zone and later, outside.

Later that night, I would smell the blood seeping from my fresh tattoos, and I thought it carried an odor of sulfur. I was slipping into hell, the place that wanted me to accept the fire as my new home and trade my soul for blazing darkness. The realization terrified me, but I had to accept my reality and my new role in it – at least outwardly. As the fresh pain pulsated under my skin, I kept repeating the Jesus Prayer, to hold on to at least a broken shard of who I was before.

CHAPTER 5

Don't Abandon Hope, Even When Falling

The brief snow melted a few days later, and we were then subjected to a harsh, chilly, and wet autumn, preceding an even harsher, freezing winter. The only good thing about the onset of cold was that the mosquitoes were gone, but it was a minor relief compared to the constant fight against the unforgiving weather.

The days were getting shorter, and morning roll calls took place under black skies, with floodlights washing the assembly ground in harsh white light. We stood rocking on our feet with shoulders drawn in and hands clenched inside our sleeves, as the moisture-laden chill seeped in under the layers of our *zek* uniforms. In a way, these chilly roll calls were worse than the ice bath I had to endure. The barrel plunge was a shock, but it struck once and released you. This other cold was relentless, chewing deep into the body, biting at my toes and fingers, numbing them long before we were finally sent off to work.

Moving helped, and as soon as we were in the forest, I worked hard with my axe to get the blood flowing and to keep my body warm. During breaks, we huddled around the campfires, and drank hot tea prepared by Artyom for both *zeki* and guards out in the work area.

I didn't envy the guards, especially those on lone patrols or manning the watchtowers. Even with their sheepskin jackets and warm gloves, it must still have been miserable to do their duty. In a way, it pleased me to know they were suffering too. Mother Nature, like true justice, was blind to whom she touched with her hand.

It was also a time when many of us, both *zeki* and the guards, succumbed to various cold-related ailments. Hundreds were affected by bronchitis and were coughing, sneezing, and fighting a fever. The camp authorities didn't care, and unless someone was delirious, they would still be sent out to work, which for too many invariably led to pneumonia and in rare cases death. But as long as *zeki* were not dropping dead in large numbers, Koralov and other bureaucrats turned a blind eye.

It was on one of those days in October that I met a person whose impact on my life is great to this day. A person whose friendship was among the few genuine ones I built as I travelled along my path.

It was a Sunday, and I was inside the barrack, sitting by the stove to warm myself up. I was down with a mild fever, and I had shivers all over my body.

Evgeny approached me with an unusual look of excitement painted across his face.

"Andrycha," he said with his eyes gleaming. "I need you to come with me to the library."

"Can it wait? I don't feel like writing another letter right now."

"There's no time, we have to go now." He urged me. "I'll explain on the way."

I stood up reluctantly, feeling a bit lightheaded, and I followed him outside.

There was an even grey ceiling of clouds over the Zone which had been the source of a steady drizzle for the past few days.

I cursed the weather and put on my hat.

Evgeny kept prodding me to move faster, while he told me what it was all about.

It was visiting day, and every *zek* who hadn't lost his privileges was allowed one visit per quarter. Just as he did with packages, Evgeny used my name as a stand-in to get an extra person to visit him. He didn't tell me beforehand, because he didn't know if they would come, but now both of us had been called in.

"It is not an easy matter. Many palms had to be greased, but now I will be able to see both my wife and my daughter," he said as we approached the library building.

There were convoy guards with rifles stationed outside, their sour faces with rain dripping off their long raincoats told their own story.

I shivered as we passed them. Partly from cold, partly from the thought of what they would do to me if they knew I stabbed Ivan.

We entered and came to a desk where our names were checked against the visitor list. After signing the list, we were subjected to a cursory search by a couple of guards. They pointed us in the direction of the *svidanka* – the visiting room.

On our way, we passed Ziya. It was the first time I met him since the day of the card game where I was tricked into owing money to Pilot.

My former comrade was walking along the hallway with a handful of papers and a pencil stuck behind his ear. His sharp, hazel eyes scanned me, and his round face flinched minimally when he saw the tattoos on my hands. He darted into one of the small rooms where the clerks and accountants worked.

I chuckled, thinking that he reminded me of a weasel. I felt an impulse to go inside and mess with him, but Evgeny urged me to the *svidanka*.

It was a long room, with a divider wall of wood and plexiglass in the middle. There were rows of eight chairs on both sides of the wall, and holes drilled into the plexiglass to allow communication. A single guard watched over the room with a bored expression on his face. When he saw us, he gave a little nod to Evgeny and pointed to a couple of women sitting on the opposite side.

"I will talk to Matryona first, you sit with my daughter," Evgeny explained quickly, "We'll switch afterwards."

I did as he said and I sat in front of the cloudy and scratched plexiglass. The chair was a simple wooden thing, uncomfortable, and creaking as I shifted on it.

On the other side was a woman in her twenties, with a round face, and a rounder belly. She was dressed in a simple brown dress, and her blond hair was tied in a braid. She had full, reddish cheeks, and her skin was clean and smooth like silk.

It felt surreal to see a woman after several months of incarceration. Almost as if she was a creature from a fantasy land, an angel that came down to the abyss to shine light on the dwellers of darkness.

We introduced ourselves, and I had to lean in to hear her through the small holes in the divider. She said to call her Lyuda, short for Lyudmila.

I was so flustered that I forgot my tongue after the introduction. She helped me, and carried on the conversation, asking me where I was from, and what I was doing before the prison. I told her my back story, and then I looked at her belly.

"When are you expecting the young one?"

"December," she replied.

"Got some names in mind?"

"Roman."

"What if it is a girl?"

"It will be a boy," she said as if the matter was already settled and I smiled at her response.

It was obvious that she hadn't got an ultrasound to figure it out, as at that time in the USSR, they were rare and expensive. She had the simple conviction of a rural woman, and I knew from Evgeny that his family lived in a village not far from Kiev.

We exchanged a few more comments about the weather, and I asked her about life in Ukraine. She said it was getting harder, and that some hoped that Gorbachev would turn things around.

Our conversation was interrupted then, as Evgeny's wife, Matryona, came over and nudged Lyuda to change seats.

I peeked at the guard, but he was blatantly looking the other way.

Matryona sat in front of me, and I had a chance to take a closer look at the woman to whom I had been writing love letters for the past few months.

She looked like a mature version of her daughter, but her face was tighter, her eyes sharper, and the first wrinkles were already carved into the corner of her eyes. She wore a light-green woolen sweater with a long black frock underneath. Her hair was covered with a navy-blue scarf on which were flower motifs, and a large cross hung in full display over the front of her buttoned-up frock.

"*Privet*, Andrycha," she said, smiling warmly. "We finally meet!"

That smile, and the kindness that poured out of her, reminded me of Mam, and I felt a lump in my throat. For some reason I suddenly felt ashamed of being locked up and of all the foolishness I got myself into since my mother's death.

"*Dobry den – Good day*," I replied simply, unable to gather my thoughts.

"Thank you for the letters," she said. "You know, you're exactly how I imagined you, I could see you behind your words."

"How did you know it was not Evgeny?"

"Oh, I know my husband. He can write down a to-do list with three items. I know he has a big heart, but you helped him when the words wouldn't come. It was a gift to receive those letters."

I felt myself blushing. It was almost too much for me. Even though the praise felt good, it also touched the parts of me that I had buried deep down in order to survive in prison and become a *vor*.

"You're a good person, in the wrong place. But it will pass," she said, seeing my reaction.

"How do you know?"

"I know, I know." She smiled with assurance. "God builds a path for each of us."

"Perhaps I landed in the right place then."

"I see more than any other woman," she said, squinting and leaning closer. "And I see that you're not well. Not in your soul, and not in your body."

"The weather is shit," I said, and bit my tongue for cussing. I muttered a short apology. "Everyone is catching colds these days."

"Yes, I can do something about that. I will get you good medicine, something that will help you through the winter, and will keep you strong."

"How? We won't be allowed any packages until next year."

"Good that visiting is still allowed, a true blessing, don't you think?" She smiled again, and there were such a strong faith and conviction in her words, that I couldn't help myself but sense some form of hope. "I am not going back to Ukraine. I have found a place nearby in Old Iskitim. I can practice my craft there and stay close to my husband. We will find a way to get you men all you need. And perhaps we'll figure out how to shorten your sentences too. Now that would be good, wouldn't it?"

"Of course," I mumbled, not knowing what to make of what she said. I was just at the beginning of my twelve-year stretch, and after joining the *vory*, my chances of parole were rather slim.

"I already talked to Evgeny about it. I'll prepare something to keep you strong and healthy in the winter. Look for St. Andrew's cross in the forest."

I gave her a questioning look, but she mused on something for a while, and then said, “As for your soul? Keep faith, Andrycha, don’t lose yourself, and one day the light will come back. “

The guard, sitting against the wall, cleared his throat loudly.

I looked at the clock hanging on the wall. An hour has passed since we entered, and I was surprised that time could fly by so fast.

The visit was over, and I bid farewell to Matryona. Soon, I was about to find out how resourceful Evgeny’s wife was. It still amazes me when I think about what lengths she would go to help her husband, and to be finally reunited with him.

But most importantly for me at that point, her words struck a hopeful chord for me and became a lifeline to which I held on to in the dark years of imprisonment. While on the one hand I built my identity as a *vor*, on the other, I kept the tiny flame of my former self flickering in the corner of my soul.

There is no better place to understand how to become successful and rich than in prison. Why Prison? If it works here, it works anywhere, trust me. It is a place of realists.

Here it shows you how strong you are. You can’t hide behind money, police, or friends. Here is how you go from zero to a hundred no matter if inside or outside of prison. Business is business.

Step 1: If you have nothing, first get a skill. A high-income skill. In prison these are: medical skills, cutting hair, fixing clothes, or technology. In real life this is a skill that pays 100 Dollars per hour and more. Take six months to learn minimum two hours every fucking day.

Step 2: Now you have money coming in. Most fools now buy a better life. In Russian prisons people get extra ration of bread, cigarettes or even worse

– drugs. Stupid. No matter how much money you make, stay humble, save your money. I give you a number: save 55% of what you make. Then go to step 3.

Step 3: Multiply. You will never get rich if you trade time for money. Remember that. You get rich when you multiply your time WITH money.

In prison the smart zeks buy more tools, more supplies, more connections. They turn one haircut into a barber shop crew. You understand?

And of course you build a team who have your back. Yes, there are still good people out there, trust me.

Step 4: Now it gets very boring, but this is where the money is. Invest into compounding assets with leverage. What does that mean? Compounding assets are things that become more valuable over time. Like real estate, gold, silver, platinum. Not your TV, new car, or phone.

Leverage means: you use the money you have now to easily get more money in the future. Prison shows how capitalism works.

It is called the "store man". A prisoner who bulk-buys commissary like ramen, tushonka, mackerel, coffee, or cigarettes. He then loans it to the broke ones who need it now. They borrow one can. They need to pay back tomorrow double the price.

The store man takes payback, buys more bulk, loans more out. This is the raw, cold game of capitalism.

In regular life do not go with this dishonorable shit. This is for Suki.

Buy real estate in places with low taxes. Rent it out to good people at decent prices. Good people and decent prices will give you a better, more steady income stream than overcharging broke people.

Honor makes you more money in the long run than dishonor.

And remember this *droog*, every century a major monetary system gets reset. That means only those people with hard assets like real estate will have something left. Everyone else's money, stocks, bonds will be devalued, they will be stolen. Look at history. And look into the future.

Grim times are coming.

Embracing my new criminal identity was not just about brotherhood, learning thieves' argot, or tattoos. I was now surrounded by people for whom stealing and violence were as natural as eating and shitting, without shame or second thoughts. Their hatred and rejection of the state went much deeper than anything I ever felt as an idealistic, and rebellious boy in the GDR.

Anyone who was not a *blatnoy*, or an *urka* – a young thug – was seen as a willing slave of the system. The *muzhyki*, with rare exceptions, were kept at a distance. They weren't despised like the *suki, kozly,* or *petukhi* – roosters, but seen as passive, and not players in the criminal game.

Among them, the political prisoners, or *politicheskiye*, were held in contempt. They were perceived as the fallen servants of the state. Once the oppressors, now the victims, which made them not only despicable, but also weak. This was of course an unfair characterization, as many of the 'politicals' were locked without any prior engagement with the state, simply for being in opposition to it, just like the *vory*. But the prejudice was there, and like it usually is, it was not based on reason.

As much as I felt some pity for the *muzhyki* who had to obey the rules of the criminals running the prison, I also knew where my loyalty was. It was not the individualized and scattered regular prisoners, with their meek politeness and dreams of equality who paid my debt to Pilot. The food smuggled to my isolation cell didn't come from them. With their lack of rules and organization, they were powerless and unable to protect themselves or others. Compared with that, the Code and Brotherhood I received from the *blatnye* were gifts. But the Code had to be embodied through action, and the Brotherhood upheld through obedience to the rules and hierarchy of the *Bratva*.

I did my part, and when Sidoy asked for something to be done, I asked only: when?

Small and big sins accumulated on my conscience in IK-22. Some I remember to this day; some became so commonplace that they were blended into a general feeling of darkness that rose within me with each passing day in lockup.

The first time I acted as an enforcer for the *Bratva* was on the day after Tsikhiy returned to the camp. He had spent weeks in the closed ward of a hospital in Novosibirsk, recovering from the gruesome wounds he inflicted on himself to defy Ivan and the other guards.

All the *blatnye* got off their bunks to greet him, as he entered the barrack and raised his left arm in a mock salute. His hand was gone. The forearm ended in a pink stump, with wrinkled scars running halfway to the elbow.

Fresh *chifir* was brewed, with extra sugar, and we sat around Tsikhiy to listen to his stories from the outside. He'd always had a low, raspy voice, but now it was rougher still, as if he'd endured far more than an amputation. His deep-set, brown eyes sat beneath dark, furrowed brows, and were ringed with heavy shadows. He looked like a ghost coming back to tell the tales of the afterlife.

His recount of the events outside was as bleak as anything in the Zone.

Ivan Rostovkin landed in the same hospital a couple of weeks after him. Tsikhiy had learned that from the *militsiya* men who came to investigate the assault on Ivan. Despite his state, Tsikhiy had been subjected to an enhanced interrogation and denied painkillers for several days, which he described with a chuckle as 'the kind of unending torture that makes you pray for sleep, even the final one'.

Such was the sense of humor among the *vory*.

I didn't laugh though. Instead, I felt a knot forming in my stomach when I heard that the investigation into Ivan's stabbing reached even Tsikhiy in the hospital. In a way I passed my initiation, but I also put a target on my back, which I felt haunting me during all my years in IK-22.

As for Tsikhiy, the *vory* welcomed him back, without pity or pretense, but a new aura of almost saintly martyrdom surrounded him now. He was already a *vor v zakonye*, but with the newly gained status, he rose in hierarchy to become the second only to Sidoy. That is why when he asked me to join him to collect his tax from the politicals, I didn't ask any questions.

In IK-22 we had a bunch of former party members who had fallen out of grace for one or other reason. Tsikhiy made it his mission to show them their place in the Zone, and he demanded a regular 'tribute' almost like a feudal lord of his peasants. When he landed in the hospital, the tribute stopped coming. Perhaps the peasants hoped their lord would not return. But he did, and he wanted what he felt he was owed.

You might think that he took me with him because he was a cripple without a hand, and he wanted a younger, fit, and eager brother by his side to protect him. Trust me *droog*, Tsikhiy was as dangerous as they came, and even with only one hand he could deliver a lot of harm. But he was now too high in the hierarchy to dirty his hands with the common *zeki*.

There was something else he had learned about me that made him choose me as his bodyguard.

"Sidoy told me it was you who handled Ivan Rostovkin." His voice creaked in a raspy whisper as we walked through the camp yard. "You did a good job, like a real *torpeda*," he said, slapping the palm of his right hand into the pink stump. *Torpeda* – torpedo – was a word we used for a hitman.

I didn't say anything, only blew my runny nose on the ground. As much as I accepted what I did, and what I was becoming, I wasn't exactly proud of it. I just hoped I wouldn't have to stain my hands with blood again, at least not so soon.

As if reading my mind, Tsikhiy added, "You don't have to be so rough with the *muzhyki*, they fall in line rather easily. But they should know their place."

I nodded and we walked on to find the first victim sitting in the communal area of Barrack 10. The guy was of average height, with a round belly, full cheeks, and neatly trimmed moustache. His name was Kovalchuk, and he used to be a director of a coal mine in the Donbas region.

He was playing chess at the common table with another inmate. The chessboard was made from two old planks, the squares carved with a knife and painted with soot. The wooden pieces were small and made with clear craftsmanship, most likely by a skilled *zek* inside the camp.

The other inmates got out of our way, as we approached the table. The two players raised their heads, but seeing us, they immediately lowered their eyes. It was not smart for a *muzhyk* to stare a *vor* in the eyes.

Tsikhiy didn't say anything, just extended his remaining hand towards Kovalchuk in a demanding gesture.

The former director scrambled to his bunk, and brought back a half bar of soap, and a pouch of dried apples, which Tsikhiy swiftly placed in his pocket. He then extended his hand again, demanding more.

"I have nothing more, Tsikhiy," Kovalchuk said, his eyes going wide and his voice as remorseful as a sinner confessing some grave misconduct. "The packages are not coming. We all barely get by here."

"Andrycha," Tsikhiy said. "Check his pockets."

I hesitated. I wasn't used to manhandling others. Tsikhiy must have noticed. He grabbed me by the arm, and I turned to him. A command was clearly written on his face, but when he spoke, his words were directed at Kovalchuk.

"Tell Andrycha why you're here, comrade Kovalchuk."

"Criminal negligence, but I was innocent!" the former director exclaimed.

"He pocketed money by signing off fake technical inspection papers." Tsikhiy drawled his words, while his eyes burned like two coals in a fire pit. "Five miners were injured in an explosion caused by a malfunctioning ventilation system. One of them got blinded. Do you think this corrupt dirtbag deserves your pity more than them?"

"They framed me," Kovalchuk protested. "They needed a scapegoat!"

A sudden surge of disgust and anger made me clench my jaw. I knew these sleazy types. I had met some on my black-market escapade with Ziya. Factory managers selling equipment stolen from the plants, foreman neglecting their duty and safety rules to skim off some falsely accounted overhead. Greedy and cowardly, they would embezzle funds with one hand, while writing anonymous denunciation letters against their political rivals with the other.

I didn't care if Kovalchuk was guilty of that specific charge or not. His attitude and body language screamed of an opportunist and a fraudster. I spun and slapped him hard to the side of the head. He fell, holding on to his ear, but he didn't make a sound.

"Turn out your pockets," I ordered.

He did as commanded, and I collected a pack of Belomorkanal cigarettes that he handed me from one of his pockets. The others were empty.

I looked back at Tsikhiy, but he didn't seem to be satisfied. His gaze landed on the chessboard. I swept the pieces off and packed them together with the wooden board. As Kovalchuk was rising, massaging the side of his neck, we left the barrack to continue the collection trip through the Zone.

We visited a dozen other politicals that evening. Tsikhiy made it easier by telling me their charges as we made the rounds. They were all embezzlers, career-ladder climbers, and former apparatchiks whom he targeted as his feudal peasants. We collected a good amount of *obshchak* tax that day, and I didn't hesitate anymore.

Adaptability is the great gift of the human species. We can survive anywhere; we can get used to anything. But this trait can also cost us everything, rob us of our morals, values and what makes us human in the first place.

CHAPTER 6

Those Who Keep Peace Can Make War

Becoming Tsikhiy's enforcer brought me recognition. Among the zeki my name began to carry weight, and I got new tattoos that told stories of violence and loyalty. I was rising within the *blatnye* ranks and with that came a deeper understanding of the power *vory* held over the camp.

The hierarchy inside IK-22 was clear, and all the *zeki* fell in line rather easily, while the guards turned the other way whenever thieves' business was conducted. In turn the *vory* kept peace inside the Zone, and we enforced the laws based on the Thieves Code.

You might think: what laws could there be among the lawless?

I tell you *droog*, there were many, and as much as the Thieves would exploit other prisoners, they also made sure that there was fairness in the Zone.

Words had to be kept, debts had to be paid, and a man's possessions and standing were protected. Disputes were judged, and infringements punished. As paradoxical as it may sound, the *vory* were considered the most honest arbiters of justice in the Zone.

The Pilot's gang at that time was also influential, but their power was purely economic. They ran the trade with the outside world and kept a cozy relationship with the guards. For that they were regarded as traitors by the *vory*, but to keep peace, both groups stayed away from each other. In the end, the guards, the Pilot's gang, and the *vory* all had something to gain from the status quo.

This uneasy balance, upheld inside the Zone by the Thieves' Code, was known as Vorovskoi Mir – which in Russian means both the Thieves' Peace, and Thieves' World. The *vory*, seen as guardians of the law, held sway among the petty criminal population. As much as they kept order and enforced their rules, they could as easily introduce chaos and retaliate if they were pressed too hard. Ivan's story was an example – touch us, and you will pay, no matter who you are.

Because of this, the *vory* were granted a fair deal of autonomy. Old Major Koralov understood the value of letting us police our own. I witnessed many incidents where guards would leave us be, despite clear breach of the official camp rules. But sometimes things got out of hand, and the fragile peace was put under pressure.

One such incident I remember clearly. What happened that day made me realize just how much power the *vory* had in our black prison. And how quickly it could spiral out of control.

It was early November, and the snow finally settled over Western Siberia, announcing a long, unforgiving winter. Tired after a workday, I was warming up by the stove in Barrack 6 or the Sixth as we called it. We kept the windows shut for winter, as the small metal stove was barely enough to keep the place from freezing. The sound of coughing, grunting and whispered curses filled the stuffy air. The dinner that day was meager, and we shared canned sardines bought in the commissary with the money from the *obshchak* – the common fund of the *Bratva*.

My nose was running like a shower, and I had to use an old shirt as a wipe to keep it from dripping all over me. Seeing me sniveling and wrapped in a blanket, Evgeny came over and squatted beside me.

"Matryona will get us some remedies," he said. "She knows how to cure everything from blisters to diarrhea."

"How? We don't get packages." I asked, miserably.

"Don't worry, *bratan*. I had a word with her during the last visit. We'll get a delivery straight into our work zone."

I wanted to ask for details, but just then the barrack door burst open and a gust of freezing wind swept in with Kamen, Aslan, and another man who looked familiar. I recognized him at once. It was the *kozel* from the Eleventh, the one who had questioned me when I moved in with the *vory*.

Kamen went to fetch Sidoy, while I wanted to greet Aslan, but Evgeny held me back.

"He'll face a hearing, your friend." Evgeny said, quietly. "Stay away from it for now. Let Sidoy decide."

"A hearing? What are you talking about?"

"Kostik accused Aslan of stealing his food. Your friend wouldn't have it and started a fight. They had to be separated. The *smotritel* from their barrack called Kamen to resolve the dispute."

"Why did no one tell me about it?" I clenched my jaw in anger, feeling betrayed.

"He's your friend. You would want to protect him, but we must keep the rules."

I swallowed a curse. Evgeny was right; I would do what I could to protect Aslan. But if he was guilty, my involvement would undermine the authority of the *blatnye* in IK-22. The *zeki* believed that, despite their predatory nature, *avtoritety* – criminal authorities – kept their word and were just. This made the *vory* not only feared but also respected, and allowed them to run the Zone inside the barbed wire.

Reluctantly, I faded into the crowd and watched.

Aslan and the other guy, Kostik, were led before the table, where Sidoy, Tsikhiy, and Kamen presided.

Sidoy sat with one arm resting across the table, the other holding a half-smoked cigarette between yellowed fingers. Smoke curled upward like a slow-moving spirit, filling the barrack with the scent of cheap tobacco and incoming judgment.

"Speak," Sidoy said flatly, not lifting his eyes from the cigarette.

Kostik stepped forward first. His voice was shaky, but loud enough:

"He stole my bread and half a tin of *tushonka*. I left it by my bunk before heading to the latrine. When I came back, it was gone. No one else was nearby, and the *smotritel* found my can, emptied, under the Chechen's blanket."

Aslan didn't flinch, but I could see his nostrils flaring with each heavy, restrained breath. He cast a furious glance at his accuser before looking Sidoy in the eyes.

"I didn't touch his food." He spoke with a voice trembling with anger. "I don't even pass near his bunk. I had my evening prayers outside. He must have planted the can under my blanket then."

"Do you have any witnesses?" Sidoy asked.

Aslan shook his head.

"I asked around in the Eleventh," Kamen said. "No one saw anything. Their *smotritel* told me the barrack was empty when he came back from dinner. He found the can under Aslan's blanket."

Sidoy put out the cigarette, and his brow furrowed. A group of four young *urki* gathered to the side. They held towels with rocks wrapped inside. Punishment awaited the perpetrator, a bloody example for the others.

The room fell silent, even the stove crackled more quietly. I realized that whatever Sidoy said next would decide whether Aslan walked away or didn't.

But Sidoy was taking his time, drilling his eyes into both the accused and the accuser. Meanwhile, Tsikhiy leaned in and whispered something in Kamen's ear.

"Was there a guard on patrol while you were praying?" Kamen asked Aslan.

"Yes!" Aslan exclaimed. "The Estonian, Tamm, would have seen me."

Sidoy looked at Kamen. Kamen gave a subtle nod and stepped out. We waited, with whispers and tension rising in the crowd. A few minutes later, Kamen returned with a tall *zek* with sunken cheeks – one of Kostik's barracks mates.

"I spoke to the guard," Kamen said. "And I brought this one with me to act as witness. Tell them what the guard said."

The small guy stuttered but finally spoke. "You asked the guard if he saw anyone in the yard."

"What did the guard say?" Kamen prompted the little man impatiently.

"The guard said he saw the Chechen praying out in the exercise area after dinner."

The whispers rose. Aslan sighed with relief, while Kostik shifted on his feet looking around nervously.

"False accusation?" Tsikhiy said in a low, rasping voice, like a barbed wire scratching on steel. "Trying to stain a man's name. That's a serious offense, even if you're just dumb and not a *suka*."

"I didn't lie!" Kostik exclaimed. "The can was under his blanket! Will you trust a guard on this?"

A few voices of support rose among the men. I heard a whisper about "dirty Chechen", and I saw Aslan's body tighten.

Sidoy raised a hand, silencing the crowd. Then he smiled, as if he found an answer to a particularly difficult puzzle.

"I can spot a liar, Kostik. Now, will you tell us the truth?" Sidoy's deep voice came almost friendly, as if he were going to reprimand a wayward child.

Instead of answering, Kostik wrapped his hands together, pleading. "Please, I didn't mean to. It's just a mistake, that's all."

"Yes, you made a mistake by falsely accusing another prisoner. You're lucky this didn't go to the guards. We wouldn't be letting you go off so easily if it did. Now it is time to pay the price!" Sidoy's voice roared with judgment as he suddenly rammed his fist into the table, making Kostik jump.

To his side, Tsikhiy gave a sign to the four *urki* with the towels.

Kostik's eyes widened in panic and he bolted towards the exit. Byk, who as always sat by the entryway, grabbed him, as the little guy tried to squeeze past. Kostik squealed like a pig about to be slaughtered, but the doorman held him in an iron grip and dragged him back.

"No, you can't do this, who do you think you are?" Kostik screamed.

"What a weasel," Kamen said. "Give him a good one, he deserves it."

Byk threw Kostik to the floor like a sack of grain, then four *blatnye* with rocks wrapped in their towels began working on him. Kostik kicked and wriggled around at first, but as the blows fell one by one, he cowered his head and folded himself into a fetal position. The screams continued though, mixed with shouting of the angered crowd. I almost felt sorry for him. If not for the fact that if his false accusation had stuck, it would be Aslan paying that price.

It must have been Kostik's desperate screams that drew in the young guard – Tamm. No one heard him approach, as the shouting had drowned out the sound of the outer door creaking open. The doorman was distracted by the action inside and didn't spot Tamm until it was too late.

"What is this, what are you doing to him you monsters?" Tamm yelled, getting everyone's attention. "Stop it right now!"

All the faces turned towards him, and the silence that fell over Barrack 6 told a tale of broken decorum. Only Kostik kept whimpering, and as the beating subsided, he crawled to Tamm and grabbed him by the leg.

"They are murdering me here, comrade!" he cried out.

"You're getting what you deserve, *suka*!" Someone in the crowd uttered.

“Leave him to us, chief,” Kamen spoke calmly as he approached the guard. “This is *vory* business, not yours.”

“You can’t do this.” Tamm’s voice cracked as he raised his rifle with shaking hands and pale eyes darting between the crowd. ”Please, stop,” he pleaded.

He must have been frightened to the bone, but I must admit, he had balls to stand there and make demands while surrounded by wolves in their den.

I saw Evgeny slipping through the shadows by the wall, and realizing what he was about to do, I stepped forward and joined Kamen.

“Comrade Tamm. This is not what you think. This *mudak* lied about something important. No one is going to kill him, but he must be punished.” I raised my hands and spoke slowly, with a calm voice. I wanted to make the guard relax and give Evgeny time to get behind him.

“You’re one of them,” Tamm said, noticing my tattoos.

“That I am,” I replied and stepped towards him, “But you’re not the one who would pull the trigger.”

Our eyes locked and I could see my old self in his. I saw the naïve border guard, as I was in the past, someone who refused to shoot his comrade, because he believed in doing the right thing.

“Just take it easy, Tamm.” I said softly and it seemed to work as Tamm lowered his rifle.

I smiled reassuringly and made a step forward with my hands raised hoping to deescalate the situation, while Evgeny crept up behind the guard.

Kostik whimpered loudly on the floor.

“Mraz, be quiet,” someone behind me spat and Tamm’s eyes began darting to the sides once more. Suddenly, as if the fear came back rushing to his head, he pointed the gun at me again.

I heard it then. The familiar scraping of the AKMs safety lever, and the click when he drove it down. His finger then slipped down and curled on the trigger.

"Everyone get back or I will shoot!" he yelled, his voice breaking.

I froze and heard others behind me shuffling backwards. This was getting out of hand. I made eye contact with Evgeny who was now behind Tamm. At this point it was no longer a disagreement. We had a live weapon pointed at us, and everyone knew what came next. Not only Tamm had interfered with business in our barrack, but he also threatened our lives. It was a breach of *Vorovskoi Mir* and now we had to deal with him.

"Come," the young guard said to Kostik, and grabbed him by the collar.

For a moment he relaxed his trigger finger, but it was enough. Evgeny yanked the AKM up and back, wrenching it free before the boy could even react.

Several of us jumped forward. In a matter of seconds, the guard was on the floor, disarmed, and held down by four men. I kept one hand on his mouth, preventing him from calling for help. He looked at me with eyes bulging with terror as I brought a finger to my lips, showing him to keep quiet.

"Kamen, go and ask for Major Koralov," Sidoy commanded. "We need to fix this before more shit rains."

The final roll-call of the day was approaching fast. We had very little time to defuse the situation. As Kamen hurried to the guard house to request Major Koralov's presence, several others and I went to the barracks to gather the lower-ranking criminals for a silent show of force.

When Koralov finally arrived, marching under the escort of ten armed guards and Captain Svietlov at his side, there was a small crowd gathered outside of the Sixth. All the *blatnye* and the inmates from our barrack stood outside. Off to the side, the thugs from other buildings formed a wide, loose, but still menacing corridor through which the guards had to pass. It was a clear show of strength, and a warning meant to frame the negotiations.

Koralov entered the building with Svietlov, and one other guard, leaving the rest of his AKM-wielding entourage outside. There was no need for many spectators.

Inside, only a few of us remained: Sidoy, Tsikhiy, and Kamen, to talk, and me to keep Tamm under control. The young guard had calmed down by now and was sitting on a chair with his hands tied behind him. His unloaded rifle, with the bolt locked back, and magazine out was laid out on the ground in front of him.

"What the hell is this?" Svietlov asked angrily, looking at me.

I kept one hand on Tamm's shoulder, and I could feel him flinch at his superior's voice.

Koralov cleared his throat and turned to Svietlov with a flat face and an unexpectedly sharp gaze. Svietlov's lips turned into a pale line as he swallowed his outrage and followed his commander's lead. Koralov moved to the table, and Svietlov followed reluctantly. The way they took their seats spoke volumes. The old major dropped into the chair, making it creak as he spread his legs, and rested his intertwined fingers on top of his round stomach. Svietlov, on the other hand, lowered himself slowly onto the wooden chair, back straight, eyes locked on us, gleaming with anger.

The seniors of the vory sat across the table with the highest prison officers, like leaders of the two Cold War nations at the brink of a nuclear exchange.

"Well, comrades? What do we have here?" The old major leaned back in the chair and folded his arms. "Assault on a prison officer."

"There was a misunderstanding," Kamen said. "We were dealing with a liar, who falsely accused one of his mates of stealing. Justice was being served when your man barged in and saw more than he should have. We took his rifle and calmed him down. No harm done."

"Justice!?" Svietlov scoffed. "You mean extortion racket?"

"Comrade Captain!" Koralov called his second in command to order. His voice was calm, almost bored, but carried the authority of a seasoned Soviet officer.

Svietlov's face went red, he clenched his jaw but backed down. The air in the room grew heavier.

"If we hadn't dealt with this," Kamen continued. "There would have been blood, and more problems for you to handle. Instead, you've got peace in the Zone, and your guard is safe and sound, not a hair missing from his head."

"This comes soon after private Rostovkin was gravely injured on a patrol. We are still looking for the perpetrator," Koralov's eyes narrowed, going over the *vory* present in the room. When they reached me, I felt a sharp pang of guilt in my stomach. Did he know? Has someone ratted already? Being involved in an incident with another guard might have put the spotlight on me. I strained myself to keep the poker face.

Then, Tsikhiy shifted in his chair and placed his left forearm on the stained, wooden tabletop. The pink scars drew Koralov's eyes away from me.

"We wish comrade Rostovkin a swift recovery," Kamen said. "But as you see, we have also suffered here."

"Right. Still, someone must pay for this," Koralov spoke, pursing his lips. He looked sideways at Tamm and me. "I can't let it slide."

"Yes, you can," Sidoy put his tattooed hands on the table, his voice carried deep and steady like a distant thunder. Everyone's attention fixed on the gray-haired *vor v zakonye*. "We had enough *shmony*, and interrogations after Rostovkin's accident. You took the packages away. The Zone is not happy. The *urki* are waiting for a reason to start a riot. Look outside. It would take one word to break them loose. No one wants that. Take your comrade and let it go."

Svietlov's face turned from red to crimson. If he could have his way, he would have put an iron fist on us all, but that would only lead to widespread bloodshed and chaos. Koralov knew that, and he looked up at the ceiling, as if weighing the costs.

"Comrade Tamm," he said out loud, "What happened here?"

"I heard screams from the outside. It sounded like someone was being butchered. I came in, and these monsters–"

"No comrade," Koralov interrupted him. "What happened is that you came into the barrack, and you slid on a wet floor. You banged your head and dropped your rifle. The *zeki* helped you up, and they asked me to talk with them, to clarify the situation."

Tamm's youthful face drooped in resignation. He looked as if his ideals were torn out of his hand, and his faith in Soviet justice was shattered.

"Do you understand?" Koralov asked slowly, looking directly at him.

"Yes, comrade Major," he uttered.

"Well. No harm done." Koralov stood. "The boy learned something today. Everyone back to their posts, we still have a roll call to do before we close this day."

As the guards left the barrack, I watched them, feeling relief. Each of them had a different story painted on their face. Tamm looked gutted, with a head hanging low while Koralov seemed unperturbed, and perhaps even amused. Svietlov's face told another tale, one of hurt ego, damaged pride, and a bitter pill he had to swallow.

The roll call followed soon after, and the *zeki* gathered on the assembly ground for the final count of the day, as if nothing had happened. The cold cut through the air, and the stars watched us with their unblinking gaze. The Zone swallowed the incident as it often did.

But my mind was troubled, as I stood there, waiting for the headcount to finish. Koralov's words kept running through my mind. They were still looking for the perpetrator of the assault on Ivan. Even though I trusted my brothers to never snitch, the thought of potential consequences kept coming back.

Then, there was more to the accusation made by Kostik. I found it unlikely that he would try to frame Aslan out of the blue. He must have been acting on someone's behalf, and I had a few suspects in mind. There were people in the camp wishing me, and those close to me harm, and I realized that I had to protect not only myself, but also others.

Meanwhile, new developments came to light that required my attention.

Evgeny announced that we should keep our eyes peeled in the work area for the signs left by his wife, Matryona. She was about to provide for us, despite the food package ban. As the winter tightened its grip over Western Siberia and IK-22, we were waiting for gifts to help us through its cold embrace.

CHAPTER 7

MAN'S ENEMIES ARE A THREAT TO HIS FRIENDS

"Look, I think that's it!" Evgeny whispered, his voice tight with excitement. "There!"

I followed his pointing finger.

Tied to a branch of a fallen cedar on the edge of the clearing was a piece of red thread with a small cross made of sticks hanging on it – just like Matryona promised. I walked closer and looked in the direction the branch indicated. About fifteen meters away, a brush pile sat low in the snow, half-covered in twigs. It looked like a good hiding spot.

I exchanged looks with Evgeny, and Aslan, tilting my head towards the pile.

"Stay here, *bratan*. Keep watch," I said to Aslan.

He nodded, turned around, and began scanning the clearing while sipping tea that steamed from his metal mug.

Evgeny and I walked to the brush pile, mugs in hand. It was the midday mealtime, and we were just strolling around, taking a break before the workday resumed. This was one of the few moments when everyone in the work zone relaxed. Even the guards were taking it easy, drinking tea, and eating dark rye bread and canned pork, instead of the prisoners' watery soup.

The current logging zone lay deep in the pine forest, an hour's march out of the colony. It was surrounded by barbed wire, watchtowers, and secured by a squad of armed convoy guards during the day. At night only two guards stayed behind to watch the logging trucks and equipment.

That gave Matryona a chance, and she took it. At first, she spent many nights mapping weak spots in the guard routines and the perimeter. She told me later about those nighttime escapades. How she watched the guards huddled by a campfire, and going on patrols along the fence. She moved through the forest in silence, testing the wire only when the guards were distracted at their posts.

She learned where the wire sagged and where the forest pressed close, and she used those places to crawl underneath. It was slow work, and it was risky. The barbs tore at her clothes and skin. Moving inch by inch through wet snow and frozen mud, becoming still whenever a floodlight swept the trees or a voice carried through the darkness. Once, she had to lie flat under a bush for nearly an hour while a guard wandered off from his comrade and into the work zone after losing a game of Seka. He sat on a nearby tree stump, muttering about his bad luck, smoking cigarette after cigarette and washing them down with vodka from his canteen. He only returned to the campfire when the flask ran dry.

She told me she came home that night on the edge of hypothermia, and it took her days to recover. But she kept coming back, night after night, and she covered her tracks carefully. Only then did she hide the contraband and mark the place with the diagonal cross of St. Andrew. Her signs were small enough to be missed, unless you knew exactly what to look for.

For the past several days, we had spent our breaks loitering around the perimeter. We were pretending to stretch our legs while looking for that red thread. When we finally saw it that day, we all felt a thrill, like kids spotting presents under a Christmas tree.

We reached the brush pile, peeking around to make sure no one was watching us. The snow around the pile was trampled and dirty, a sign of it having been stacked during recent operations. I crouched beside it, putting my mug in the snow, and scanned the tree line.

The barbed wire was visible, stretching at one of the work zone edges, but all the watchtowers were obscured by pine trunks. It was a good spot for clandestine activities.

Evgeny and I began looking around the pile, and shortly after, I saw another thread, this time black, tied to a twig at the bottom. I dug into the compacted snow beneath the thread with my gloved hands, until I reached the rough and rigid texture of a canvas bag. I brushed off the snow and dirt from the top of it, and looked around again to make sure no one was watching, before extracting the bag from its hiding place.

There was another one beneath it. I quickly gave one to Evgeny and took the other one myself.

The bags were flat and long and had string looped at two opposite ends. I took off my gloves, lifted my jacket, and placed the bag around my waist, tying the strings together over my belly, so it worked like a belt. It felt cold and wet to my body, but I barely noticed, nervous and eager to hide the contraband quickly.

As I was pulling my jacket back down, I heard Aslan's loud voice coming from behind the fallen tree. I looked over the brush pile and saw the foreman walking in our direction. Aslan was moving to cross his path.

Evgeny was still struggling with the string, his fingers numb from the cold. I rushed to help him. We were squatting behind the brush pile so the foreman could not see us unless he got closer. Evgeny held the belt-bag close to his stomach while I tightened the strings and made a solid knot to keep it together. I then pulled his jacket down.

We both put our gloves back on and grabbed our mugs, before standing up and walking away from the commotion which had erupted between Aslan and the foreman.

As we circled around, I noticed guards running and Aslan standing with his hands up in the air. The foreman was lying on the ground.

Bells rang, and the first guard who reached Aslan tried to hit him in the head with the butt of his rifle, but Aslan ducked, and the guard stumbled.

The other guards came in and pointed their AKs at my Chechen friend. He froze and I felt a pang of worry as the muzzles could spit death in a blink of an eye. I was glad that Ivan Rostovkin was no longer in the colony. The other guards didn't share his bloodlust and ordered Aslan to lay on the ground with his hands behind his back.

As soon as he dropped to the ground, a couple of the guards jumped in and began beating him. Nothing out of the ordinary in the Zone, just the regular brutality to which we were accustomed. After venting their frustration and making sure Aslan was pacified, the guards dragged him away.

Everyone in the work-zone was called in for a head count, after which the break was over, and we were sent back to work. The labor continued as if nothing happened. Just a short disturbance in the operation of the dark machine.

We learned later, the foreman had been on his way to mark new trees for cutting when Aslan got in his way. Our Chechen friend cursed the foreman loudly for being a cunt, alerting Evgeny and me. To prevent him from getting too close to us, Aslan attacked him and knocked him down.

He knew his life was at stake, and severe punishment a certainty. We were a team, and we all knew the dangers of our secret operation.

If the foreman had spotted Evgeny and I, while we were grabbing the contraband, all of us would be in trouble. We would lose our supply line, so Aslan decided to sacrifice himself to buy us time.

As I continued working the fallen Siberian pine with my axe, I saw the infirmary UAZ roll into the work zone. The guards dragged Aslan toward it, his hands cuffed behind his back, his steps unsteady but proud. He didn't look at us, he didn't need to.

The doors slammed shut, and the truck drove off in a cloud of exhaust and snow dust. Work resumed immediately, as it always did. Trees were felled, logs were stacked, and the forest kept quiet about what it had just witnessed.

When Aslan returned from the infirmary days later, he was sent straight to isolation. He got two months, without any appeal, without mercy. He took it like a man and never spoke of it.

I managed to get some food delivered to him through back channels, just as I had once been helped during my own time in the isolator. Every day in the work zone, I felt the lack of his presence. I missed his jokes and his steady resolve. It was a reminder of the price he paid to keep our lifeline going.

After the evening roll call, Evgeny and I sat down on his bunk, and we emptied the belt-sacks onto the rough, woolen blanket.

Inside were handmade bags, filled with dried herbs and powdered tree mushrooms: chaga, turkey tail, and reishi, among others. All of them were gathered, cured, and packed by Matryona herself. There was also a small leather pouch with several folded papers inside. On them, we found handwritten instructions: which herbs to use for what, how to brew an immune-boosting mushroom tincture, and how to apply certain powders or poultices for cuts, infections, or swollen joints.

I already knew the power of Matryona's remedies. The blister ointments kept our hands and feet from splitting, and the mushroom potion Evgeny made for me brought me back to life after isolation. I recovered faster, had more energy, and I didn't catch a cold even once while I was on it. But the supply ran out quickly, and without food packages, we were left hanging, until now.

You must know, *droog*, that chaga, reishi, and turkey tail were common in village medicine long before anyone bothered to give them Latin names. Russian and Japanese scientists caught up with the old traditions already in the 50s, exploring health benefits of the substances hidden within fruiting bodies of these fungi.

They grew on sick or dying trees, almost like the Grim Reaper of nature, who comes and takes out the valuable ingredients, compounds them into a mushroom and makes them available to the other creatures of the forest. The closing of the circle of life.

The dark brown chaga was cut from birch trunks and brewed for stomach ailments and inflammation. Reishi was prized for strengthening the body after illness and calming the nerves. Multicolored turkey tail was used to help wounds heal and to steady men worn down by fever or exhaustion. Matryona believed the mushrooms worked together, rebuilding what hunger, cold, and stress had taken away. In a place like the IK-22, that was exactly what we needed.

With the new smuggling channel established and the first contraband in our hands, we came up with a plan. We could make medicine following Matryona's recipe and stop the outbreak of bronchitis in our barracks. There were a few kilograms of dried mushrooms in the sacks. It was enough to make liters of tincture and keep everyone in the Bratva healthy. All we needed was alcohol.

Hard to obtain and in high demand, booze inside the Zone was as good as money. Some zeki brewed their own rotgut – fermented slop from bread, sugar, and fruit peels. But that stuff was garbage. You couldn't make a real tincture with it. What we needed was clean spirits, and that meant smuggling it in.

Asking Matryona in a coded message was an option, but it would be much harder to smuggle many liters of vodka from the work area to the camp.

It took us a few days to think it over, until we came up with a better idea.

We would buy the alcohol from Pilot's gang, through Artyom, the cook. This way we would not get involved personally with the collaborators, but we could use their channels to our advantage.

With this plan we came to Sidoy, to ask for his blessing, and access to the *obshchak* to fund the project. We told him what we had and what we could make out of it. We told him how everyone in the Bratva would benefit from the endeavor.

Evgeny left me to do the talking, and I did my best to present our case in a good way, but without exaggeration. Among the *blatnye* there was no room for half-truths and flashy marketing.

This was my first business pitch ever, and I tell you droog, my palms were sweaty, but I kept my voice calm. I laid out our case and I explained that with the tincture we would produce, we could make all the *blatnye* in Barrack 6 healthier, and stronger. Some of them, like me, had already tried Matryona's elixir, and they backed us up.

Sidoy, who was responsible for the *obshchak* – the common fund – listened in silence. He then told us to give him time to think. I know he met with other seniors later, and the next day he gave us his answer.

We had a deal.

The *obshchak* would fund the vodka. Evgeny and I would be responsible for the production, but we could count on the help of our brothers. The first batch of the medicine would go entirely to the *blatnye*, not to the *muzhyki* or the *suki*. If it worked, we'd keep going, buying more vodka, brewing more medicine.

We shook hands with Sidoy, and that same evening, Evgeny and I went to find Artyom. We caught him in his barrack playing dice with a couple of sleazy types. Evgeny gave him a nod. The cook got the hint and stood up abruptly before following us outside. His two comrades murmured with frustration, but when they saw us, they looked away and continued their game as if nothing happened.

"What's up? Something wrong with the food again?" Artyom asked, eying me wearily.

He was the cook in our work brigade, making tea and the watered-down soup we ate during the meal breaks. His job came with two perks: access to food and ties to black-marketeers from Pilot's gang. He wasn't one of them, but he moved in their shadow, and he'd been my go-between before. Once, he had helped me cut a deal with Klerk for extra rations for our brigade. The deal ended with me owing Pilot money after getting conned. I didn't hold it against Artyom, he did what I asked him to do. Pilot was the one who played me, maybe to have a payback after I'd taken his cash in a high-stakes Seka game.

"We need vodka Tyoma, a few liters," Evgeny said, using an amicable Russian short for Artyom's name.

This bit of friendliness seemed to have eased our cook a bit

"I thought you bosses don't drink." Artyom smiled sheepishly, but seeing no reaction he added, "Fine... It will cost."

"Don't worry about that. Can you get it?" I pressed.

"Yeah, I know a guy," Artyom said, shrugging. "When?"

"Yesterday," I told him.

"Of course," Artyom chuckled,

We settled on a price and shook hands. I remember Artyom's palm was cold and sweaty. The guy seemed always on the edge. Like a mouse trapped between foxes.

"I'll have it by the end of the week." Artyom said before going back inside.

When the time came, he delivered the tightly wrapped bottles, ready for hiding. We paid him with tobacco from the *obshchak*, plus a little extra for his trouble.

As I tucked two bottles into my waistband, Artyom spoke.

"Andrycha, a word?"

I looked at Evgeny. He shrugged and drifted off, leaving us alone.

"Tsikhiy's back," Artyom said. "We had... problems in the logging area."

"Soup problems?" I asked.

"Yeah. Maybe you could... say a word for me? To ease things up?"

"Sure. You're a good *muzhyk*, Tyoma." I patted him on the shoulder.

"Thanks," he said, and then looked around, as if double checking that no-one was listening.

"Anything else?" I asked impatiently.

"I heard something you'll want to know. I learned from my guy in Pilot's gang that Kostik had a debt to Klerk for a while now. The debt was settled after he accused your friend Aslan."

"*Suka*," I spat.

"Figured you'd want to hear it."

"Somehow, I am not surprised. Thanks, Tyoma."

I went back to the barrack with the vodka bottles pressing cold against my stomach, and a hot anger building up inside of my chest.

What Artyom said made sense. Klerk couldn't touch me since I became a vor. So, he acted like a snake, and used his influence over Kostik to hurt me, by hurting Aslan.

I knew something would have to be done about it, but Klerk was one of Pilot's men, so I had to find a smart way to deal with him.

But first, Evgeny and I had work to do. We needed to prove to the *Bratva* that Matryona's elixir was not a waste of the *obshchak* funds. With freshly delivered vodka, we could start on the same day.

The process of brewing Matryona's potion was slow, as it required the powdered chaga, reishi, and turkey tail mushrooms to steep in the alcohol-filled jars for many weeks. It was mid-November when we began hiding the jars beneath the stove, under the floorboards.

To keep our operations secret, Sidoy ordered all the *muzhyki* out for 'a walk'. By that time, I had learned enough to not be surprised by how quickly they followed commands of a *vor v zakonye*. Obedience bought them peace, while defiance or disrespect towards a *vor* led to a brutal punishment. Some of the things that I saw over the years, things done to the *zeki* who went against the *blatnye*, will haunt me until my last breath. But back in the winter of 1985 I was a neophyte – dedicated, and proud to serve the *Bratva*.

After six weeks we took the jars out, and then filtered the heavy, brown alcoholic liquid into old flour tins, provided by Artyom. The leftover mushrooms we cooked in our *chifir* pot on the stove. When the water extract was ready, we mixed it with the alcohol tincture. The end result was almost ten liters of Matryona's potion.

Following her instructions, we gave each of the *blatnye* three drops in their morning tea. Evgeny and I guarded the stash and were responsible for doling it out.

At first there were no effects, and after a few days, some of the *vory* complained that the medicine didn't work. Lop seemed eager to express his disappointment.

"You wasted perfectly good *samogon* – moonshine – on witchcraft," he scoffed.

But as the weeks passed, the coughing in the barrack dropped, and there was no more sneezing. The atmosphere in the Sixth began to change. From a subdued feeling of a hospital ward, it turned to a lively place, with talk, laughter and energetic movement filling the space. As if the summer had returned earlier. Even some of the older guys began moving easier and with more vigor, as if the rust in their joints had loosened up. Some of the hardened blatnye came to us to say thanks in private, which meant a lot to me.

I could feel the benefits myself. My feverish state from the past couple of months had completely disappeared, my nose stopped running. I could work harder, sleep better, and even my head was clearer.

Still, not everyone was happy, and as we crossed into the new year of 1986 and Orthodox Christmas approached, I came into conflict with Lop over who could use our potion.

Aslan had just come out of the isolation, and he looked like a ghost. After two months he had lost a lot of weight and his pale, sunken cheeks contrasted strongly with his straggled black beard. On top of that he was coughing like an old man.

I brought him food and tobacco, and when I hugged him, I felt the bones through his coat. He laughed and joked like nothing was wrong.

"It wasn't so bad," he said. "At least I could pray in peace."

I admired his attitude, but he was in a bad state. I went back to Barrack 6 and filled a small bottle with our potion so I could bring it back to him.

I told Evgeny what I planned but Lop overheard and jumped off his bunk to confront me.

"Why waste our stuff on a *muzhyk*?" he asked loud enough, so that everyone could hear.

"Why is this your business? You didn't lift a finger to help with any of it." I turned to him, feeling blood rushing to my head.

"I do what has to be done for the *Bratva*." Lop stepped closer, clenching his fists. Other *blatnye* got off their bunks and a small crowd began gathering around us. "I contribute to the *obshchak*. I won't have our share pissed away on lowlifes."

"Aslan is not a lowlife, you..." I bit my tongue before cursing Lop in front of everyone. The words we speak carry power, and in prison they can lead to violence and even death, especially among the *vory*.

Lop had hated me since the time of our baptism, and he was one of the strongest opponents of using moonshine for making the potion. Seeing that he wanted to provoke me and that there was no point arguing with him, I turned to Dima Sidoy.

He was sitting on his bunk, back against the wall and with a book in his hands. It was a tattered copy of 'The Brothers Karamazov'. His eyes were running along the lines on the yellow, crumbling pages. He seemed lost in it, unaware of what was going on around him.

"Sidoy, what do you think about this?" I asked him. "Aslan risked himself for us. Without him, we'd have been caught, and there would be no potion. We have plenty now, and he deserves a bottle to help him recover."

"But he is not a *vor*. And it was our common fund that was invested to make this work," Sidoy said, without looking up.

Lop raised his head at that and smiled triumphantly. He thought the matter was settled.

"True," I replied quickly, "but he is an honorable man. And we owe him."

Sidoy didn't move, and I felt my arguments were not convincing anyone. I saw several others nodding at Lop's words. It was then I had another thought.

"What if we could help *Bratva* profit from this?" I asked.

Sidoy slowly put the book to the side and frowned at me. "What's on your mind, Andrycha?"

"There are other *zeki* struggling with the winter conditions. Many barely function because of bronchitis. We have enough potion to keep us going for months, and we will make more as soon as we receive the next batch of ingredients. We could turn it into a business. Use what we need and sell the rest to the *muzhyki*."

Lop laughed hysterically at that suggestion.

"Are you kidding Andrycha? No one is paying for your forest tea when they can get high by buying dope and moonshine from Pilot, and your old friend Ziya."

"Let me worry about that," I said without breaking eye contact with my mentor. "Sidoy, together with Aslan I can find customers for our potion. Not everyone in this place is a complete degenerate, some hold on to life and to honor. Give me a quarter of what we have. I'll move it with Aslan, and the *obshchak* will grow."

Sidoy looked into the empty air, lost in thought. I waited patiently but after a while he just picked up his book again and returned to reading it.

Lop chuckled and pursed his lips in a mocking grimace.

"Go for it, Andrycha," Sidoy's voice came deep and low from behind the book cover. "But it better work like you say."

CHAPTER 8

Dignity Binds Men Stronger Than Fear Divides

Lop was right. Most of the *zeki* were not interested in bartering to get the remedy.

They had little trust in life, or in the future. The only thing that mattered to them was the pain they were going through. The everyday hunger was barely quenched by the camp kitchen meals. They had to suffer the mosquitoes in the summer and cold in the winter, the backbreaking labor, the uncaring and often ruthless guards, not to mention the violence among the inmates themselves.

Many were mentally crushed by these circumstances, living in a stupor like ghosts. They would trade future happiness just to get rid of the pain of the moment, to feel something else, something better, even if it was just an illusion. Drugs and alcohol were in high demand among those who couldn't take the pain, but who could afford to pay for the alternative. Sometimes even those without means indulged, but they didn't last long, like poor Seryozha.

It was a difficult market, but Ziya taught me that all you needed was sufficient demand for your product, you didn't have to sell it to everyone. Aslan and I just needed to find the right group of people. Prisoners who cared about themselves, and who were focused on the future despite the darkness around them.

As I returned to Aslan with a bottle of the potion, I explained to him how to use it, and what my plan was.

There were still some Muslims and Christians in the Zone who stayed away from booze and drugs. There were *zeki* whom we met in the training ground each Sunday. There were a few political prisoners with good lives to go back to, and resources coming from outside.

Since I was now a *vor* I asked Aslan to act as our frontman. He was respected among the inmates, and I believed they would trust him more. He would also insulate me from direct dealings with the lower castes, much like a *smotritel* who isolated *vory* from direct interactions with the guards.

Aslan took time in the evenings, meeting with potential customers, pitching the idea of a powerful medicine. He was the walking proof of it working, he would tell them, as now after just a few days of using Matryona's potion, his cough was gone. He was gaining weight, and doing better on the exercise yard.

It took him a couple of weeks to gather a group of twenty zeki to come and try the potion. He told each of them to meet us in the exercise yard, on a Sunday after the morning roll call.

That morning, I went with Aslan to the meeting, the cold pricking at our cheeks and snow crunching under our boots. We did some light exercise on the bars to get the blood flowing, and our bodies warmed up. I was hanging around to make sure no one fucked around with Aslan. As a *vor*, I was the authority to the gray mass of *muzhyki*; even Pilot's guys, and *kozly*, didn't dare to get in my way.

We waited and I remember feeling excited about getting our little business moving forward. I smoked a cigarette, sitting on a bench with a bottle of the potion tucked into my trousers. Aslan leant on the wooden post a few meters away, looking like he'd never been to the isolator.

I still smile when I think about it. We were like two gangsters on a street those days, but instead of poisonous drugs, we sold a fighting chance to those who had hope and who wanted to carry on.

Yet time passed by and no one showed up.

"Are you sure you told them this Sunday?" I couldn't hide impatience from my voice.

"*Bratan...*" Aslan said, giving me a meaningful look.

"Sorry, but this feels wrong." I looked around, my guts clenched. "Something must have happened."

Two guards stepped from behind the library, walking straight at us.

"*Suka blyat,*" I cursed.

The guards closed in quickly, one of them keeping his rifle at the ready while the other approached Aslan.

"What are you doing out here in the cold?" he asked.

"Waiting between sets, chief. Need to stay in shape," Aslan replied.

"Hands up, prisoner," the other guard commanded.

Aslan lifted his arms, and the guard began patting him down. Slowly, deliberately, eyes watching Aslan's face.

I remained silent, but I was fuming inside. Someone ratted on us.

Finding nothing suspicious on Aslan, the clearly frustrated guard drove a fist into his ribs. Aslan flinched, and the other guard shuffled nervously with his rifle.

I had enough of it. I stood up from the bench and took the last drag of my smoke, before squeezing the butt in my fingers, and flicking it so that it landed at the guard's boots.

He looked at me but didn't come closer. He knew better. I didn't say anything, but with my arms folded, my chin lowered, and my gaze fixed on the guard I was showing him that I was ready for a confrontation.

"This is exercise space, not a lounge," the guard told Aslan, before marching away with his comrade.

Aslan and I exchanged looks. We didn't have to say anything. We knew someone informed the guards.

"What do we do now?" I finally asked, my mind racing.

"If the mountain won't come to Muhammad, then Muhammad must come to the mountain," Aslan said with a grin. "Let's find out why the guys didn't show up."

I agreed and we went to Aslan's barrack. We found one of the would-be customers sitting on his bunk. His eyes widened when he saw us.

"Apologies," he muttered, starting to rise.

Aslan's hand landed on the guy's shoulder, pressing him back down. I sat on one side, then Aslan on the other. My palm rested on his forearm and squeezed it. The veins and tendons on my hand shifted beneath the Grim Reaper on my skin, and it moved as if brought to life. The *man's* eyes dropped to it, and he shuddered.

"You said you'd meet me today," Aslan whispered. "Why didn't you come, *droog*?"

The *zek* swallowed and then spilled his guts. He told us that there was a rumor circling, that Aslan is involved with the *vory*, and sells dope for me. Nobody wanted to be near that.

We left him pale and sweating on his bunk. Outside, I looked around, and only when I saw there was no one in sight, did I curse and punch the wall of the building with pointless fury. The pain dimmed my anger, and I realized I was heaving. I calmed my breath and turned to Aslan.

"Klerk!" I spat. "This time we settle it."

Dealing with Klerk wouldn't be easy. We needed help and advice, but I didn't want to go straight to Sidoy and admit I was already struggling to get the business started. I thought it over, and instead pulled Evgeny, Tsikhiy, and Kamen aside after dinner.

I trusted each of them for distinct reasons. Evgeny was like an uncle to me, Kamen hated Pilot's gang more than anyone, and Tsikhiy was fond of me and owed me even if he'd never say it out loud.

We stopped between two barracks, using them as cover from the wind that howled across the yard. It was cold and snow dust stung our faces, but at least we had some privacy. I pulled out a pack of cigarettes and offered it around. Then I lit one for myself and told them the whole story.

My deal with Klerk, and how he had helped Pilot put me in debt. How he cornered me with his friends, trying to turn me into a rooster.

No one reacted, as this kind of stuff was nothing unusual in the Zone. They just listened, exhaling smoke, with faces tightened by the cold.

But when I said Klerk had made Kostik lie about Aslan, Tsikhiy's mouth twisted, his thick brows drawing together until his eyes turned into black holes And when I told them he'd gone to the guards saying Aslan was pushing dope for me, Kamen's stone-carved face twisted into a snarling grimace of disgust. He spat into the snow.

Evgeny just nodded slowly, scratching the hard stubble under his flattened nose. Then he muttered: "You have to get him, before he gets you."

"Mudak crossed the fucking line. Stick him good!" Tsikhiy hissed. "Get some blood, like you did with Ivan."

"No," Kamen cut in, shaking his head.

Tsikhiy squinted at him. "You? Letting a *suka* slide?"

"It would only make him bolder," Evgeny added.

"Slide? No way." Hatred seeped through Kamen's words. "But spilling blood would mean a war with Pilot. Better to send a message no one here will forget."

"What message?" I asked.

"Talk to Artyom. You've used him before," Kamen explained. "Tell him to lure Klerk to the commissary with an offer of a sweet deal. Set the meeting during work hours. Tsikhiy and I will handle this while you and Aslan will have an alibi."

"You'll just beat him up?"

Kamen grinned like a predator, and a shiver of more than cold ran through me.

"Enough to soften him for the show," he said. "But first I'll make a deal with the Rooster King."

Even Tsikhiy winced at that. "Be careful. That dirt sticks."

"No worries, *bratan*, I dealt with such creatures before. I know where to stand."

When Kamen explained the details of his plan, another shiver ran through my body. Everyone agreed on the execution, but I felt that dark cold grasping at my throat. Another person would fall because of me. Like with Ivan Rostovkin, I understood that it was either him or me, but still it was a weight on my conscience.

Later that same evening, after roll-call, I caught Artyom walking to his barrack. I told him that I wanted to organize a delivery of extra food for our brigade.

"Sorry, but Klerk won't sell to you anymore," Artyom tried to excuse himself.

"Don't mention my name. Say you have a buyer with a fat commissary balance. Tell him to meet tomorrow in the store to settle the deal. You won't have to worry about him after that."

"This sounds bad..." his face soured.

"Do it, and you're paid. Don't do it, and..." I let the rest hang in the air.

He was silent, then nodded and scurried off.

The next day, I went to the logging site as usual. As we crossed the gatehouse, and waded through the ankle-deep, fresh snow on the forest road, I glanced towards the far end of the Zone. The library building loomed there, with a few windows casting an orange glow into the dark winter morning. On the other side of the assembly ground stood the mess hall, and the commissary store. It was a place of trade, where the *zeki* could buy food, tobacco, and other basic supplies to make their life a little easier with the money balance deposited there by their kin outside. The long *banya* stretched in between. If Klerk was to take the usual route from the library, he would pass right by the *banya*.

Work was lousy for me that day. My mind wasn't in it. I had second thoughts about the plan, and I worried about everything that could go awry. At some point I struck one tree at a wrong angle, and the axe bounced, almost hitting my leg. Aslan swore at me for that and told me to keep my head straight.

We were the first group to return from the logging work that day. Some of us walked to the *banya* and lined up for a quick shower. The steam clung to my skin as Aslan and I waited for our turn. I wondered whether Tsikhiy and Kamen managed to get things done.

Suddenly from somewhere down the corridor a scream cut through the normal commotion. People went to check; the sound was coming from the mop closet. Someone swung the door open. In there, between buckets, brooms, and mops, lay Klerk, butt-naked, with his arms tied and a wild expression on his face. Two roosters, also naked, lay there with him in a tangle of limbs and rags.

"Get me out of here," Klerk yelled, panic flooding his voice. He looked confused, with his face bruised and swollen.

The crowd froze. Then a murmur went through the gathering like a wave, as the news spread among the *zeki*. Klerk rose to his feet shakily, but some-one pushed him back in with a broom.

"Stay there, *petukh*," a voice from the crowd barked with disgust.

"Come closer and I'll smash your teeth," another one spat.

I looked for a short while as Klerk cowered, trying to stand, only to be hit by brooms, and kicked back down. There was no going back. His old life was lost. People witnessed him among the roosters, and that was enough. He was one of them now. An untouchable, a downcast, lower than dirt for all the other *zeki*.

Later, Kamen told me he had met with the Rooster King, an informal leader of the *petukhi* in IK-22. The very fact that there was a hierarchy even among the outcasts was a weird curiosity for me. In the end, the roosters got a bag of tobacco, and three cans of *tushonka* for arranging the spectacle. Cheap price for erasing a man. I counted it as an extra cost for my business, but at least I knew that Klerk would never trouble me again.

The camp buzzed with rumors of what happened to Klerk for a while, but as the new reality settled in, even his old friends from Pilot's gang shunned him as a rooster. The rules of the Zone were unwritten, but still organized the mass of the *zeki*, setting boundaries and forcing hierarchy. Pity was in short supply, as everyone struggled to survive in the inhumane conditions of imprisonment and forced labor.

With what we had seen as an obstacle to our business endeavor gone, Aslan and I went back to work on it. But even among those who seemed to be potential clients, the hesitancy was still strong. There was little trust in prison, and no *zek* would give away a can of *tushonka* for something that could very well be 'snake oil'.

Realizing that, we changed the strategy. We were being bad-mouthed as dope pushers, so we decided to act like ones. We gathered a group of a couple dozen *zeki* who suffered most from bronchitis, and who were interested but hesitant. We told them they could get the potion for free for two weeks, and if they liked it, they could come back for more and pay.

Aslan handled distribution, three drops for each guy on our list, each night, after dinner. The guys came eagerly to get their share of the potion, as long as it was free. With little to lose they were ready to give it a shot.

Two weeks later we waited for them to come back with a payment. It was one thing to receive free samples, but to put your money in the game was a different thing. It was the real test of our medicine.

I remember it very well, for it was one of the most meaningful days during my lock-up.

It was well past dinner time, and no one had showed up. I felt disappointment as we had used up almost a quarter of what I took from the *blatnye* stash, and I knew there were other men like Lop who wanted to witness my downfall. I was learning that even among the brotherhood of the *vory*, there were those who felt threatened by others' success.

Suddenly, a group of *zeki* broke out from the larger crowd leaving the mess hall and headed our way. I looked at their faces and counted them as they came closer. It was all the people we gave the potion to for free. Every fucking one of them.

I was astonished, and I had to stop myself from smiling. Standing to the side, straight and menacing, I watched them like a wolf as they approached Aslan. One thing that struck me was that no one in the group was coughing anymore. In the time when camp's air was thick with hacking and wheezing, that alone was worth witnessing.

One of the group, a political prisoner named Boris, moved to the front with a cloth-wrapped parcel in his hands. He nodded to me and then turned to Aslan.

"Boss, your medicine works," Boris said. "We all talked about it. Everyone feels better. Even the work goes easier. We want to continue, but not all of us can pay that much. This is all we've got this time."

He placed the parcel on the wooden bench and unwrapped it. There was a small bag of tobacco, and at least a hundred hand-rolled cigarettes, some sugar, and a few cans of food.

I looked at it and considered what they brought. This was no ordinary business, nor were we a charity. I had my obligation to the *Bratva.*

Still, I was moved by the fact that these men, regular *muzhyki*, forced by the camp to fend for themselves, came together and decided to help each other. What connected them, I wondered?

They came from diverse backgrounds. There were Muslims from Tajikistan, and Azerbaijan, there were Christians from the Urals, and some ex-party members from Moscow. There were strong, young lads who exercised a lot, and some intellectual types with wiry bodies hardened by the camp labor and the power of their will.

I couldn't fully grasp it at that point, but I thought about it frequently over the next few years, especially when the situation among the *vory* deteriorated, and I saw dishonor among their ranks.

These men were connected by a common thread of dignity and a will to survive, which was stronger than the pain they suffered. Meeting as a group regularly to get our medicine brought them closer. They could see there was something that they shared. The bond they formed was strong enough to make them stand together when the payday came.

The goods they brought were not much, but enough to cover the *obshchak* expenses. No profit in it for me, and Aslan, but at least we hadn't failed.

In the end, I nodded my head, and Aslan began distributing drops of the potion to the gathered crowd.

The winter months continued and the men from that first group came with their friends, and other *zeki*, to whom they spoke in confidence about our enterprise. We got more supplies from Matryona and began making the potion in regular batches. At some point Aslan recruited Boris, and a few others to help with distribution.

By the next winter there was a small but steady group that became our customers. They kept coming back, and they paid what they could. Some months we got more, some less, but the *obshchak* was getting regular contributions. Sidoy was satisfied with that and Lop stopped circling me like a vulture.

As strange as it sounds, these were the best times in the camp for me, and I recall them fondly. Perhaps it is because I tend to remember the good things more than the bad. But during that time, I felt I was doing something positive, that I was making a difference. It was the first business I started, and I was proud of myself for bringing value instead of destruction to some of the oppressed.

Aslan regained his strength, and when Kamen got sent to the isolation after a brawl with one of Pilot's men, Aslan joined the *Bratva* and stepped up as *smotritel* for Barrack 6. Meanwhile, I learned more about the Thieves' Code, and built myself a reputation both among the *vory*, and the general population of the Zone.

Matryona and Evgeny were also busy not only with love letters and the smuggling operation, but also with a plan to cut short his stay in prison. That resourceful woman wasn't going to wait fifteen years for her man. She was determined to get him out of IK-22, no matter the cost.

As the years went by, she gathered resources and influence needed to achieve her goal. I learned all about it two years later, when the time came to make the move, and Evgeny asked me to join him. He laid out the details of what she had prepared. It was risky but I wasn't going to pass up a chance to shorten my own prison sentence there. We began preparations on our side of the fence, staying in touch with Matryona through our smuggling channel in the forest.

When I think about Matryona back then, I admire her perseverance and determination in moving towards a seemingly insane objective. The patience and strength needed to do it showed a dedication we rarely see today.

She gave herself completely to the task, moving step by step, to finally enjoy the bitter-sweet taste of reunion on her lips.

Sometimes people ask me, how do I start a successful business? I owned many enterprises, but the one we ran with Aslan in IK-22, selling Matryona's potion, was the first one and it taught me a lot. I understood then that a Grim mindset is the foundation of business success.

I will give you five Grim rules.

Number 1: Stop fooling yourself. The first step is being sincere. The problem is – people follow their passion, but does their passion also follow people?

Test and find out if what you are building is something people actually want. Don't build something you don't love. And don't build something people don't love. Test early. Test sincerely. Talk to your potential customers. See if their eyes light up. If you don't find real passion inside you, and inside them, build a different product.

Number 2: Thunder is your friend. Grim comes from the Slavic word "Grom" which means thunder. Thunder does not wait for perfection. Thunder strikes. No matter if thunder hits or misses, it strikes again.

Start small. Build a prototype. Ship Fast. See what works. Change what doesn't. Strike again. Build the smallest usable version, get this into real users' hands. Speed and iterations beat 'perfection' every fucking day.

You polish forever in secret? Competitors have already taken the market. Good is better than perfect, remember that. Because good lets you strike.

Number 3. Focus on one core problem. Life is grim. Harsh. Cold. That's the problem. And the problem is your friend. Good startups do one thing well. They focus on one problem. And solve it. Distraction kills early companies faster than competition. Filter without mercy: If your product does not solve the problem – cut it. No extra features. No side quests. No shiny shit. Fall in love with the problem, not with the solution.

Number 4. Build a culture of radical honesty. Grim means earnest, serious. No games. Inside your team, truth is oxygen. No politics. No egos. No hiding mistakes. Founders who don't like hard conversations destroy their own enterprises. Speak directly. Eye to eye. And always with respect. But speak honestly. Bad news now is always cheaper than bad news later.

Number 5. Keep on walking, grim. Take care of your energy. Take care of your people. Startups die when teams die. And teams die when founders burn out.

Sleep well. Train the body. Take silent days. Be a brother, not a colleague. And always, always keep walking.

Not those people make it, who are the smartest, or the best connected. But those who keep walking, through the fire. Together. Alone you go fast, but together you go far.

Remember, these five rules of building a business.

Sincerity. Thunder. Focus. Team. Endurance.

Times are grim but in grim times the opportunities are the biggest. Because weak people give up quicker than ever. But you are a Grim. You don't give up, you get up.

Be honorable.

Part 2

1988

CHAPTER 9

Liars Are Poison To Your Inner Circle

There are times in life, when everything happens all at once, when everything changes, and through the chaos and turmoil a new reality emerges for a man as he is forced to make hard choices. For me, and many others in IK-22, a storm broke in the middle of '88.

After three years in the penal colony, I was already a seasoned *vor.* I became ruthless, and resilient, matching the fierce rejection of all external authority that the *blatnye* upheld. There were matters I got involved in and things I did of which I will not speak of here. The oath still binds me to silence. The scars and stories in ink on my body speak loud enough of my service to the *Bratva* in IK-22.

At the same time, and perhaps as a small redemption, I kept brewing and distributing Matryona's potion. Even if the business was not as profitable as selling dope or booze, it was one of the few things that gave me a feeling of satisfaction, instead of pangs of bad conscience. Besides fearful looks of the *zeki* seeing me as one of the wolves, I was getting quiet nods from those whom the potion helped. As I see it now, self-respect was the currency I gained in that exchange, and it was worth much more than the rubles or dollars I made with Ziya before our incarceration.

But the situation in the Zone was deteriorating and the colony was becoming an ever-tightening noose.

Everything was getting worse as the Soviet Union itself was in steep decline, nearing its spectacular collapse. At that time no one suspected that the end was so close, but the signs of the machine breaking down were clear. The entire country was barely operational, and the penal system was at the bottom of the priority list for the apparatchiks trying to salvage the wreck.

As the country-wide shortages began to intensify, the living conditions in IK-22 decreased rapidly. By the spring of 1988, the food in the camp was so scarce that even the guards were looking for ways to get extra rations. The packages sent to the *zeki* either went missing or were delivered with the contents plundered. I had seen men crying over an unwrapped package where instead of long-awaited sustenance was just a loaf of stale bread, and only a smell of dried sausage lingering on the paper.

At the same time, Pilot was pulling more young convicts into his ranks as they were easily lured by the promise of quick money and power. While the ranks of collaborators grew, we had to stand together against the guards, snitches, and the growing menace of Pilot's gang.

The tensions were high, and all the groups that had some power leveraged it to survive, with the *muzhyki* at the bottom suffering the most.

As for the *vory*, we kept the *Vorovskoi Mir*, however the balance of power was shifting, and we were losing influence. We still brewed our potion, but with the supply of moonshine cut off, we had to reduce the process to cooking alone, which produced a less potent infusion. The food supplies we had accumulated as part of the *obshchak* were dwindling and the potion itself was not enough to keep everyone going.

People like Tsikhiy and Lop were willing to squeeze the *muzhyki* dry and leave them starving, while Sidoy wanted to keep the extortions at 'reasonable' level. He said that if you take everything from a man, and he has nothing else to lose, he might snap back at you. I knew how right he was.

After all, I had joined the *vory* when everything was taken from me, and death became an acceptable outcome. Sidoy was respected, and most of us followed him like a father, but a sense of uneasiness was growing within the *Bratva*, and the first cracks of division began to show.

Captain Svietlov increased the tension by giving more privileges to the *kozly* and pitting them against us. More scuffles broke out, and both the infirmary and the isolation cells were soon running at capacity. No one realized this was part of a larger plan the ambitious officer had for the camp, but everyone could feel that the foundations of the old order were shaking, like ants in a jar, and that the threat of a bloody riot hung in the air.

It was during those trying times, on a warm, steamy midday in August, when I witnessed a dark omen of the coming hardships.

Aslan, Evgeny, and I were sitting in the logging area. It was raining for a few days, and now the sky was covered by a thin layer of clouds. The mosquitos kept swarming around us but were reluctant to bite – as we rubbed our skin with the juice of freshly ground tansy plants we collected on our way to the work zone. Our shirts were soaked with sweat, and we had to deal with the odor of our unwashed bodies mixed in the air with the bitter smell of tansy.

The midday meal was barely enough to keep our stomachs from grumbling. We shared one small can of mackerel from the *obshchak* between the three of us, before flushing it down with the camp issued soup.

"Not bad," Evgeny smirked, holding up a string of fat and meat on his fork.

"Lucky you," Aslan said before slurping his own soup straight from the tin.

Evgeny bit down, and we all heard a crack. He grimaced in pain and spat into his hand.

"*Suka*," he uttered, holding his mouth. "I broke a tooth."

Amidst the hodgepodge of half-chewed food, I saw shards of his tooth and another bony object.

Aslan reached out and picked the thing up. It was a yellow fang, big as my thumbnail, rotten through with dark pits.

"*Paskuda*!" Evgeny cursed. "Artyom, *suka blyat*! What the hell is this?"

"Leave him," I said, "He just cooks what they give him."

"Are things so bad that they feed us dogs now?" he said with a sigh.

"Maybe a goat?" Aslan shrugged, trying to make a joke. "One with teeth in the wrong place."

No one laughed. One after another we emptied the tins onto the forest floor.

Evgeny rinsed his mouth with some tea. "Not a good sign. I am done with this slop."

"How are things with Matryona?" I asked.

"Collecting ingredients for the mixture. But it should be ready soon."

I nodded. "We need to figure out the routine of the new convoy guard, Kolesnikov. There can be no fuckups when the time comes."

"I'll watch him," Aslan said. "You work the cook."

"This can wait until the last minute," I said. "I trust his fear, but less talk, less risk."

Evgeny and Aslan muttered their agreements.

I looked around. Others kept eating their soup, unaware of the content. The guards were at their posts, following routines that we had studied for months.

The time was coming soon to leave IK-22 behind us or to be buried in it.

We walked back to the camp with stomachs grumbling, and our moods darkened. Evgeny kept running his tongue over the cracked molar tooth and cursing under his breath.

As the clearing of the camp and the double fence surrounding the Zone appeared in front of us, we noticed some commotion around the guard barracks outside. When we reached the gate, we could see a group of guards, perhaps a platoon-size detachment, getting drilled by Captain Svietlov. These were unfamiliar faces, with fresh uniforms and riot gear. It seemed that somehow, despite not being able to feed the zeki properly, the system could still find enough resources to try to keep us down.

"More dogs to guard the cage," Aslan remarked.

"Like we didn't have enough mouths to feed," Evgeny spat.

"Or enough problems," I sighed.

The presence of new guards stirred some worries in me, and I wondered what the purpose behind it was, but soon I had to focus on new developments inside the Zone. After passing the gate, another group of convoy guards caught our eye, gathered outside the library building. The muffled sound of bombastic music and a propagandistic voice-over told us there was an orientation session ongoing. Fresh meat had arrived.

I recalled the time I first came to IK-22 and crossed the gate, becoming one of the *zeki*. The processing, the shaving of our bodies, and the itching and burning after being sprinkled with the disinfectant powder – all of it still felt vivid in my mind. After all that manhandling, we got our assignments and were accompanied by the guards to the big hall in the library. There we had to endure a speech by a Party apparatchik followed by mediocre prop-agit movies, meant to instruct us on our way to reeducation. It was a joke.

Now the newly arrived *zeki* were going through the same process, and I was excited to see if there were any potential brothers among the newcomers. These days we were looking for recruits to strengthen the ranks of the

Bratva, and I was curious what kind of material we would get from this new group.

I washed myself, and together with Aslan, we checked each other for ticks. The little bastards were plentiful this summer, and each day after staying in the forest, we would find a few already feasting on our blood. I learned to pick them out cleanly just with my nails, but there are places on a man's body, where he can neither see nor easily reach with his fingers. I can tell you, *droog*: fighting pain and struggling together brings men closer, but having your brother pick ticks from your ass makes you family.

After finishing the cleanup and tick-check, we walked to the Sixth, to hear what the *vory* learned about the new arrivals.

Sidoy and a few others were already going through the list, which they got from a *zek* who worked as a cleaner in the mess hall. He eavesdropped on the work assignment process and noted down names of those who would be of interest to the *Bratva*.

"Anyone good?" I asked while sitting down with the seniors.

"A few," Sidoy said, tapping at the paper. Some names were crossed out, and some underlined.

I skimmed through the list and smiled seeing some guys with serious charges. These were good candidates, ones who knew violence and pain already. Ones who rejected the authority of the state as a matter of principle. I felt hopeful. I thought the *Bratva* would gain strength, just in the time when it needed it. I just didn't expect that it would be the first time that I witnessed a fake *vor* being dealt a bloody punishment.

When the list was ready, Aslan and Kamen were sent to get the word out. The guys we selected were supposed to show up in the Sixth to stand in front of the *vory* council. It reminded me of my own audience with the *vory*, and the time when I still rejected their authority, thinking I could make it on my own. Such a foolish boy I was back then.

The evening came, and a group of five gathered outside, waiting before they were let in by our doorman. Byk ushered them in and measured each of them with a solemn face that spoke of countless fights and promised violence to trespassers.

Aslan and Kamen would do the talking since they were the Watchers. I sat near the table with four other *blatnye.* Our job was to gather attention of the candidates, and make them feel judged, while the real decision-making process was happening among the seniors.

Sidoy, Tsikhiy, Evgeny, sat to the side, mixed with the rest of the inmates and watching with seeming lack of interest. While a *smotritel* was talking, those three would observe and make the final decisions. Who would be invited, who would be discarded, and who would be punished ruthlessly was determined by these experienced, clever men.

There were simple reasons behind the arrangement. Sometimes, when you are engaged in a conversation, you might miss something, a small detail of speech or body language that could betray a person's true character. We show much more with our behavior than with our words, and people like Sidoy had a keen eye for those tell-tale signs. I was always learning much from him.

One by one the potential prospects came forward. They were asked who they were and their bodies were scrutinized for tattoos. Three were turned away as their answers didn't satisfy Kamen, and Sidoy had nothing else to add.

The fourth one was a youngster from Kazan, nineteen years old, with a wide grin on an almost baby-like face. He was tall and lean, with large hands, and a scar over one of his blue eyes.

The lad introduced himself as Misha and he took off his shirt without being asked, revealing a pale but muscular body. He was clean, without any sign of ink, but with a lot of fresh bruises. Just as I was when I first arrived at IK-22.

"Who are you, Misha?" Kamen asked.

"I'm a fighter," the young lad replied, raising his fists to his chin in a boxing stance.

"We heard you beat a man to death. Why?"

Misha's smile evaporated in an instant and he lowered his hands.

"He hurt my little sister." His voice was dark, and I could see pain in his bright eyes.

"Why didn't you let the state handle him?" Kamen pressed on.

"Fuck the state! They wouldn't do shit," Misha snarled. "A man has to fight for his family."

"Would you like to embrace a new family, Misha the Fighter?" I chimed in. I liked his attitude. He reminded me of myself, of a young Andrej – full of ideals but lacking in knowledge.

"Only if it is honorable." Misha looked me in the eye and a smile returned to his face.

"Watch your words, *patsan*," Kamen scolded him, and looked at Sidoy, who gave a slight nod. "It is you who will have to prove your honor. Come back with your things. We'll have a bunk ready for you."

"Andrycha will be your mentor." Sidoy pointed at me. "Talk to him when you come back."

I knew it meant that I was now responsible for Misha's conduct. I had to get him up to speed on everything and help him with his prospect task, whatever that would be.

Misha bowed his head theatrically and left the building.

The last of the newcomers was still waiting. He was in his thirties, short, but brawny and with a face showing signs of a recent beating. His lips were swollen, and one of his eyes had a deep blue bag underneath. Clean shaven otherwise like all the *zeki* straight from initial processing, he looked quite unassuming until he removed his shirt. His chest was adorned with a tiger's head baring its fangs, and beside some smaller tattoos that I couldn't read from a distance, he wore depictions of military epaulettes on his shoulders.

"Greetings, *bratan*," Kamen said, "what is your *klichka*?"

"I go by Afi," the man replied with his head raised high.

"Afi, like *afiora – a* conman? Is that what you're in for?"

"I am just an innocent man," Afi smirked. A few guys in the crowd chuckled.

"Where do you come from?" I asked.

"Yekaterinburg."

Silence ensued. It was almost as if everyone was holding their breath. This was not something the *vory* expected to hear from one of their kind. When asked where he is from, a real vor names the prisons he's done time in, not his city. A novice might say something like that, but not an anointed *vor*, with authoritative ink on his body.

"Are you a *vor*," Sidoy asked, raising himself up from his bunk. His face was unreadable, but the very fact that he stood up during the questioning meant trouble.

Afi was unaware of that and he began nodding, but as he opened his mouth to speak, Sidoy raised his hand and cut him off. "Wait before you speak. Let me first explain what happens to those who falsely pretend to be a *vor v zakonye*. They die."

Sidoy's words cut like a sharp knife through the otherwise silent space of Barrack 6.

"I ran with a gang in Yekaterinburg," Afi said after clearing his throat.

"That is not what I asked." Sidoy walked closer but kept a safe distance from Afi, as though he were a leper. "Were those epaulettes ordained by a *vor v zakonye*? If so, where and by whom?"

Silence again. Afi weighed his words and looked around as if looking for an answer in the tense faces of the *blatnye* around him.

"No," he finally said, "but we follow the code. My gang and I."

"If you had followed the code, Afi the Conman, you would have known that only a *vor* can make another *vor*. This is how it works, and you are an impostor." Sidoy took a step closer and, in the blink of an eye, retrieved a knife from his sleeve.

Afi jumped back, but Sidoy turned the knife handle to him, nudging him to take it. I knew the blade; it was the same I used on Ivan.

"We will not kill you." Sidoy's deep voice carried a new verdict. "But you will have to remove your tattoos. They are a lie, and we won't allow them in our camp."

"Remove, how?" Afi asked sheepishly, pretending he didn't understand.

"Use the knife, *suka*." Sidoy spat and dropped the knife at Afi's feet. "And if you have problems with reaching all the way behind your shoulder, we have a new prospect who can help you with that."

A short silence ensued, and Afi swallowed heavily, looking at the darkened, pitiless faces around him.

A knock on the door sounded like the judge's hammer, settling the sentence. As if summoned by the dark spirits, Misha barged into the room carrying his belongings, and a bright smile on his face. It faded quickly as he saw the mood inside was grave, and he stopped in his tracks.

I walked to him slowly, and as I took his bundle from him, I explained what he was tasked to do. Misha's face went pale, but he nodded, and we returned to Afi, who now had a long and painful night ahead of him.

I must say, he took his punishment like a man. He might have been a liar, and an impostor, but he was also tough. Maybe it was fear of the alternative that drove him. Sidoy was not joking, and death was hanging in the air.

All the *blatnye* closed in, forming a tight circle, while the few *muzhyki* curled up in their bunks. The doorman placed himself firmly in the entryway – lessons had been learned after the incident with Tamm.

Afi sat on his heels and picked up the shank. It was the same blade I used on Ivan. A long piece of steel, with a razor-sharp edge, and a thread wrapped around one side as a handle. Not your typical camp shiv, made from a long nail, or an old spoon sharpened on a piece of concrete.

No one spoke, but the air was heavy with intensity at what was about to happen. In that thick air and under the gaze of the gathered *vory*, Afi took the knife to his chest. His hand shook at first, and he let out a brief sigh as the blade cut the skin around the tiger's head. He clenched his teeth and looked back at us with a fire of anger in his eyes.

Blood ran down his chest in dark lines, and color left his face, as he continued circling the blade around the tattoo. Heavy drops of sweat were hanging on his forehead, and his lips were trembling when he lifted the skin with the blade and grabbed it with shaking fingers. He closed his eyes and jerked a strip of skin off his chest. A short scream cut the air and reverberated in my ears as the silence returned.

My stomach lurched as I imagined the pain, but I felt neither pity nor blame. In a way, what was happening was normal to me now. A transgression met justice; the payment of blood had to be made to avoid the loss of life. Afi reminded me of an animal trapped in a snare, willing to bite off its own leg to break free.

He continued his grizzly self-punishment, tearing his own skin off, bit by bit. When he was done with the tiger head, he began cutting around the epaulettes on his shoulders.

At some point he looked up at Misha, who stood beside me, and extended the blood-covered blade to him. Misha's eyes were wide, but he didn't hesitate. He took it and went to stand behind Afi. He took the knife and with one hand on Afi's neck, began carving clumsy lines into the tattooed shoulders. Afi flinched with each pass, biting down his own fist.

Tsikhiy, who was in front of him now, squatted and studied his eyes. He was passing his own judgement, it seemed, or maybe he was just interested in the pain itself.

When Misha was done with circling the epaulettes, he looked up with a question in his eyes.

"That's enough," Tsikhiy whispered to Misha in his low, raspy voice. "Let him finish."

Afi's fingers found the edge of the skin on his left shoulder. He closed his eyes again and pulled. The screams followed. Tears mixed with sweat ran down his contorted face. His fingers slipped on the bloody skin. He grabbed again, and pulled, this time getting a large piece of the epaulette off. Strip by strip, he ripped out one epaulette, then the other. His screams had turned to whimpers, then he collapsed to the floor and passed out.

I checked his pulse; he wasn't going to die today it seemed. While a few of us wrapped his wounds with clean rags, Afi woke. He seemed delirious with pain, and as the blood seeped through the bandages, he must have had dark thoughts about his future in the Zone. We handed him his clothing and told him to leave, his false status as a *vory* gone.

Kamen ordered a *petukh* from our barrack to clean up the mess on the floor. The rooster crawled in and began scrubbing the blood, head bowed while people passed around him like he was filth.

Meanwhile, Afi left the barrack on shaky legs. His eyes were glassy, but he understood enough when we warned him: no infirmary until morning, or worse would follow.

I showed Misha to his new bunk; we always kept one or two free for a freshman. He was pale, but steady, and soon a smile returned to his face.

"Is it like that every day, boss?" he asked me.

"Every fucking day," I winked and patted him on the back. "You can call me Andrycha. And we'll figure out a good *klichka* for you."

"Misha the Fighter, I liked that one," his grin widened.

I rolled my eyes.

"So be it, Boyets," I said.

Boyets means 'fighter' in Russian, but it also sounds like the word 'boy' in English, and both suited him well.

CHAPTER 10

After Victory, Reflect On Who Else Benefits

I began mentoring Misha, who, even though shaken by his first bloody experience in the Zone, adjusted quickly. The boyish grin stayed on his face most of the time. It was easy to like the young boxer, who combined the discipline and maturity of a man with the light-footed mischief of a street jester. He was handsome, and spoke about women a lot, making some of those who listened jealous, but most of us liked his stories as they brought back good memories from the world outside.

We had him assigned to my work group and together with Aslan, we taught him to fell trees. All of that reminded me of my own first summer in IK-22, and it made me think how much I had changed since then.

What happened to Afi was in no way shocking to me anymore. I had seen it as a natural expression of the Thieves Code. For the same reason, I developed an attitude of superiority towards regular prisoners, and the fate of roosters no longer made me cringe. The bright idealism which got me in trouble back in the GDR, and which I carried with me into imprisonment, was gone by that time. Or perhaps not gone but transformed into a sense of pride from being a *vor*, and loyalty I felt for the *Bratva*. It defined me, and it gave me strength to do what had to be done. With rising tensions in the camp, we had to be more ruthless than ever.

Just as Afi was cast aside like a piece of trash, unfit to carry his ink, Misha had quickly proven himself to be as loyal and dedicated as any weathered *blatnoy*. As my young mentee, he followed me and Tsikhiy on our taxation runs. The *obshchak* was dwindling, and we were squeezing the regular inmates harder, to keep the Brotherhood fed. The resistance among some of them grew, and violence had to be used to keep them in line.

Pilot's gang was becoming a bigger problem too. They were struggling as their sources of contraband outside were drying out. Encouraged by the camp officials, they began encroaching on our territory, demanding tribute from the regular prisoners. We learned about this for the first time in early September.

That month the *zeki* got new funds on their commissary balances and whatever rations remained from the food parcels they had received over the summer. Normally, they would come over to the Sixth to pay their tribute directly, to show their allegiance. But as everyone was struggling, and Pilot's gang was gaining strength, some decided to take their chances.

Each barrack had a *smotritel* working as our eyes and ears. From them we got a list of those prisoners, who despite getting money and supplies from the outside didn't come to the Sixth with their tribute, as was customary. The list was growing each month, and it was impossible to chase down every delinquent, so some had become overconfident about not paying.

But the hand of the *Bratva*, although sometimes slow, was also sure and uncompromising. Each month, we made visits to those who failed with their payment obligations. Usually, the very sight of us walking into a barrack was enough to get the offenders to jump off their bunks and come with apologies and excuses. Some would get off easily, with a word of warning, after contributing what they owed. But those who tried to avoid us got punished, to give example to others. It was a dirty business, even though at the time I found rationalizations for it.

On that evening, Tsikhiy, Lop, Misha, and I were on a tour around the barracks. With Lop I had bad blood from the past, but we had come to an uneasy peace and sometimes we both helped Tsikhiy.

That night was the harvest time for us, time to get our share of what belonged to others, in exchange for keeping peace and order. Or that's how I explained it to myself back then.

We were about to finish our round and go back to the Sixth, when the *smotritel* from the Third came over running.

"Tsikhiy, there are Pilot's guys in our barrack!" he told him, gasping. "They're saying it's their territory now and demanding tribute."

We all cursed and looked at each other. This was serious.

"We need to handle this right now," Lop growled.

"Get more *blatnye* from the Sixth," Tsikhiy ordered the *smotritel*. He then looked back at us. "Let's go. We need to remind those *mudaki* where their place is."

We marched quickly and when we entered the Third, we had our eyes around us and our fists ready. There was a commotion in the dormitory area, someone was crying out, and a loose crowd of the *zeki* was spread around, watching. Those who saw us quickly stepped out of the way, and soon we were in the middle, pressing between the double bunks. A *zek* was laying on the floor, holding a bag to his chest, while a group of Pilot's men were kicking him and demanding he give it to them.

"I can't," the zek pleaded, "I promised Tsikhiy I'll have something for the *blatnye* this month."

"Fuck *Blatnye*, we rule this place now!" A tall guy said, while punching with one hand and trying to get the bag with the other. He was one of Pilot's enforcers, called Zhiraff – Giraffe.

One of his pals noticed our arrival and gave him a sharp warning. The entire group faced us, and the place went silent.

Zhiraff whistled and a few more of the Pilotovtsy stepped in from the crowd. We were surrounded. With around a dozen of them against the four of us, the odds were not exactly in our favor.

Tsikhiy didn't seem bothered. He folded his arms and looked at Zhiraff with his lips curled downwards in a mix of disgust and hatred.

"Say it again, *suka*," he said through clenched teeth.

Zhiraff smirked and stepped forward between the bunks, waving for the rest of his gang to get closer. Regular prisoners scooted out of the harm's way, jumping over lower bunks or squeezing between them and the men coming at us from all sides. The guy with the bag crawled under his bunk and went still. The atmosphere in the room became charged like a stick of dynamite, waiting for a spark to explode.

I took my place beside Tsikhiy, while Misha and Lop turned around to cover our backs.

The tight space between the rows of bunks worked to our advantage. Pilotovtsy couldn't use their numbers to gang up on us easily. They moved closer, and now Zhiraff was standing a few steps in front of Tsikhiy.

"Fuck *Blatnye*!" He spat on the floor and repeated. "We rule this place now."

Tsikhiy didn't wait, he sprung forward with the stump of his left forearm raised in front of him like a shield. In his right hand a shank materialized seemingly out of nowhere.

Zhiraff's eyes went wide, and he tried to grab Tsikhiy's knife wielding hand with both his palms. A mistake, leaving his side open. Tsikhiy pulled the right hand back and smashed his stump into the side of Zhiraff's face.

The tall guy stumbled, and I helped Tsikhiy drop Zhiraff to the ground. I jumped over his body and confronted the two guys directly behind him, while Tsikhiy stomped the sprawled Zhiraff.

I kicked the guy directly in front of me in the knee and as he lowered his guard, I surprised him with a few crosses and jabs. He staggered, and

I pushed him hard into the other one. Both went down. Before I could kick either of them, someone grabbed me from the side.

That guy had jumped over the nearby bunk, grabbing me around the waist and trying to topple me. I smashed my elbow onto the back of his head several times, and he released me. I lost him as more blows fell on me from the side.

It turned into a blind crush of fists, elbows, and bodies. I punched at the men in front of me and at those trying to get at me from the side. It was total chaos, and from that haze I now remember only bits and pieces. Me driving my fist into a man's nose and feeling bone crack beneath my knuckles. A stinging pain in my arm when a sharpened piece of wood stabbed into me. The frantic struggle to stay on my feet as two men nearly toppled me.

I received hits, and I did my best to give some back. Most of them didn't even register, I was so full of adrenaline. At some point there were four guys coming at me, two in the front and one from each side. I was losing and retreated to Tsikhiy's side.

Zhiraff lay curled on the floor, unconscious, Tsikhiy stood over him, his chest heaving, eyes glossy with fury, and blood dripping from his knuckles. Behind him Lop and Misha, side by side, fought against five other guys. It wasn't going well for them either. I saw Misha getting hit with a wooden club in his face and swaying on his feet.

I struggled to catch my breath; my heart was beating like a war drum, and my lungs burned with fire. I felt there was not much more fight left in me.

"*Raz rodila mat, raz nam umirat.*" Tsikhiy gasped.

It was a rhyme we often used when things were getting hairy. It means something akin to 'Born once by your mother, die once, like no other.' We were ready to face our end, but as the Pilotovtsy regrouped to continue their onslaught, the doors to the barrack swung wide open.

"Get the *Suki*!" Evgeny yelled as he rolled into the dormitory waving a chair leg in his hand. Behind him a stream of blatnye from the Sixth, at least twenty of them, some with makeshift weapons, others with their bare fists and lust of violence painted on their faces.

The Pilotovtsy wavered. Some of them turned, trying to prepare to defend themselves against our new reinforcements, while the four of us used that opportunity to attack. I dashed forward, punching the guy in front of me. He punched back fiercely, and we managed to hit each other many times. At some point a *vor* came behind him and dragged him to the ground. We both kicked him until he stopped moving.

I took the moment to look around, feeling a fierce buzz of the fight heightening my senses. The few of the Pilotovtsy who were still standing, now were being chased around the barrack, and cornered by groups of *blatnye*. One by one they were dragged down and had the shit beat out of them.

A loud bell began ringing outside. Yells of the guards quickly followed, and we knew they were coming here soon. The *vory* left their victims on the floor, and we gathered in the living area of the barrack. Everyone was catching their breaths, as if we all participated in a marathon. Tsikhiy patted me on the back, Misha grinned despite a swollen lip and blood dripping from his nose. While Lop looked like he was ready to fight the guards, with fists still clenched and a tense body. Someone wrapped an arm around my shoulders, it was Evgeny.

"Next time you go against *Suki*," he said with a satisfied smile. "Don't leave me behind. You need someone to watch your back, Andrycha."

The guards barged in, a whole bunch of them, waving their batons and screaming at everyone.

"What is going on here?" A Sergeant yelled at no one in particular.

"Nothing chief. Why so worked up?" Tsikhiy said, wiping blood from his knuckles into his trousers.

Zhiraff and the other Pilotovtsy were slowly scrambling to their feet, while others were standing with swollen, bloodied faces. To the guards, they said that they had tripped and fallen, or that they didn't know what had happened.

Everyone agreed that things were fine. The *muzhyki* from the Third were especially convincing, saying emphatically that nothing was going on in their barracks.

The Sergeant was not convinced.

"This is a riot!" he screamed, and the guards began hitting the *muzhyki* with *dubinkas*. Poor prisoners, who didn't even participate in the scuffle, were now getting punished for it. The guards didn't dare to beat any of the *vory*, but we were pushed and ordered to leave the barrack and line-up.

Outside Captain Svietlov was waiting with another detachment of guards in a semicircle around the door. They all wore helmets, some carried riot shields. Most had their batons out, but a few pointed rifles at us as we gathered outside. Three distinct groups lined up, the *blatnye*, the *muzhyki*, and the Pilotovtsy.

Everyone was frisked and asked about their barrack number. Nothing was found on anyone outside, but the parallel search of the Third revealed several shanks, and other improvised weapons that the combatants left behind.

Svietlov inspected the proceedings from the side, taking notes.

In the end, several guys from each group were pulled for a trip to the isolator. The rest of us were warned about severe consequences coming if another fight breaks out. Svietlov said that "time for jokes is over," and that "real justice will be enforced". After that, we were ordered to get back to our barracks.

The Pilotovtsy slowly limped and staggered away in defeat, helping each other on the way to the Second. While we marched through the Zone straight-backed and proud. A group of more than twenty *vory*, with scars and bruises, but with a sense of winning a battle. Everyone knew what happened. The prison elite gave a show of force, but the peace with Pilot and his gang was over and Svietlov's warning hung in the air.

Still, we felt good at that moment. We had won and we had shown the *Suki* who's ruling the camp.

We even had a celebration in the Sixth that night. We recalled moments of the battle, we shared *chifir*, and food from *obshchak*. Tsikhiy took the spotlight, talking in detail about how we fought off the Pilotovtsy until reinforcements arrived. Everyone laughed when he described how he folded Zhiraff like a sheet of paper.

Sidoy remained silent though. He must have felt that something was off, that things were changing, and this was just another escalation bringing us closer towards total chaos. When blood was spilled between the *zeki*, it was the guards who benefited.

The next morning, during roll-call, Major Koralov announced that visits between barracks were limited to a single person, and all assemblies of more than five *zeki* in the yard were prohibited. Guard patrols were increased, and new rooms were assigned as isolation cells in the guards' barracks.

Whoever ended up there, had to undergo daily beatings and people came from there with horror stories that reminded me of my stay in Saratov's police station and pre-trial detention center. We also learned that the guard detachment we saw drilled by Svietlov was a new unit, meant for crowd control and suppression of riots. They were the ones responsible for the beatings, and they patrolled the Zone now, in larger squads, enforcing new rules with fresh brutality.

The balance of power was shifting. Even though we still felt in control, the feeling of tension was growing among everyone.

'*Divide et impera*' – 'divide and conquer', the old Roman rule for subjugating people, worked on us like a charm. I realized later that it was all planned by Svietlov. He manipulated us to fight each other, to weaken both

Pilot's gang, and the *vory*. To create strife and uncertainty, that he could then exploit.

Just like the guards of the modern invisible prison – corrupt politicians, financiers, and the mainstream media – turn us against each other, creating divides across racial, cultural, and political lines. The polarized society can't stand together against the tyranny of the few.

It is easier to see such things in hindsight when the fog of war lifts and the perspective widens. But when we are in the midst of turmoil, when we need to survive in the moment, and are blinded by petty grievances, we easily fall prey to the trap of division. When we see the guy next to us encroaching on our rights, we rarely ask ourselves if he is acting of his own will, or if there is some other force behind him. We need to deal with the problem, or so we think. The only thing that matters is to resolve the threat, to regain control, and the deeper thinking is suspended, until it is too late.

Look at your own adversaries today, *droog*. Are they opposed to you by their own will? Maybe someone else has pitted them against your cause, to keep you busy from seeing the invisible prison you're in.

CHAPTER 11

Before You Break Free, Secure The King's Blessing

It often happens in our struggles that just as we are about to do something important, the entire world seems to turn against us. Carefully crafted plans are stressed under changing circumstances, hard tasks become increasingly difficult as environments shift and our assumptions no longer hold. As if the universe was trying to test our resolve and commitment to what we want to achieve. To make sure that we really want it, and that we will not abandon our path just because things are getting tough.

The time of our planned escape just so happened to coincide with all these nasty developments in the camp. As if the idea of risking our lives in a daring, precarious operation was not enough to keep us awake at night, now we also had to deal with the period of the worst unrest since I landed in IK-22.

But we were committed and wanted out no matter what. Evgeny for the sake of his love for Matryona. Aslan to see his family in Chechnya. And me, to save some of my youth, and to have what I always wanted, but I couldn't get before – freedom.

We kept our plan to ourselves, even among the *blatnye*, and worked on it for months. It created a new level of camaraderie between the three of us. We became sensitive to each other's body language and facial expressions and often could communicate without speaking. Like conspirators in a revolutionary plot, we made sure no one was around when we discussed it during breaks in the work area.

Many iterations of the plan brought us finally to a version that seemed to have good chances of success. We kept gathering information and items needed for the operation. Matryona was our helper on the outside, and she was to provide us with the poison mixture necessary to neutralize the guards. The time was coming for us to receive that last bit of supply.

With everything falling in place, the day came when we had to share our plan with Sidoy. He was the respected leader of our *Bratva*. Evgeny felt that, since Sidoy was something of a mentor to me, I would be the best one to do it. Somewhere deep down, I hoped that he would join us and we could break free together.

I came to him one evening, and I respectfully asked him to join me on a walk.

He looked at me with a frown. It was usually him who would tell me to walk with him. After a moment, he nodded and got up from his bunk in the swift moves of a man who kept himself in shape despite his age.

A group of *blatnye* was sitting by one of the tables in the living area – Tsikhiy, Lop, and a few others. I felt their eyes on my back as we crossed the room with Sidoy. A pang of guilt hit me for hiding things from my brothers, but I knew by that time that we couldn't trust anyone with our plans. One word reaching the wrong ears could put all that careful planning and work at risk.

When Sidoy and I were out in the open, I checked that no one was following us. The yard was clear, just like the slowly darkening sky above us. I took a deep inhale of the crisp air and I told him about our plan. A chilly, wet breeze carried the smell of wet forest, and the first signs of autumn.

Sidoy walked quietly, gazing at the barbed wire fence, and I waited for his words.

"Your escape will bring trouble to the camp," he said, looking me directly in the eyes. "The guards won't like it."

A knot formed in my throat. He was right. We would bring further restrictions, and crackdown from the guards on all those we would leave behind. Recognizing this fact felt almost like a punch to the gut. All the work we had put in, all the hopes and efforts would go to nothing.

Sidoy laughed. "*Harasho*! – Good!"

I looked at him, surprised. His face was brightened by a mischievous smile.

"Let them get mad, *mudaki*!" Sidoy hit a fist into an open hand with a loud clap. "If you can break out, it will only prove their incompetence. It will show that no prison can hold a free man down."

"Will you join us then?" I asked with rising hope.

"No, Andrycha. I am a *vor*. I have stolen before and outside I will steal again, just to be locked up again."

"I am a *vor* too."

He gave me a sidelong glance, as if I was stating the obvious.

"Yes. But you have more to look for outside. I had my adventures already, and I have no home to go back to. Here, I am of use."

"Should we warn the others?" I asked.

"No. You did good by staying quiet about it. I have bad feelings about some of the *Bratva* lately. Talking about your plan would cause more difficulties both for you and for me. There are whispers about taking Pilot out. Not to deal with the *suka*, but to take over his business. But that would only make us into *suki* ourselves."

He spat.

I was not surprised. There were cliques in the *Bratva*, and not everyone had the same values in mind when speaking of the Code.

"How will you handle this?" I asked. "Can I help?"

"I will keep a lid on it, and I'll make sure anyone breaking the Code will be put to justice. Do what you have to do for yourselves. It will prove to the camp once again that *Bratva* is in control. No barbed wire, and no guard with a rifle can stand in our way when we decide to be free."

"Thank you, Sidoy." I said with deep emotion.

A new feeling came over me. One of gratitude for having this man as my mentor. I wondered briefly how my life would have been, if my father had cared and understood me as much as this aged criminal did.

"There is one thing you can do for me. I might be too old to break out of this place, but Misha is too young to rot here. Take him with you, he is a good prospect and will make a good *vor*. Outside you will need men like him."

I thought about it as we turned around. Sidoy was right. There were few men as eager and reliable as Misha. Even though he was still a freshman in the camp he had already proven to be as tough and as honorable as a *vor* can be. In recognition of that, his baptism was scheduled to come at first snow.

"I'll ask the others. There are risks involved," I finally answered. "If they approve, I'll talk to him."

"Boyets is as bold and daring as they come. I know how he'll answer," Sidoy chuckled and wrapped his hands behind his back. "Now, have you convinced the cook to help you already?"

"Not yet, Sidoy. I left it for the last moment. He's our weakest link."

"Bring him in when you're ready, we'll work on him together."

I thanked him, and we walked back into the Sixth in silence. I was relieved. Not only did I get the blessing of the Vor v Zakonye. He also gave advice and offered to help me, even if it meant more pain and difficulties for him and others in the camp.

The *vory* look at pain differently than the regular men. We embrace it, we make it our ally. That's why it is so hard to break or corrupt a *vor* with threats or torture. But we all have breaking points, even the hardest of us. Now was the time to test how much we could bend Artyom, the cook, to our will.

I shared Sidoy's thoughts with my co-conspirators. Both Evgeny and Aslan took the news with nods of approval. We were relieved that Sidoy not only was allowing our escape but would also support our effort. We all liked Misha, so we were happy to take him along, but we decided to keep him in the dark until his initiation. The day was coming soon, as the temperature was dropping every day, and the cold drizzle could turn to snow at any time.

It was one of those wet September evenings, when we sat together, Evgeny, Misha, Aslan, and me, discussing our observations from the workday, and noting them down. Sidoy then joined us and listened in, puffing on a rolled-up cigarette.

"Kolesnikov was in the watchtower the whole time. He got his tea in a thermos, delivered by Karimov. I saw him drink it with his ration a short while later," Misha said in a conspiratorial tone.

The young lad didn't know what we were up to, but he followed my commands without asking questions. I just told him we wanted to know the routines of the guards in case we had to conduct some 'business' in the work area.

"What about Tsuladze?" I asked about the radio operator.

"He was playing chess with Akhmetov," Aslan reported. "They drank the tea as they played."

"Why are you so concerned when they drink their tea Andrycha," Misha asked me.

"I like to know all the small details, Boyets. You never know what might be useful when you need to make a move. Now, go and bring Artyom here."

Misha got up and I turned to Evgeny, who reported his observations. Everything was mostly in line with the intel we had gathered over the previous months. The monotony of camp life and its tight schedule worked to our advantage. IK-22 operated like a machine, and both *zeki* and the guards were cogs in this hungry mechanism which devoured our lives at a steady pace.

We discussed the rest of the plan as Misha went to fetch Artyom. The cook was the last missing piece, and we needed to convince him to do something risky for us. It would be the first time I have witnessed the comfort-discomfort method applied to a person. Sidoy and Evgeny were to do the talking, while the rest of us would create the atmosphere necessary to persuade Artyom.

Presently, Misha came back with the cook, who had a frightened look on his plump face, and his eyes darted nervously between the gathered *vory*.

Sidoy pointed at the bench on the opposite side of the table from him, and we made space for Artyom to sit down.

"How are you doing these days?" Sidoy asked.

"Not that great, Sidoy." Artyom made a sour face. "People blame me for the bad food. But what can I do? The guards are giving us scraps, then Pilot grabs the best pieces, and I am left with little to work with."

"You won't have trouble with us," Sidoy said, "We understand your situation."

"Where are you from, Tyoma?" Evgeny asked out of the blue.

"Leningrad." Artyom sighed and looked up, as if recalling a pleasant memory.

"What were you doing back there?" Evgeny's voice was unusually friendly.

"I was a chef in a proper restaurant. I was the best. Had good money, good connections, and girls..." Artyom drifted off.

"How was Leningrad back then?" Evgeny asked, musingly, as if he cared.

"Ah, Leningrad..." Artyom's face softened, and he looked up as if transported to a faraway place. A faint, blissful smile appeared on his face when he began talking. "It was paradise for a man like me. Money flowed like water. The finest food, the best drinks, women who'd do anything for a taste of luxury. I had the connections, the power; life was sweet. I could walk Nevsky Prospekt, and it felt like I had the world in my hand. The smell of fresh bread from the bakeries, the sound of music from the cafes, and the women... They were elegant, classy, like something from a movie."

"Why were you locked up then?" Sidoy's words snapped Artyom out of his daydream.

"They accused me of poisoning the food when the local Second Party Secretary got sick after a dinner at my restaurant. The bastard had an affair with my wife, but I didn't do anything. He had a weak stomach, that's all." Artyom babbled now, as if trying to vindicate himself.

We looked at each other. It sounded like he was the man for the job.

"There is something we want you to do for us," Sidoy said, giving a sign to Misha, who was standing close by.

Boyets turned on his heel and disappeared inside the barrack.

"What is it?" Artyom looked between Sidoy and Evgeny. "I won't be able to get more food. No matter the price, there is just nothing to be had."

"We want you to put something in the tea that you make for everyone in the work area." Sidoy said, leaning in, looking him in the eyes.

Artyom stared back in silence. He straightened, and his face adopted a fearful but calculating look.

"This is risky business you're talking about," he said. "I don't know..."

As he was trying to come up with an excuse, the door to the building crashed open.

One of the roosters responsible for cleaning the urinal and the washing area in the barrack appeared carrying a bucket. As he was going down the stairs, someone kicked him from behind. The rooster fell face forward, spilling the contents of the bucket on the ground. Some of it splashed on him, and he slowly raised himself from a muddy puddle. He collected the bucket and looked at us with eyes emptied of life before he went away to the *banya*.

We made sure to sit Artyom so that he would see the entire spectacle.

"Ahh... Tanya," Evgeny said with a mix of pity and disgust. "She used to be a big shot, back there, outside."

Some roosters got female nicknames after being cast down and were used by those with uncontrollable urges. The Zone was unforgiving, and vicious for the weak.

Artyom followed Tanya with his eyes, and I could see one corner of his mouth twitching involuntarily. I knew then that he understood the stakes. He swallowed, and turned back to us, with a cunning smile.

"You are planning to escape," he said softly, but we remained silent. "What good will it do, that you poison the guards? You still have nearly a hundred miles of taiga to cross." He paused and put a finger to his mouth, as if considering different options. "Are you going to use the trucks? Where are you going to drive to?"

"We just want you to put some extra spice in the tea," Evgeny said with a harsh tone, cutting off the questioning.

"I want to go with you." Artyom put both his hands on the table and leaned towards Sidoy. "I have five years left. I won't make it. Pilot, the guards, and you, boss. Everyone is pushing me, and it's only getting worse. I'll do what you need, and more, but I want in on your plans."

We looked at each other. The plan was made for four people, as Matryona planned to pick us up with a passenger car. One more would be more complicated, but maybe still doable.

"We'll think about it. You can go now," Evgeny said with a frown. He then leaned in and looked Artyom in the eyes. "And keep your mouth shut, or you'll envy the life Tanya currently has."

Artyom got up, and as he walked away, he passed a couple of guards on a route through Zone. They carried their rifles at the ready. The times were difficult, and everyone was on the edge, including the guards.

As Artyom passed them, one of them yelled at him and I recognized the voice. They were more than fifty meters away and it was getting dark outside, but I recognized the familiar bulky frame, and the square jaw of a caveman. It was Ivan Rostovkin.

"What the fuck is that son of a bitch doing back here?" Evgeny growled.

"Nothing good," I said, looking down at the Grim Reaper on my left hand. 'I am here, and I am waiting.' – the tattooed letters read. It taunted me, and suddenly I wanted to get going with the escape as soon as possible.

Ivan Rostovkin came back with a batch of fresh recruits who were supposed to reinforce the ranks of the IK-22 guards. Later that week, I learned what Captain Svietlov's plan was. With the extra forces, and fomenting conflict between inmates he intended to turn the camp around. He wanted to put all the *zeki* under the thumb of the authorities, transforming the penal colony from Black – run by the *vory* to Red – fully controlled by the guards.

The new recruits were mostly young thugs with a penchant for brutality and violence. They were led by a few seasoned *omonovetsy* – members of the state riot police, OMON. Even the regular guards seemed to be apprehensive of the new group, which became known as Svietlov's Dogs. Their detachments roamed the Zone and aggressively punished any perceived misconduct on the part of the *muzhyki*.

They still stayed away from the *blatnye*, knowing that going against us could lead to a serious backlash. But their encroachment was increasing day by day, and now, with the return of the psycho-sadist, Ivan, I knew that blood would be spilled again soon.

With Aslan and Evgeny, we all did our best to keep a low profile, and act as politely as possible with the guards. Getting any one of us in the isolator would dismantle the entire plan, and in any case, we would not leave a brother behind.

I felt increasing anxiety each time I saw Ivan, and I wondered why he'd returned to the same prison where he had been so viciously assaulted. I worried he was out for revenge, and that sooner or later he would realize it was me who served him justice.

The time to face him came in shortly, and it was exactly in the worst moment, when I was trafficking the poison meant for our escape plan.

For the third day in a row, we used our midday break to loiter in the work area, searching for the hidden package.

Together with Matryona we developed a system, both for communication and smuggling. We stayed in touch through coded messages left in concealed spots in the forest. A tree hollow one week, an old fox lair the next. We kept changing our mailboxes and marked them in subtle ways that looked inconspicuous to anyone else – a thread tied to a branch, a small pile of pinecones.

Matryona often used a simple diagonal cross as a marker. She would carve it into the white bark of a birch tree or fix from two bound twigs hanging on a thread. Finding her signs took patience. More than once, we spent several days roaming the work area during breaks before we spotted them. But the system was as secure as we could hope for, and we were careful never to be seen placing or retrieving the messages or contraband.

On that day we used Misha and Aslan as decoys. Misha complained loudly about the quality of food. A common occurrence, but he made enough of a show to draw the attention of both guards and inmates.

"I can't work like that!" Misha cried out, with theatrical despair. "I am young, I need some real food."

As people gathered, focused on Misha, Evgeny and I slipped deeper into the work zone, to the place where we noticed a cross sign earlier.

"The boy won't grow properly if you won't feed him," Aslan remarked as the guards came over to silence Misha.

"He's grown enough, *blyat*!" The radio operator, Tsuladze barked.

"Shut your traps," The Corporal concluded from his chair. He was reading a newspaper and didn't even bother to look up at the commotion.

Meanwhile Evgeny stood watch, as I fished out a jute pouch filled with a new mixture from Matryona. This one was not meant to keep us strong and healthy, but instead it was the key that would open the gate out of the work zone for us. I tucked it in my underpants, and we walked back to the field kitchen.

When Misha and Aslan saw us approaching, they let go of their protestations, and sat on the ground among the other *zeki*, grumbling under their breath. Just another day in the Zone.

I worked the remainder of our shift, with the pouch hidden in an uncomfortable spot.

As we marched back to the camp, I made an effort to walk normally, despite feeling my manhood squeezed. The pouch was tucked tight in there, bringing pain and irritation but there are more unpleasant ways of smuggling goods in and out of prison, trust me, *droog*.

Back in the camp, we walked through the gate house one by one. Normally we would give our name to a guard sitting behind a barred window, while another guard would frisk us. This time, to my surprise, there were two of the Svietlov Dogs inside, and it was Ivan who did the frisking.

When I saw him, I felt a knot forming in my stomach, but then I thought about the night of my first job for the *vory*, and how Ivan fell to my blade. I thought about the *Bratva*, and that I was no longer the boy that snuck behind the guard to prove himself. I was the authority now, with fierce men, ready for violence if a guard raised his hand against me.

With that feeling I stepped forward.

"Aleksander Lenkov, Barrack 6," I told my fake name to the other guard, who marked me on his list.

Ivan waved for me with his baton to come closer.

"Raise your hands, scum," he grumbled in a deep, hateful voice.

"Sure, chief," I raised my arms slightly.

Ivan got closer and looked me closely in the eyes.

"I remember you," he said.

"Good." I turned my palms so he could see my tattoos. "We remember you too, Comrade Rostovkin."

He glared at them with sudden recognition. I saw something new on his face. His eyes were darkened, and his face looked thinner than it used to be. The injuries I gave him must have been hard to heal.

His mouth twitched, and I knew he was aching to unleash some anger on me. He pushed me to the wall and raised his *dubinka*.

"Rostovkin. Don't you see he's a *vor*?" The other guard raised his voice from his post. "Remember what Captain said, you oaf."

Ivan didn't like to hold back; I knew that from my first days in IK-22. But surprisingly, he just twisted his mouth into a diabolical smile and pointed with his baton at the door leading to the Zone.

"One day, Sasha," he whispered in my ear as I moved past him. "You thieves will pay. One day."

With the threat hanging in my mind I joined the others, waiting for the whole brigade to gather for the final count before we were dismissed. Misha was behind me in line, and when he left the gatehouse, he was walking hunched and had a pink sign of a dubinka hit on his cheek.

Back in the Sixth he said that Rostovkin smashed him several times with the baton, without giving any excuse. Just a silent beating, seemingly for no reason. Ivan must have let go of his anger on the young Boyets, who had no ink on his body yet to mark him as one of us.

It angered me to see a friend once more mistreated by the same man. Ivan's threat bothered me less than I would expect. By that time, I was ready to go, one way or the other, and the Grim Reaper on my hand felt more like a friend than an enemy now. But what the other guard had said bothered me, I felt something bad was going on. It was becoming clear that Svietlov was planning something, though we didn't yet know the extent of his plan.

CHAPTER 12

It Takes One Spark To Ruin A Fragile Peace

I told Sidoy about my concerns, and he held council with the other seniors. Tsikhiy was satisfied that Svietlov told his men to leave the *vory* alone. He perceived it as a sign that our power increased. Sidoy was more reserved, and he told us to watch our backs and be careful with the guards.

Following the 'divide and conquer' rule, the guards left us alone and for a few days focused on the weakened Pilot's gang. I had seen his men getting beaten in the yard by Svietlov's Dogs. Some of the *vory* cheered at that but when I heard that Pilot himself was stopped for wearing his pilot's cap, and confined to the isolation cell, I knew things were going to escalate soon.

I just had no idea how much.

Things took a turn from bad to worse on Misha's initiation day. IK-22 was a dark hellhole, but on that day it became darker. I clench my teeth when I think about it, even now after so many years.

It was the middle of September. The first snow came early that year, but the temperature didn't fall below zero. The Zone was a mix of black and white, with dark, wet surfaces jutting beneath the thawing snow. The walkways became muddy with slush and dirt, and with constant cloud cover, the camp was sinking in the gray, moist air.

I stood with my hands in my pockets to keep them warm, while Misha, the only prospect to be baptized this time, got undressed.

We stood in a semicircle around him and the barrel. There were about forty of us, *blatnye* from Barrack 6, the unofficial elite, and grey eminences of the IK-22 penal colony.

I thought how close I had become with many of these men, and how the best, youthful years of my life were spent among them. Aslan, Evgeny, Sidoy, and Kamen were the closest friends I had. We went through real hardships together, and knew we could rely on each other.

With most of the other *blatnye* I had good relations, as the code and mutual respect kept us from working against each other. It was a tough brotherhood, one formed in darkness and tainted by it. No other could survive the misery and oppression of the Soviet penal system.

Dima Sidoy began the ceremony and asked who spoke for Misha.

I said that he was a true fighter and deserved to join the *Bratva*. Soon, Misha was in the barrel, neck deep in the icy water. Our young *urka* was fierce and had worked hard to prove himself. He had a big mouth and liked to brag, but besides that he was dependable and did whatever he was tasked with.

I looked on with pride as he took deep breaths while dealing with the bitter cold. Just like I taught him, just like Evgeny taught me.

Sidoy pushed Misha's head under the water, and when it was done, Boyets got out of the barrel. As he stood in front of us reciting the oath, the sound of a whistle pierced the air.

"*Pizdiets,*" someone in the crowd cursed. "Guards coming."

"Svietlov's Dogs, *suki,*" another voice added.

People turned, and I looked in the direction the sound came from.

A group of a dozen guards, some with batons, others with AKMs were walking straight towards us. Ivan Rostovkin was at the front, carrying a rifle and baring his teeth in a wicked smile. His stance was tilted to the side and he now walked with a permanent limp.

By his side strode an *omonovets* named Vasilenko, whirling a short dubinka on a cord attached to his wrist. It was a type of baton with a metal core, a more serious weapon than the regular long, purely rubber *dubinka*. While the rubber was used for a beating that was supposed to cause pain but not do much permanent damage, the *metalicheskaya dubinka* could easily break bones, and crush skulls.

Sidoy didn't turn around and instead continued the ceremony.

"I will accept no authority, except that of the senior *vor v zakonye*," Sidoy's voice boomed in the cold air, and Misha repeated the words.

The guards were close by.

"Disperse, right now! Get back to your barrack you mongrels," Vasilenko yelled as they approached our gathering.

"I will never cooperate with the state, and I will always help a *vor* in need," Sidoy spoke the last line of the oath, and Misha again repeated the words.

As Sidoy moved to embrace Boyets and tell him that he was now a *vor*, we heard the sound of an AKM's bolt being racked. More curses came from the guards, who positioned themselves around us.

Kamen walked out of our group and confronted Ivan.

"Chief," Kamen said. "This is not the right time for this nonsense. You don't want to interrupt the *vory* in their business."

Without breaking stride, Vasilenko whirled the metal *dubinka* in his hand and struck Kamen on the head.

Our *smotritel* staggered backwards and a few *blatnye* from the crowd caught him before he fell. Blood flowed from his scalp.

"*Tver*, don't get in our way," Vasilenko yelled in a drunken voice.

The Svietlov's Dogs must have used vodka to inspire the courage necessary to confront us. A few more bolts were racked by the guards who spread out around us.

Ivan and Vasilenko walked on, and the crowd reluctantly made space for them.

I could see hatred and anger in the eyes of the *blatnye*. This was sacrilege, and a breach of an agreement between the *vory* and the camp authorities.

"What is going on here? Don't you know we have new rules? You should all be in the barracks, you fucking simpletons!" Vasilenko's voice rang out in our midst. He walked towards Sidoy and Misha who was now putting on his clothes.

"What is this? Are you having fun with the boy, old man?" Vasilenko stopped a few steps short of Sidoy.

Ivan stood by with his finger on the trigger of his rifle, his eyes darting to the sides. He kept smiling, but when his eyes met mine, the smile turned into a sour grimace.

Aslan stepped forward, ready to speak for the *vory*, but grey-haired Sidoy raised his hand and turned to the guards himself.

"Ivan Petrovich Rostovkin from Sosnovka and Stepan Oleksandrovych Vasilenko from Poltava. You are not welcome here. Leave before bad things happen." Sidoy's voice carried authority, and he stood with his head held high. He was the leader of free men, and he acted as if it was he who had a group of heavily armed thugs at his back.

Ivan's smile disappeared in an instant, and Vasilenko seemed to have lost his tongue. Sidoy held them in a steady gaze, while Misha buttoned up his shirt.

"You're not allowed to be here, by order of Captain Svietlov. There are no gatherings of more than five *zeki* allowed," Vasilenko barked as his face went red. The vodka gave him courage but didn't help with his thinking.

"Why don't you fuck off," Misha said, as he put on his jacket, and straightening up beside Sidoy.

This set Vasilenko off and everything after that happened very fast, almost as if the whole situation was a spring trap, armed and waiting for the slightest touch to be set off.

Vasilenko rammed his baton in Misha's face. The sound was sickening, and Misha staggered back, spitting out teeth. Vasilenko swung, but this time Misha leaned back, making the guard miss him narrowly, and instead grazing Sidoy on the leg.

Sidoy reacted in an instant, stepping forward. The blade of his razor-sharp knife flashed as he stabbed Vasilenko in the neck. Before he could pull it free, a burst of rounds from Ivan's AKM tore into him, throwing his body backward. A few stray bullets whizzed over our heads and struck the wooden wall.

Blood gushed from Vasilenko's neck, and he collapsed into the mud.

More shots from the firearms echoed as the guards around us fired in the air, yelling for us to drop to the ground.

One by one, to the noise of furious, broken screams from the drunken guards, we lay down, putting our arms behind our backs.

Vasilenko gurgled on the ground, as one of the other guards tried to stop the bleeding, but he was drunk, and I could see he had no idea what he was doing.

I looked at Sidoy, who lay sprawled on his back beside the barrel, his eyes open and looking at the sky, his chest still moving. Ivan stepped closer, looking around with complete madness, like a rabid dog.

"I dare you to stand up!" he screamed.

"Rostovkin, that's enough," another guard yelled at Ivan.

Clenching his teeth in a mad grin, Ivan ignored him. He walked over to Sidoy and pointed his gun down at my fallen mentor. With eyes filled with rage, Ivan Rostovkin emptied the rest of his magazine.

Sidoy's body convulsed on the ground as the bullets tore through him, raising pink mist with each hit. His head exploded like a watermelon, hit by several projectiles and I felt pieces of bone hitting my side.

When the thunderous echo of the shots died down, the silence that fell over the Zone was as deep as a tomb.

Sidoy's body lay mutilated on the ground, his blood splattered across the white snow, mixing with dirty water.

I looked at what remained of him, stunned, unable to believe what had just happened. I remember clutching at the slushy mud with my bare hands, feeling the wet cold in my palms, and the acrid smell of gunpowder and blood.

Ivan changed the magazine and turned around to see if there were any other targets.

We remained on the ground as Svietlov's Dogs kept their muzzles pointed in our direction. Soon, more guards came running from the guardhouse. The sound of a bell announced the end of the *Vorovskoi Mir* in IK-22.

There was no more room in the isolation cells, so the guards locked us all in the barracks. The Zone went into lockdown, with armed men posted everywhere and we were warned that anyone disobeying would be shot on spot. The time dragged as the significance and pain of what had happened sank home.

I sat with Misha, who lost two front teeth to Vasilenko's *metalicheskaya dubinka*. His lips were swollen, and he kept spitting blood onto a rag, but he had to take more pain. Sasun, the tattoo artist, worked on his chest, carving the first ink into the young fighter's body. It was part of the initiation, and even while grieving Sidoy's fate, we were determined to live by the Code.

I watched the drops of blood run down Misha's skin, mixing with the dirty prison ink. I was stunned, losing track of time as I stared at those black-red drops, thinking of Sidoy's blood spilled into the dirt of the Zone.

Before the day was over there was a banging on the door, and guards yelled that they were coming in. We lined up in front of our bunks as a large group of regular guards entered, rifles aimed at us. Major Koralov himself showed up and asked for the remaining seniors to sit down with him.

The mood was as somber as a funeral, and everyone was on edge. The guards and the *blatnye* looked at each other across the room, while the seniors gathered to hear out what Koralov had to say. Tsikhiy took the lead, with Kamen and Aslan at his sides. Kamen had his head wrapped in a makeshift bandage. A faint blood stain marked the spot where he was struck.

I stood close by with Evgeny, Lop, and others. Everything felt sharp, balanced on a knife's edge.

Koralov took a deep breath and ran a finger over his grey moustache.

"What happened today was highly regrettable," he began. "But we should work together to avoid further bloodshed. Everyone will suffer if we can't keep peace."

Tsikhiy's jaw clenched at that and he whispered in Kamen's ear.

"We don't work with you or for you." Kamen said.

Koralov sighed loudly and looked up over Tsikhiy's head, measuring the line of faces behind him.

"Private Vasilenko died in the infirmary. This creates a big problem for all of us. I could keep the camp in a lockdown for a long time. You must understand the seriousness of this situation."

"You have to keep your quotas," Kamen responded. "Lockdown will hurt you as much as it will hurt the *zeki*."

Koralov pursed his lips and scoffed like a gambler whose bluff was called.

"The quotas are important, but keeping order in the colony is my priority. If you won't cooperate, more incidents will happen." He leaned back and crossed his arms. "Captain Svietlov told me he can handle a riot if necessary, and trust me, he won't go easy on anyone."

"All I want is to get to my retirement without any more blood," Koralov said looking up, as if trying to imagine a life far away from the camp.

I thought then that he was as much a prisoner of the penal system as we were.

"We don't want to see any of the Svietlov's Dogs in the Zone. They were the ones who caused the trouble," Kamen conveyed another message from Tsikhiy.

Koralov mused over this.

"This can be arranged," he finally said. "But be careful. No more leniency, rules must be followed. We need a new peace in the camp, one that will benefit all."

No answer came back. Tsikhiy and the others sat motionless, like iron statues.

Koralov got up and left us with the silence which persisted for a while after the guards shut the door locked for the night.

We were allowed out the next day, and during the morning roll call Koralov talked about 'the unfortunate 'accident', which shouldn't distract us from working hard toward rehabilitation.

With blank faces, the *zeki* listened to his calls for peace and cooperation, though everyone knew that the situation was not going to get better anytime soon.

At least Svietlov's Dogs were pulled back to the guard barracks outside the Zone, kept there to prevent more trouble. Still, their presence close by was a threat enough. At any moment they could be unleashed upon us again.

It was under these conditions that we finally decided to stop waiting and execute our escape plan as soon as we could. Evgeny, Aslan, and I sat with Misha, whose grin was now marked by two gaping holes in his otherwise pristine front teeth. I told our freshly baptized brother about our plan, and I mentioned that Sidoy's wish was for him to join us.

Misha nodded thoughtfully, as his tasks from the past weeks made more sense to him now. His face tightened with seriousness when he thanked us solemnly for the offer, and he swore that he would do his best to help us get out of the prison hellhole.

Together, we put our plans in motion.

On the following day we left the coded letter to Matryona in the marked hiding place in the cubbyhole of an old tree. We urged her to be ready to receive us in the coming days. The escape had been planned between us over many months and she had everything prepared, including transportation.

All we had to do was leave the work zone in a truck and get to the meeting point in the forest, ten kilometers west of the work area.

To find the right spot we had crude maps drawn by Matryona as she had spent many days wandering the forests around IK-22. She used these hikes to search for ingredients for her remedies as well as to gather information necessary for our escape.

The last thing we needed was a confirmation from Artyom.

I met him inside the library. He had fresh bruises and scratches on his face. Someone must have manhandled him. It was true that he was under a lot of pressure these days. Being the cook, he was an easy target of frustration for those who suffered from hunger.

I told him we could take him along, but that he would have to obey our authority and do exactly as he was told.

"Do you give me your word that you won't just ditch me after I put your 'spice' in the tea?" he asked after I gave him the pouch with the poison we'd gotten from Matryona.

"I give you my word. If you do what is needed, we'll take you out with us."

We shook hands, but as I was turning away, Artyom grabbed me by the jacket sleeve. I pushed him off, angrily, and looked him in the eyes. He had guilt written all over his face.

"There is someone who wants to talk to you," he said, nodding his head towards a bookshelf on the far side of the room. "Behind that shelf."

Then he dashed off like a scared rabbit.

"*Suka*," I muttered, checking that the shank I had hidden at my waist was within easy reach before moving in the direction Artyom had indicated. Keeping my right hand on my belt, I carefully leaned forward, peeking behind the shelf.

Ziya Pashayev was standing there with a book in his hands. Seeing me, he put it away and smiled. I looked around. There was no one else in this part of the library.

"Andrej," he extended his hand.

"Ziya," I said, pretending not to notice his outstretched palm. "What do you want?"

"Don't be angry at Artyom, he wasn't the one who told me about your plans. I just asked him to arrange this meeting between us."

"My plans? What do you mean?" I kept a poker face, but my gut was tight with anxiety. Was he going to interfere with our escape? A thought crossed my mind that I should use the shank and get rid of the threat right then and there, but I composed myself. I had to learn how much he knew, and what his angle was.

"Let's say that I figured out you're on your way out of this shithole," Ziya said in a businesslike manner, "I don't blame you. Especially now, when your *Bratva* is falling apart under pressure. It is smart to abandon a sinking ship before it is too late."

I clenched my jaw, ignoring the insult. He was baiting me, but I needed answers.

"I don't know what you're talking about," I lied. "Things are getting worse for everyone."

"Not for me," Ziya said, smiling, "With Pilot in isolation, I took on more responsibility within our organization. I am using my contacts outside to get on the good side of Koralov. He is a reasonable man, not like that stick-up-the-ass Svietlov. I'll help him manage the *zeki*, and maybe my sentence will be reduced."

"Good for you," I spat. "Shit always floats to the top."

"So good to talk to you again, *bratan*." Ziya kept the smile on his face, but for an instant I saw a flash of anger in his eyes. "Now let's get back to business. I know you're up to something. You and your pals have been procuring weird items all of a sudden. Rubber gloves, wire cutters, it doesn't take a genius to figure out you want to bail."

He paused, watching me.

"I know what's going on around the stores," he continued. "And I treat information like that as currency. I won't cause you trouble."

He winked at me, but seeing no reaction he finally got to the point. "For my silence, I want you to do something for me."

He reached under his jacket and pulled out an envelope.

"I suspect that if you manage to survive your little escapade out there, your path will sooner or later lead you back to Berlin." He held it out the envelope. "I want you to deliver this letter."

"Why would I do anything for you?" I glared at him.

"Andrej, no need to get nasty. We have our differences, but I tried to be fair with you. I told the *vory* that the drug business was mine. And I didn't tell anyone who you really are, and that you served in the GDR military. You should know by now that this would not fly with the honorable *blatnye* and their code."

I swallowed, realizing that he was right. *Vory* shunned those who served the state and among the strict code followers there was no place for ex-military or policemen.

"Besides," Ziya continued, "If I wanted to hurt you, I could just spread the word that you're planning to escape. I am pretty sure your plan doesn't include waiting to get out of an isolation cell. All I am asking for is that you do what you've been doing all along, but instead of writing a love letter for me, I want you to deliver one."

"What? Is that it, a love letter? Why don't you just send it yourself?" I asked, confused by his request.

"I've been sending letters to her for the past three years. Never got an answer. Maybe she changed her address, or maybe the letters were confiscated. I can't be sure. But you're a resourceful guy, you can find her for me and deliver the letter in person. As much as I think your 'honorable' ways are naïve, and childish, I do trust that you would keep your word on that. That is all I am asking for."

At the end, the arrogant smile left his face, and his voice actually sounded genuine for a change.

I considered his request. It was true that he could harm me, and as much as I hated being blackmailed, it didn't sound like an unreasonable demand.

"Under one condition," I said, "You'll give me contact details for the people we dealt with in Berlin, Poland, and Ukraine. If I get out, I will need to start an operation. It will be good to have someone I could work with."

Ziya snarled, and scratched his chin, looking at me sideways.

"Fine," he said, reluctantly. "I'll give you the contacts, but whatever business you do with them, I'll want to get a thirty percent cut when I am out."

"If we live that long." I said, then grabbed the envelope.

"Good. We have a deal. On the envelope you'll find the name and address of the girl, Elsa. She studied journalism back when I dated her in Berlin."

He paused, and for a moment his face took on a distant look. "Ahh. You remember, the day we met, the flowers, how you helped me with the van?"

"The contacts?" I pressed, unwilling to go down the memory lane with him.

"I will write them down and have them delivered to you before curfew. Take care Andrej, and I'll see you on the other side."

"No need for that," I said, turning my back to him, and walking away.

Sometimes people ask me how to deal with enemies. My best friend in life became my biggest enemy. Only God can forgive him. And me. One day.

Be thankful for your enemy. He will teach you everything that you need to know about your mind, your life, and your death.

Number 1: You are not a rock. You are an ocean. A good enemy will teach you that before strategy, before words comes control over the ocean that is inside of you. Is it storming? Then better not go and sail towards your enemy, *bratan*.

He wants you to crash into the rocks. He wants you to be swallowed by your own waves. Do not engage with your enemy in anger. An enemy wants a reaction. Rage. Fear. Impulse.

You will not give him that. Suka. The silence is your shield. Silence is your sword.

Number 2: Reduce yourself. Limit exposure. Limit information. Limit emotional availability. The less access an enemy has to your time, data, and energy, the weaker they become.

Number 3: Build boundaries around your ocean. State clearly what you will accept and what you will not. Once. Calmly. Respectfully. Without explanation. Then enforce through consistency, not outbursts.

This way you will calm not only your own ocean inside you but even his.

One boundary is: never fight in public. It turns disagreement into big theater. Trust me, I know what theater is. Egos rise. Faces must be saved. Positions harden. Silence again is your master.

Number 4: Stop personalizing, start analyzing. Do not take things personally. You are not the center of the world. You do not really matter. Most enemies are not driven by hatred towards you. They are driven by their own fear, status, resources, insecurity.

Ask yourself: What do they gain by opposing me? Then remove or neutralize that gain. You don't defeat enemies by insults. You defeat them by making opposition unprofitable.

Number 5: Document. Memory can lie. Paper does not. Write down facts. Dates. Words. Actions. Not with emotion. With precision. Documentation is quiet power. It protects you when stories shift and narratives are rewritten. The calm record outlives the loud accusation.

Number 6. Generosity. Follow the rules of Silence, Boundaries, Ani-Personalization, Analyzation, Documentation and then in a sudden moment – your biggest weapon to diffuse the enemy is honor. Be generous to your enemy, use it like a weapon. Trust me, it has worked many times in my life with enemies that pursued me for many years.

Number 7: Remember Death. Your enemy will teach you an important lesson. When death greets you all you have is who you have become. If you have become full of hate, then you take this into the afterlife. Don't do it.

No matter if you come to good terms or not with your enemy – forgive him. So, your soul is not burdened anymore. So, your soul can fly. And maybe his too, in the end.

CHAPTER 13

In Chaos, The Path To Freedom Can Be Forged

It was close to the end of the midday break, when the first *zeki* began to succumb to Matryona's poison. This was one of the most bizarre days in my life, and the few images of it I have in my mind remind me of surrealistic, infernal paintings by Hieronymus Bosch.

The day was grey, with low overcast clouds, and the taiga woods were wet with recent rain. The leaves of the few birch and aspen trees had already turned yellow, and they stuck out in the otherwise dark-green, coniferous forest.

I moved to my post, close to the tent where the radio was located, with Misha at my side, while Aslan and Evgeny loitered around the trucks where the drivers sat.

The work area lay about five kilometers down the dirt road from the camp. It was a square, roughly two hundred meters each side with barbed wire spread on the perimeter, and four wooden watchtowers, which reminded me of deer stands that I would often see in the East German forests. Guards manned the towers, with clear sight of the perimeter.

The *zeki* were forbidden to go anywhere close to the barbed wire, and the guards were allowed to shoot without warning. This left the inner part of the work area under the control of eight more guards, one of whom was positioned on a smaller watchtower beside the base of the operation. Tents were erected there for the field kitchen and the radio, and the generators rumbled nearby while the logs were loaded onto heavy-duty, offroad trucks.

This was the area we were focused on, especially the guard on the central watchtower, the radio operator, and the truck drivers. To get through the checkpoint on the way out of the forest, we needed one of the drivers, so Artyom filled the lucky guy's thermos before adding the poison to the large pot where the tea was brewing.

The tea itself was one of the few luxuries that both the prisoners and the guards enjoyed. It was a dark-brown brew, with added sugar and whatever spices Artyom was able to procure. Though not as potent as *chifir*, the tea still had a kick, and everyone partook in it. Knowing that, we've chosen it as a delivery method for the poison prepared by Matrona, and we made sure that all the guards drank it on an everyday basis.

When the break started, we lined up with the rest of the eighty *zeki* from our brigade to get our rations. Artyom doled out watery soup into canteens and filled mugs with tea. He looked sick, he was sweating despite the cold, damp weather, and his face was pale.

I gave him a reassuring smile when my turn came, but it only made him more jittery. I cursed him in my thoughts, but I was stressed myself.

The plan wasn't perfect, and we had to trust that the stuff Matryona prepared for us would work as promised. Many things could go wrong, and I kept thinking about the possible complications. It was too late though, we were committed, and if we failed, our fate back in the camp would be even more miserable.

Mine especially, given what Ziya had said. I had no doubt he would hold his blackmail over me going forward and that would make my situation much, much worse. Perhaps even get me killed. Our escape had to succeed.

The guards got their tea first, and they sipped it while watching the distribution.

I peeked at Kolesnikov, on the central watchtower. He was leaning on the railing, smoking a cigarette, and scanning the area lazily from his vantage point. His thermos with the tea inside, stood beside him, unopened.

I squatted close to the tents with Misha, and we pretended that we were playing dice, while watching closely what the guards were doing. I focused on the radio operator, a Georgian, named Tsuladze. As usual, he was playing chess with his comrade, a Crimean Tatar named Akhmetov.

Misha cleared his throat. I looked at him as he glanced towards the tower. I followed his gaze and saw Kolesnikov pouring tea from the thermos into the cup. I sighed with relief as he was taking longer than usual and most of the other guards had already drunk their tea.

I returned to watching the chess players. Their mugs stood beside the chessboard, steaming into the chilly air. Akhmetov sat with his brow furrowed, keeping one elbow on the table and resting his cheek on his clenched fist. It looked like an intense game. They were both lost in it, to the point where they had forgotten about their drink.

I decided to make a move.

"Keep an eye on Kolesnikov," I whispered to Misha, and I then stood up. With the mug in my hand, I strolled to where Tsuladze and Akhmetov were playing. They were still so engrossed in the game that they didn't even notice me standing nearby, until I spoke.

"Who's winning," I asked, sheepishly.

Akhmetov remained focused on the chessboard, while Tsuladze looked at me and cursed.

"The Soviet Union is winning over the enemies of the people, that's what, *blyat*," he growled.

"It will lose if he moves that knight," I replied, trying to break their concentration.

This got Akhmetov to take his eyes off the chessboard as well, and now both of them were glaring at me.

"Are you looking to spend some time in the infirmary?" Akhmetov asked, casually.

"Sorry chief, I just haven't played chess in a while. I always get so involved, even just watching." I raised my mug in toast. "To your health comrades and let the best man win!"

I then pretended to take a sip, watching them over the rim.

It is hard to explain the relationships that formed between the guards and the prisoners, especially in a place like IK-22, where official authority for years worked in parallel with that of the *vory*. The mutual hatred was muffled by the fact that we were all, in essence, forced to live in that hellhole, bearing the same shitty conditions, and seeing each other daily, which over many years created a weird sense of familiarity.

Inside the Zone, *vory* were the authority, at least until recently. That made most guards treat us with a reluctant respect, compared to the mass of *muzhyki*. Seeing me raising my mug, and making a toast to their health, they seemed to suddenly be reminded of their own drinks. They reached for their cups, and each took a swig, and as the tea warmed their bodies, they kept sipping on it while I walked away.

"To the glory of the Soviet Union," Tsuladze made his own toast.

"*Oohpah, chai* is strong today," Akhmetov exclaimed, as he returned to furrowing his brow over the chessboard.

With that I was certain that all the guards had drunk their tea, as the ones on the outer watchtowers got their thermoses delivered to their posts first. I knew from our prior observations that they warmed themselves up with hot tea as soon as they got it.

The only thing was to wait and hope that the poison worked as intended. I walked around the tents and smoked a cigarette, while keeping eye contact with Aslan who sat on a trunk beside the trucks, and Misha who was positioned close to the tower where Kolesnikov was stationed.

Matryona wrote in her note that the first effects should start after fifteen minutes, with the full onset of symptoms between half an hour and forty-five minutes, depending on the person.

As I continued to observe the *zeki* and the guards, I could see a certain sluggishness to their movement now. A few minutes later the weaker of the *zeki* began drifting away. I could see them sitting by the campfire, with their arms wrapped around their knees, and heads resting on them, as if they were taking a nap. I heard one of them saying: "I don't feel so well," before he rolled up and lay on his side on the muddy litter which covered the ground. More of the *zeki* were hunching down, holding their stomachs. Some staggered towards the field latrine with a growing sense of urgency.

The next minutes were going to be crucial and most risky.

I picked up my axe and I strolled casually behind the tents, as if going to relieve myself before the end of the break. I glanced up at Kolesnikov. He was looking the other way.

A wire ran from an opening in the tent roof over to an antenna mounted on a lone pine trunk nearby. It would have been best to cut that wire, but it was too high.

I looked down at the thick power cord running from one of the generators into the tent. I squatted beside it, close to the canvas wall of the tent, and I raised the axe. I had to cut it in one go.

I was prepared. In the past weeks, I had practiced on small, wet branches lying on the ground. The axe blade was sharp, I'd made sure of it that morning. The handle was damp with moisture, but I was wearing rubber gloves I had bartered from a *zek* working as a cleaner in the kitchen. Over my shoes, I wore standard rubber galoshes. I hoped it would be enough to protect me if the current bled through.

Still, my hands were slick with sweat in the rubber gloves, and my heart hammered like it was trying to break free from my chest.

As I took aim, an angry shout came from the front of the tent.

"Artyom, *suka*!" someone cursed loudly. "Food is bad, you *tver*!"

It was starting – the literal shit was about to hit the fan.

I whispered a quick prayer, and I struck the cable with all my might.

The blade bit into the cord, but not cleanly. Sparks sprayed up my arm, sharp and hot, and for a heartbeat the generator coughed instead of dying. Exposed copper sparked and hissed against the wet ground.

I dropped the axe and reached for the wire cutters in my pocket. They were too small to sever the cable outright, but enough to finish what I'd started. My fingers went numb inside the gloves, as I cut the remaining strands. The machine choked once more and finally fell silent.

I grabbed the axe and snuck around the tent to see the commotion spreading.

More people were on the ground, both *zeki* and guards. Some held on to their bellies, spitting curses and grimacing in pain, while those not fully affected yet were helping out their comrades or running with great urgency towards the latrine.

There was a queue already outside of the three wooden stalls, where we got to relieve ourselves over holes dug in the ground. The men in the queue looked almost as if they were dancing, stepping nervously from one foot to the other, shaking their hands, or holding them tight to their underbellies. Some were giving up, and walking at a fast, awkward pace to the bushes.

I pretended to be sick as well, and I hunched over as I walked into the crowd, with my left-hand clutching my stomach. I passed the Corporal who was vomiting on a tree. People were moaning, others shouting. Someone was calling Artyom's name.

"Tsuladze, call in backup, something is wrong!" Kolesnikov yelled from his watch tower. "I need to get down. My head is spinning."

"Stay on your post, *blyat*!" Tsuladze shouted back as he ran into the tent. "There is no power, the generator is down!"

"I'll start it up." Akhmetov grabbed his AKM and glanced around as if looking for someone. "Artyom, I'll get you, *suka*!"

I moved through the chaotic crowd, with people crawling and stumbling around me. Some were vomiting, others shitting their pants while moaning hysterically. It looked like most of the effects of the poison were kicking in, and part of me pitied the *zeki* who had to go through this, but at least I assured myself that it would not kill them.

I saw Misha sitting on his heels underneath Kolesnikov's tower. He was rocking back and forth, pretending to be sick. I gave him a sign with my fingers to watch Akhmetov, who was walking to the generator. Misha followed the guard while I entered the tent where Tsuladze was sitting over the radio.

His back was turned to me. I closed the distance in two steps and wrapped my arm around his neck, locking it tight the way Aslan had taught me.

Tsuladze jerked in surprise and slammed backward into the chair. It toppled, skidding across the floor, and the radio set crashed down with it. He clawed at the controls out of reflex, but the panel stayed dark.

I dragged him down, tightening the chokehold, and locking my legs around his waist. He bucked once more, kicking out and scraping the floor with his boots. When he finally went limp, my arms were burning with the effort.

"I turned on the generator. Radio the camp!" Akhmetov barked as he entered the tent. "*Kakogo chyorta?*" he snapped when he saw me, my arms still wrapped around his Georgian comrade. "Let him go, or I'll shoot. Now!"

I released Tsuladze and raised my hands. Akhmetov was grimacing in pain, his stomach must have already started playing up, but he was still aware enough of what was going on. He kept his rifle pointed at me. "It is all your work, *yebanuty*. What have you done to us?"

"Chief, I have an antidote, just put the gun down, and I'll give it to you." I said standing up with my hands raised.

"The fuck I put my gun down," Akhmetov said, his voice strained. The tea must have been taking hold of him. "Give it to me now."

"Just don't shoot me, or you won't get it." I pleaded, patting my jacket like I was looking for it and trying to calm him down.

He frowned but he lowered his gun.

It was enough.

Misha, standing behind him, struck the back of Akhmetov's head with the axe handle. The guard dropped to one knee, and I rushed in to wrestle the rifle from his hands. He tried to get up, but Misha hit him a couple more times before he collapsed on the ground.

"Kolesnikov?" I asked.

"Still in the watchtower."

I went back to Tsuladze, and together with Misha, we used the cords we'd each been carrying for this very purpose to bind his hands and feet. Then I slapped his face until he came to his senses and looked at me with returning clarity.

Misha was pointing Akhmetov's gun at him, and I put my finger to my lips warning him not to scream. Outside, the noise was building as the poison's effects took hold.

"Call Kolesnikov to come here," I told Tsuladze quietly. "We just want to get the fuck out of here. No one else needs to get hurt."

He looked at me with hatred and spat on the ground.

I punched him once, lightly, but enough to get his attention. I then pulled a knife out of my boot and crouched beside him.

"Tsuladze," I said, pressing the blade to his ribs. "We have nothing to lose. Call him in, and I promise none of you will be hurt."

"Kolesnikov!" Tsuladze yelled.

"Tsuladze, it's a fucking hell out here. I feel I am losing it," Kolesnikov yelled back.

"Come here, we need help," Tsuladze commanded.

"The others are down," Kolesnikov replied, his voice shaking. "Crawling like bugs with the *zeki*."

Tsuladze hesitated. I leaned in and pressed the blade harder.

"Get down here," he barked. "Now!"

There was a pause. Long enough to make my jaw tighten.

"I'm coming," Kolesnikov said at last.

I smiled and again put my finger to my lips. With the axe in my hands, I positioned myself beside the tent entrance.

Soon I heard approaching footsteps outside, and then Kolesnikov barged in with his rifle hanging on a sling from his shoulder. He came face to face with the muzzle of the AKM held by Misha, and as he raised his hands, I disarmed him and pulled him further inside.

He was frantic with panic in his eyes, his face twisting with pain and almost green in color. As Misha kept pointing the gun at him, he bent over and a loud sound of defecation was followed by a foul smell filling the tent.

"*Suka,*" I cursed, bringing him down to the ground, "Don't move!" I ordered as I tied him up, while wrinkling my nose at the stench. We tied Akhmetov up as well and used rags to gag all three of them. We put on their jackets, and caps, and armed with two rifles we walked out of the tent.

Where just fifteen minutes ago *zeki* were relaxing under the lazy gaze of the guards, was now a scene of total, surreal, and unimaginable chaos. The ground was covered in people in various stages of psychedelic delirium, crawling, stretching their arms out towards the sky, rolling in their own vomit and shit, or just laying still, with their bodies twisted and contorted, like toppled, deranged statues.

I counted the remaining five guards among the crowd; their weapons stuck in the mud. A few people were still standing, leaning on trees, or bits of heavy equipment. A couple of *zeki* staggered through the forest, talking to themselves.

I looked for Aslan, and Evgeny, and I saw them beside the trucks. Aslan waved at me and gave me a thumbs up. They had the driver.

Only Artyom was missing.

"Find the cook, and let's get the fuck out of here," I told Misha. We split up, crossing the clearing and looking for our accomplice.

The feeling of uneasiness struck me as I glanced at the faces of people writhing on the ground. Some of them were scared, others grimaced with pain. The smell of feces was overwhelming and it made me gag.

Back then the only thing I knew about the poison was that it would make people delirious and sick to their stomach to the point they would become incapacitated, but I hadn't expected this degree of turmoil.

Matryona later explained to me that she had used a combination of liberty caps, raw fly agaric, and baneberries. She adjusted the dosage for the thirty-liter pot of the tea shared by close to a hundred people. She was always very meticulous with her potions, and she hit the spot with this one.

Both baneberry and fly agaric cause severe food poisoning, resulting in debilitating diarrhea and vomiting. Fly agaric, also known as *Amanita Muscaria*, on top of the food poisoning, causes hallucinations and confusion, which were further enhanced by the liberty caps, commonly known as 'magic mushrooms'. That combination led to both physical and mental anguish in all those who consumed the poison.

To this day I feel sorry for what the *zeki* had to endure for us to escape, as it looked like they were stuck in a living nightmare that must have lasted for hours. But I knew that if we had only poisoned the guards, there would be fighting among the *zeki*, and we would have never gotten through the checkpoint. I cared a bit less about the guards, but to some extent felt sorry for them too.

Sometimes, I still relive that day in my nightmares. In them, I am one of the poisoned *zeki*, my intestines writhing in pain and my mind lost in hellish visions.

But back then, my adrenaline driven focus was only on getting away.

I searched for Artyom's plump face among the *zeki* on the ground, but then I heard someone loudly shouting his name. Following the voice, I reached the edge of the clearing where freshly fallen trees lay. There, a *zek* – naked except for rubber boots and an ushanka – was wildly swinging an axe over a fallen pine.

"Come out, Artyom. Come out, I won't hurt you!" He kept saying, while hitting the branches around the tree trunk with his axe. His moves were erratic, and he was swaying on his feet, but he could still pose a danger.

"Did you see Artyom?" I asked, trying to sound casual as I walked closer.

The *zek* turned to me. I didn't know his name, he was one of the new arrivals, a big, healthy-looking man. That's probably why he was still standing despite the poison messing with his head and body.

"*Mraz* is hiding under this pine. Help me and we can get him together!" the naked *zek* spoke, twisting his mouth in a weird way.

"Sure," I said slowly, walking closer. I kept the rifle at the ready, but I didn't want to use it on the madman.

"Artyom, are you there?" I whispered loudly.

"Andrycha, for fucks sake," came Artyom's voice from beneath the pine branches. "Help me, this lunatic wants my head."

"Sure, I do!" the *zek* said, squinting at me as if he had trouble seeing me properly, "You fucked up the food. I'll get your head and put it on a spike, like in the old days."

"We will get him together, *bratan*," I said in a calm voice, trying to reassure the *zek* as I closed in on him.

"Wait," he said, as if hit by a sudden realization, "You two know each other?"

Before he could raise his axe, I hit him in the stomach with the stock of the rifle.

The strike folded him, and he vomited all over Tsuladze's jacket I was wearing.

I hit him in the temple with the stock, and when he dropped on the ground, I took his axe and threw it aside before taking off the soiled jacket and moving to help Artyom.

The cook was well hidden beneath the pine trunk among the branches, and it took a while to get him out. His face and arms were scratched, and his clothes were torn.

"I came to hide in the ditch behind this tree after giving out the tea." Artyom mumbled, as I walked him towards the trucks. "But that guy came running over here, throwing his clothes around before taking a shit in the forest. He saw me on his way back and recognized me, so I hid under the tree. *Chort*, this was close, he almost got me with the axe."

"Don't worry, we are almost done here," I reassured him. "Everything worked out as intended. Now we just need to pass the checkpoint, and we are fuck out of here,"

We ran into Misha on the way back, who, like me, had been looking for Artyom. Then together we ran to the trucks, where we met up with Aslan and Evgeny.

The drivers were also there, lying bound on the ground, with two of them writhing in agony, their eyes wide with terror. The third one was fully conscious and he gave me a frightened look.

"All good?" I asked Evgeny.

"Yes. No problems. The cargo area is ready, and comrade Talgat here will give us all a ride," he replied, kicking the conscious driver gently as if to wake him up.

I squatted beside the man and leaned over his face. He was young, with short black hair and dark, narrow eyes. A Buryat, or a Mongol perhaps.

"Is that right, Talgat?" I asked, looking him in the eyes. He nodded and we began hasty preparations for departure amidst the cacophony of chaos and disorder.

The truck was a KamAZ-4310, used for carrying heavy equipment in and out of the work area. Unlike the Zil logging trucks with open cargo spaces, this one had a tarp that could be spread over the cargo load. There were some large crates in the back that Aslan and Evgeny emptied and dropped to the ground, leaving space for them to hide.

They and Artyom squeezed between the remaining boxes in the back, and Misha and I covered the whole cargo with a large tarp. We then took Talgat inside the cabin and tied one of his legs to the metal frame underneath the chair, giving him enough room to operate the pedals, but short enough to prevent his escape.

Together with Misha we squatted on the floor in front of the passenger seats. Misha kept the AKM pointed at the driver, while I put a hand with a knife on his right thigh. On that day we all got out of the camp with our shivs. There would be no coming back through the gate and body check for any of us.

"*Bratan*," I said to the driver. "All will be fine if you take us through the checkpoint. Say whatever lies you need to tell and be convincing. Otherwise, we will all die here, but I will cut your balls off first."

Talgat didn't say anything and just nodded at me again with a grave look on his face. He was young, but not a wimp and I felt it would be seriously regrettable if we had to hurt him. He started the truck and drove it out of the work area.

I peeked out of the cabin as we passed the barbed wire and one of the watchtowers on the perimeter. There was a military jacket hanging on the fence and as we turned into the road leading to the checkpoint, I saw a guard in his fatigues on the road to our right. He was walking in the main camp's direction and was less than fifty meters away. His body was twitching and he reeled on his feet moving like a zombie.

"Stop!" I yelled and the truck came to a halt as Talgat obeyed immediately.

The guard turned around, and seeing the truck, he waved at first, but when he saw Misha opening the door he opened his mouth as if he had seen a ghost. He then turned around in a wide arc and ran, clumsy and panicked, his legs barely obeying him.

"Should I get him?" Misha asked, ready to jump out of the truck with the AKM.

"No." I glanced at the watch I had taken from Tsuladze. "We need to pass the checkpoint. Gunfire would alert them. Even if he manages to keep the pace and goes straight to the camp, we still have at least thirty minutes. We should meet Matryona in ten."

I then turned to the driver. "Drive and be quick about it."

The engine rumbled and the truck lurched forward on the uneven forest road. Talgat kept his eyes focused on the path ahead, while I took a last peek at the guard running back to the camp in a mad frenzy.

Together with Misha we stayed as low as possible in the truck cabin while Talgat drove us towards the checkpoint a few miles down the road leading out of the forest.

"We are getting close. I will have to stop soon," the driver said in a strangely composed manner, as if he was trying to reassure me. "I will get you through, just be still."

I couldn't keep myself from admiring his composure. He knew the stakes and the risks, and yet he kept calm. He acted almost as if all that was happening was a normal, everyday occurrence. With that attitude, he stopped the truck and rolled down the window on his side.

"Out so soon, Talgat?" A voice came from outside.

"I need to bring fuel for the generators, they are running low," our driver replied in a casual manner.

"Mind bringing us some bottles on the way back?"

"Sure, comrade, but you have to pay first," Talgat said, extending his hand through the open window.

I stiffened and pressed the blade to his underbelly. I was fearful that he wanted to delay us or give a sign to the guard. I could see the side of his face, and it remained stoic. A muffled curse came from outside, but soon Talgat retrieved his hand with a banknote.

"Two bottles, and bring the change back," the voice outside grumbled.

"Of course," Talgat replied, and rolled the window back up. I could then see the boom barrier rising in front of the truck, and we drove away.

"Relax," Talgat said, keeping his eyes on the road, "He would be suspicious if I didn't ask for the money. I don't want to get caught in any crossfire."

I withdrew the knife and showed him the map we got from Matryona.

He took us along the forest road to the crossroads close to the meeting point. I didn't want him to see our escape car, or Matryona, so I told him to stop there. We tied him up, and left him in the cabin, continuing on foot.

Our galoshes sloshed and squeaked as we walked along the tractor road, crossing puddles and wading through mud. Apart from the noise we made, the forest was quiet.

I looked around and felt strange. There were no guards with rifles, no barbed wire to keep us in.

After a few minutes of walking as fast as the mud allowed, we reached another crossroad, with a clear, grassy meadow surrounded by bushes. That was supposed to be our meeting point, but no one was there. No sign of Matryona or the getaway car.

"Is it the wrong place?" Evgeny asked.

"No," I looked at the map. I traced my finger from the checkpoint where Talgat got us through, and north towards the crossroads where we left him. "It must be here."

"She bailed on us! Or maybe she was stopped by the militsiya?" Artyom's voice rose in a high-pitch. He was still shaking from the previous shock, and now his eyes went even wider.

"Quiet," I reprimanded him, putting a finger to my lips.

Aslan put an arm over Artyom's shoulder. "It will be fine, Tyoma," he said.

Evgeny wrapped his hands together and put them to his mouth, making a whistling, birdlike sound. No answer came.

"We can't just stand here like a bunch of ducks. Let's hide and wait." I did my best to keep my own voice calm, but I felt sudden despair squeezing the breath out of me. What if Artyom was right?

Shortly, we were sitting in a thicket, observing the road from behind low hawthorn bushes. The leaves were dark green, and the red fruits growing in clusters reminded me strangely of Sidoy's blood splattered in the muddy yard. To my side, Misha was caressing the AKM, as if holding on to the lifeline that would lead him to freedom. Was that it? I thought. A moment of freedom, just to be found in the forest and fight for our lives?

We waited in suspense. Time dragged mercilessly. I kept looking at the watch. Every minute was marked by rising tension and fear. We were running out of time. Back in the logging zone someone might be coming to their senses. The poison should hold for at least half an hour longer, but as we had seen, some people were less affected than others. The runaway guard could reach the camp in fifteen minutes if he kept his pace. We should have been out of the forest and driving down south by now.

I took a few deep breaths, and I prayed.

The trees rustled over us, the sun pierced through the clouds, and the forest had the autumnal smell of mud, wet leaves, and decaying undergrowth. As my mind stopped racing, the moment felt almost peaceful.

Suddenly, I heard a branch cracking behind the bushes, deeper in the forest. We all stiffened, looking in that direction. Another one followed, and soon, we could hear some muffled steps and sounds of brushing through the leaf-covered branches.

Evgeny whistled again. A mistake I thought immediately. The sound of footsteps stopped. And a similar whistling sound came from the forest.

"It's her." Evgeny whispered, and we rose to face the sounds.

Matryona came out from between the bushes with a wicker basket full of mushrooms. She was just as I remembered her from the visit, although dressed in more practical clothes with a khaki raincoat and long rubber boots.

She looked at us calmly, as if five men in worn-out, dirty *zek* uniforms standing in the middle of the forest were nothing unusual. Then her eyes met Evgeny's, and they both smiled and walked toward each other.

The rest of us stood in silence as we watched husband and wife reunite after three long years of separation. They embraced each other, whispering tender words. Matryona kissed his face all over and hugged him tightly.

I think it was then that I felt real hope returning for the first time since my arrest. We were still not out of danger but for a moment, I simply enjoyed my newfound freedom. We were barely out of the penal colony. It was time to get away and find a safe place where we could start a new life.

Matryona gave Evgeny one last kiss, holding his face in her hands, and then turned to us. Only then I saw her hands trembling. Something was wrong.

"*Zdrastvuite, patsany* – hello boys," she said with a strained smile, "I had to leave the car elsewhere. The road here was blocked. A truck was stuck in a ditch. Come, we've wasted enough time."

We hurried through the forest. It took us precious minutes to reach the access road. It was sandy, with large puddles, and deep ruts formed by the heavy trucks driving the lumber out of the forest.

A car was parked on the side of the road. It was a dark blue Lada Niva that looked like it had seen better days, with fading paint and patches of rust on bumpers and around the doors.

"Let's get you out of here, but first you need to change what you are wearing."

She opened the trunk where several bundles of clothes were stored. She picked up one and gave it to me.

"*Spasiba*." I thanked her. Then, I took it and began undressing in haste.

Aslan and Evgeny got theirs too. Matryona knew our sizes and prepared accordingly. For Misha and Artyom, she had some middle-sized attire. Aslan couldn't hold back a chuckle when he saw them dressed up in their new civilian outfits. The clothes were a bit too small for Misha, who was tall and broad in shoulders, while too baggy for Artyom who was much shorter, and rather scrawny. At least they didn't look like *zeki* anymore.

The first problems came up as we began getting into the car. There were only five seats inside, and Matryona insisted we shouldn't look too cramped if we had to pass some people. Someone had to go in the trunk, which was rather small in the Lada.

"Artyom, you get in there." I pointed at the trunk.

"Why me?" he moaned, hunching down.

"You're the smallest," I said, feeling frustrated with his attitude. "Just get the fuck in!"

He didn't like it but squeezed into the trunk anyway and I slammed the lid shut.

"Look!" Aslan said, then throwing in some Chechen curses. He was pointing to the east, towards the work area we had just left. A red signal flare was slowly descending over the treetops, flickering in the gaps between the branches.

"We need to get going," I said, urging Misha and Aslan to get in the car.

"Leave that thing behind. I don't want it with us," Matryona said to Misha, who was holding the AKM.

"What if they come after us?" Misha asked, not happy to leave the weapon.

"They will have many more rifles and bullets. That one will not make a difference. Just leave it here," Matryona insisted with a voice that said she was done arguing.

Misha looked at me, and I gave him a nod. The gun rattled as he dropped it to the ground.

We all got in, with Matryona and Evgeny at the front. Misha, Aslan, and I squeezed together in the back, with the basket full of mushrooms on Aslan's lap. We drove for a while and as we passed one of the side roads, I noticed a large logging truck in the distance. It was tilted to the side, with a group of people gathered around. I thanked God, they didn't block the access road.

After a few more minutes we reached a gravel country road and Matryona sped up.

Tension slowly left my body as we traveled, but my eyes were still searching, looking for any sign of danger. I watched the birches pass by as we drove and I relished the thought that with each minute that passed, we were getting farther away from IK-22.

The engine rumbled, the suspension squeaked, and the car clattered on the uneven road. We left the forest and for a while we drove through a more open taiga landscape, where towering pines thinned out, giving way to a patchwork of uneven terrain covered with lichen, moss, and low shrubs. We passed through the village of Malinovka, and continued through another forest, with a wide river to our left.

Matryona kept looking across to the other side, and at one point, she turned onto a dirt path on the left. After a short distance, she pulled over on a clearing overlooking the river. She took out a pair of binoculars from the glovebox and walked towards the embankment.

We let Artyom out from the trunk and then we all joined her in silence.

There was a small town on the other side of the river. Wooden houses, painted in various colors and covered with corrugated sheeting, looked homely and inviting. Smoke rose from many chimneys, and brown, freshly plowed fields stretched to the edge of a dark forest beyond the village. Matryona swept the area with binoculars until her gaze stopped on something, and her face tightened.

"*Blyn,*" she cursed. "There is a militsiya checkpoint on the bridge."

I took the binoculars and looked along the river and towards the bridge. There were two yellow-blue patrol cars at one end with militsiya men in their dark blue uniforms strolling around.

"Can't we just continue on this road, without crossing the bridge?"

"This road continues to Iskitim. There will be checkpoints there for sure. I was hoping to go south from here and reach Altai on the country roads." She sighed in clear disappointment. "But we are too late. The militsiya is already on the look-out. It will be worse near bigger towns."

"What do we do?" Artyom's voice shrilled with panic.

I almost slapped the cook in anger but I stopped myself. I gave a silent chuckle, thinking how much prison had changed me. My younger self would never have hit someone, but my older self knew the usefulness of violence now.

"I need to take a closer look, but first I'll bring you to my dacha. It is safe there," she replied, ushering us back to the car. "We might have to go with plan B."

We scrambled back in with a rising sense of urgency. The militsiya's presence complicated things, and I saw Matryona struggling to stay calm under this new pressure.

CHAPTER 14

MERCY IS LOST WHEN VENGEANCE BLINDS

She drove back to the main road, then continued. After a bit further, she turned onto a small forest road. It was almost like a tunnel, with tall aspen trees growing on both sides. Their branches, covered with yellow leaves, stirred in the wind over our heads. Grass and weeds grew up in the middle of the road, and I could hear them scratching against the chassis.

After some time, we reached a clearing with a small dacha, deep in the forest. We left the car and walked to the building, which had to have been quite old as the logs it was made of were grey, like ash.

We all grinned as we stretched the kinks out from the trip. Even sour Artyom was smiling. We went inside following Matryona and the first thing that hit me when I crossed the threshold was the intense smell of herbs. Dried yellow tansy flowers formed a garland around the doorway, and there were various dried plants hanging from the rafters and on the walls.

The dacha had a single room which was perhaps thirty square meters. There was a wood-burning kitchen stove in the corner, a bed beside it and a camping table with four chairs in the middle. A map lay on the table, held down by candles in tin holders, with papers covered in notes scattered around. Wooden cabinets and boxes stood beside the walls, and the few, small windows let in little daylight, making the living space dim, and filled with shadows.

"So, what's the plan?" Artyom asked while stretching his shoulder after a bumpy ride in the trunk.

"I was hoping to immediately drive through the town," Matryona said, keeping her eyes on Evgeny. "But the flare meant that the camp discovered your escape sooner than we had hoped. Militsiya will be on the lookout. I will go to the town and see what the situation is. You stay here. Don't walk outside. Eat, drink, and recover. I will be back soon."

With that, Matryona left the dacha and we heard the Lada rumble away.

It felt strange to be ordered around by a woman. Even though I knew Matryona from her letters and visits to IK-22, and had deep respect for her, it wasn't something I was used to. Neither of us was. Still, I knew we had to trust her, and there was no time for squabbling, so we did as she said.

"Artyom, why don't you make us something to eat?" I asked, sitting by the table.

"Yeah, I am starving!" Misha exclaimed.

"I am not your servant," Artyom crossed his arms and looked at me with defiance. "We are out of prison. Free men can make their own food."

Evgeny turned and raised his finger at Artyom.

"We took you with us because you were useful. We all have things to worry about. Stay useful, and do what you're good at, *blyat*!" His gruff voice carried a threat that made Artyom move back a step.

"Come, Tyoma, I'll help you," Aslan offered, putting a hand on Artyom's shoulder and they began firing up the stove.

I sat at the table with Evgeny and Misha, and we looked at the map that spread out before us. It was a topographic map of the area, with Novosibirsk to the north and Iskitim in the center. IK-22 was not originally on the map, but it was marked there with a red pen. Different work sectors we labored in had been marked with pencil. They had dates scribbled beside them, as after clearing an assigned part of the forest we were moved to a different one.

I looked at the dates, and with them came memories of those places where I had toiled. There were twelve of them in total across the three years we spent in IK-22, and the latest, marked June 1988, was underlined. The meeting point where we found Matryona was also marked and underlined, with arrows pointing at different routes and with additional notes.

As I went through the notes, I was beginning to understand the amount of work and preparation Evgeny's wife put into our escape. Her sheer determination and total commitment were evident in her meticulous writing. She wanted her husband back, and she was willing to risk everything to accomplish it.

I felt lucky to be Evgeny's friend and to have the chance to escape with him, but we weren't out of the woods yet, so to speak.

The smell of butter and fried onions reached my nostrils, and I glanced over at Artyom dropping eggs into a cast-iron pan sizzling on the stove, while Aslan poured hot water from a kettle into a teapot. Soon, each of us got a portion of scrambled eggs with herbs, mushrooms and onion, and a piece of bread to go with it. I hadn't tasted fresh eggs in three years, and I felt my taste buds bursting with delight at each bite.

"Thanks, Tyoma." I said with my mouth full, turning to Artyom, who sat with his plate on one of the beds. "This is fucking delicious."

Others murmured their agreement and we ate away, cleaning the tin plates dry with pieces of bread. In the end, every crumb was devoured, and we sat, sipping tea with a generous amount of sugar when we heard the car pull up outside.

Evgeny looked through the window, and from his vague smile I understood it was Matryona.

She walked in moments later with a serious face, but before talking to us, she went to Evgeny and embraced him. He patted her on the back and whispered something in her ear. She was a strong woman, but with her husband, a more fragile nature came to the surface.

"We can't drive," she said, releasing Evgeny and walking to the table, running her finger along the road leading south. "I drove to the town. There were patrol cars and checkpoints on all the access roads. Bastards acted quickly. There must have been a lot of pressure coming from the top. It's not every day people escape from a penal colony."

"What is plan B then?" I asked.

"We walk." Matryona tapped her finger on a pencil-drawn arrow going west, and then pointed to a marked spot on the Berd River. "We avoid the roads and go through the forests and taiga here. There's a ford in the river where we can cross. We then continue west, south of Iskitim. There we can catch a cargo train to take us farther south. I know people in Altai who will help us."

"Walk?" Artyom came closer and looked at the map. "How far?"

"Fifty kilometers, give or take," Matryona said matter-of-factly. "It will be rough terrain, and we will have to cross the river twice. Five days, perhaps a week."

"That's harsh." Artyom protested, "I thought we were taking the logging truck to get away."

"*Durak*," Evgeny snapped. 'You wanted to drive the truck straight back to Leningrad?"

"Who is that?" Matryona asked, eyeing Artyom cautiously.

"Artyom, the cook," I explained. "We wouldn't have gotten out without his help."

"Maybe we can wait here until they remove the checkpoints?" Artyom asked, almost pleading.

"It is too risky. Sometimes people come knocking on my door, asking for help." Matryona explained. "There is a manhunt ongoing and a reward for your capture. If someone sees you, we will be in trouble. And if we wait too long, the winter will be here and it will be much more difficult to survive outside. We must go, and we must go as soon as possible. Today we sleep here, then we gather supplies and leave tomorrow."

We remained silent, looking at the map. She turned to Evgeny. "*Harasho*?" she asked.

They exchanged glances, and Evgeny finally nodded: "*Harasho*," he confirmed, settling the matter.

Artyom stared blankly at the map, as if he could see dragons and trolls hidden between the river bends and in the forest ravines.

I was tired, the food made me sleepy, and I didn't pay much attention to the frightened look on his face. He wasn't the bravest man I knew, but I wasn't expecting what was about to happen. I was still young, and despite being hardened among the *vory*, I still had a lot to learn about people.

If only those lessons were not so painful.

We all went to sleep early, the adrenaline which had fueled us during the escape left us exhausted, and everyone crashed. Matryona spread four bedrolls on the floor, while she and Evgeny tucked themselves under a woolen blanket on the bed. I could hear their whispers, and gentle shifting of bodies muffled by the thick wool.

Aslan soon started snoring, covering the sounds of their intimacy.

I drifted away and had nightmares about German Shepherd dogs dressed as penal colony guards, chasing me through a dark, dead forest.

I woke up feeling a draft of cold air on my face. I opened my eyes, and I saw a figure in the doorway, it was Artyom. I made a sound, and he turned to me. His dark silhouette was looming with the backdrop of a moonlit tree line.

"I need to shit," he whispered and I watched him close the door gently behind him.

I turned over and went back to sleep. The next thing I remember was opening my eyes to the bleak, blueish twilight of the morning. I yawned and stretched, inhaling the fragrant, spicy smell of the drying herbs. I sat up, and I noticed that Artyom's bedroll was empty. I looked around, and my eyes met Evgeny's.

He was sitting on the bed with his back to the wall. His body was naked, putting his life's story on display. On his stomach, he had a tattoo depicting a portrait of two cats, a female and a male, with their muzzles touching affectionately, and a garland of flowers surrounding them. I knew what it represented, but as I got to know Matryona better and saw how much of a 'cat' she herself was, my comprehension grew deeper.

"*Dobre utro – Good morning*," I whispered, my greeting.

"*Zdarovo*." Evgeny's voice croaked with morning drowsiness. "Where's Artyom?"

"I don't know, I just woke up," I replied, standing up. "He went outside to take a shit in the middle of the night."

I went to Artyom's bedroll and I touched it inside. It was cold.

"*Pizdiets*." I cursed, softly. Then louder to everyone, "Wake Up!"

Misha and Aslan were up on their feet in seconds. Misha even had a shank ready.

Matryona got out of bed in a long night shirt and began dressing.

"What's wrong?" Aslan asked.

Before I could answer, I heard the sound of a car engine closing in outside. I looked through the small window.

It was a yellow-blue militsiya UAZ. It stopped beside the Lada Niva and two uniformed men got out of it.

"*Suka*," I uttered as one of the militsiya officers dragged Artyom out of the car, and the three of them began walking towards the dacha.

"Natasha Nikolayevna," one of them shouted. "Step outside for a minute, would you?"

"Coming out," Matryona yelled back. It seemed the locals knew her by a different name. She hurried, putting on work trousers, and a dark blue tunic.

"I know these fellows. Let me handle this," she said, seeing us getting our knives ready.

"We should have taken the *avtomat*," Misha complained and I felt he was right about the rifle. We trusted Matryona, but now we were trapped in the dacha, with armed militsiya men outside.

My mind was running wild and I was thinking about how to best handle the situation. I exchanged glances with my brothers. We were not going down without a fight. Perhaps we had a chance to get close enough to the policemen so that we could charge them and overpower them before they could use their guns.

Matryona walked past Misha on her way to the door and smacked him on the back of his head.

"*Avtomat*!" she scoffed. "You've watched too many movies. Now, put those stickers away and come with me," she ordered.

I looked at Evgeny, who nodded with a slight smile. I understood at that moment that he trusted his wife fully. It made me relax, at least slightly.

We hid the knives in our pockets, and the four of us—all seasoned criminals, and authoritative thieves—followed Matryona outside. There was something about her, she had her own authority; and her presence was strong and grounded.

We walked out into the open with Matryona in front and the four of us spread in a line behind her. The knives in our pockets were calling for blood, and we were ready to sprint and take the militsiya men out.

They stood beside the UAZ, less than fifteen meters away. One of them had an AK hanging casually on a sling underneath his arm. The other one was holding Artyom by the collar of his jacket. The leather holster of his pistol was unbuttoned and his other hand hovered around the grip.

Matryona went forward and stopped a few meters from the two militsiya men, who eyed us suspiciously over her shoulders.

Artyom looked miserable between the two officers, like a fox caught in a trap. His eyes darted between us and the militsiya men, as if he was confused and hadn't yet grasped what was happening.

I kept my hands in my pockets and I squeezed the handle of my knife tightly, feeling tension building up in my body, waiting to be released in a violent outburst.

"Gleb Yaroslavovich," Matryona nodded to the one holding Artyom.

He bowed his head slightly and I felt the tension releasing its grip on me.

"Yuriy Arkadyevich," she greeted the second officer. "How is Nadia?"

"She's good, fully recovered now."

"And little Masha?"

"She's crawling around like a cockroach," the officer smiled involuntarily. "She laughs a lot too."

"I am glad to hear that," Matryona said in a warm, motherly voice. It felt as if she really cared about these people.

"Listen." Yuriy Arkadyevich stepped from one foot to another, as if uncertain what to say. "This little rat was walking on the side of the road, and when we stopped him, he said that you're harboring the escaped prisoners. He thought he would get a reward and reduced sentence for the information. I see here that he was telling the truth."

I stiffened, and in the corner of my eye, I could see Aslan moving ever so slightly forward. Fucking Artyom betrayed us. But the militsiya men made a mistake. They allowed us too close. It was just a matter of seconds to reach them. I also shuffled forward, ready to spring and deal with the one closer to me.

"Those are just distant relatives on a visit," Matryona said, dismissively. She turned her head and gave each of us a look. We were like a wolf pack, sneaking on its prey, but her words and her gaze stopped us in our tracks. "They are a bit nervous when they see strangers," Matryona continued, "and the one with you is the retarded cousin. He talks nonsense when he gets scared."

"I see," Yuriy mused, looking at the four of us standing behind Matryona. "Let me tell you something. I'll leave your 'cousin' with you. You take care of him. And then you leave and never show yourself around here. I owe you the life of my wife and my daughter, but with this, the debt will be paid in full."

"No!" Artyom screamed, "you can't leave me with these criminals!"

The militsiya man holding him, punched Artyom in the stomach. It must have landed hard on the solar plexus, as Artyom fell to his knees and began coughing and spitting bile.

"We will go now Natasha Nikolayevna," Yuriy said, watching us carefully. "Leave today, and avoid the roads. Good luck."

With that the two officers returned to their UAZ and drove away into the foggy, morning forest.

The dawn was approaching, drops of dew glittered on the grass around the dacha, and thin stretches of mist hung over part of the meadow. I cursed Artyom in my mind, the coward displayed his full colors and now we had to deal with him. Evgeny and Aslan walked towards our former comrade, who was sitting on his heels with his head hanging down. His left hand rested limply on his thighs. His other was inside of his coat pocket.

"Why the fuck did you do it Artyom?" Aslan asked.

"We were supposed to escape in a car, not cross forests and rivers like some animals," Artyom said without raising his head. He seemed resigned. "I wouldn't make it in the taiga, and you would cut my throat and leave me there, I know your kind. No mercy for the *muzhyki.* Treating us like slaves and cattle."

Aslan and Evgeny stopped beside him.

"You've proven us right, you fucking rat," Evgeny said, looking down at Artyom. He grabbed the cook by the clothes, wanting to raise him up.

Artyom reached inside the folds of his jacket. A long, thin blade of a kitchen knife flashed in his hand.

"Knife! Watch out!" I yelled as I sprang forward with Misha right behind me, but we were too far.

As Evgeny pulled him up, the cook drove the knife upward, hard, just under the left ribs. Evgeny gasped, and staggered backwards. Aslan was about to grab the cook but Artyom slashed at him, grazing Aslan's leg, and forcing him to take a step back.

Matryona screamed Evgeny's name, as her husband held a hand to his stomach, wavering on his feet.

Artyom had a wild, terrified grimace on his face. His eyes were glossy and bulging, and he breathed heavily through his clenched teeth.. He raised the knife high and he started backing off into the forest.

Aslan followed him slowly, with his hands in front of him, ready to intercept the knife hand if Artyom decided to attack him further. At the same time Misha and I charged from the side.

Artyom spun as I closed by. I was stopped in my tracks as he slashed with the knife. The thin, silvery blade had blood on it, and I could see dark droplets flying through the air. Artyom raised it again, but then Misha ran into him with a measured frontal kick. The blow was powerful, all of Boyets' weight behind it, and it drove Artyom backward.

His feet rose into the air, and he hit the ground hard.

We descended on him without mercy. I kicked the knife off his hand and Misha struck him hard in the back. Aslan joined and the three of us stomped and punched, as he curled on the wet grass. I have no idea how much time passed, we were unleashed, raging at what he had done.

Matryona's voice dragged us out of the rage. Evgeny was lying on the wet grass with Matryona by his side. Her hands were on his stomach, pressing hard, her fingers slick and red.

"Andrej, bring me my medicine bag. You'll find it to the left of the entrance. Hurry!" Matryona's voice was trembling, but her commands were clear.

"Tie him up." I told Misha and left him to take care of Artyom while Aslan joined Matryona.

When I came back with the bag, Aslan was pressing down the wound, while Evgeny's wife grabbed the bag from me, and tore it open.

Aslan leaned his weight into the wound, both hands planted, his back straight, muscles on his neck standing out from effort.

"Stay with us, Zhenya," he muttered. "Breathe, bratan!"

Matryona worked quickly, retrieving a bottle of alcohol and gauze from the bag. She motioned for Aslan to lift his hand, and she poured alcohol over the wound without warning. She then packed gauze into the wound, one roll, then the next. Evgeny jerked, his face contorted by pain, then sagged again.

"Pressure! Don't lift your hands," Matryona commanded, and Aslan's hands returned to the wound, strong and steady.

Blood soaked through almost immediately, spilling further over the sides of Evgeny's torso.

His breathing turned shallow and uneven. Each breath strained, shorter than the last. His lips had gone pale, almost gray. His eyes kept slipping shut.

"Open them," Matryona said sharply, shaking him. "Look at me. Breathe."

As he was fighting for his breath, a sudden cough rattled his body. Dark blood bubbled from his mouth, spilling down his chin.

Matryona froze, then reached back to the bag, picking up more gauze and yarrow herbs meant to help with bleeding.

"Knife went in from below," she said, more to herself now. "Left side, high. Liver."

The blood kept coming.

Evgeny's eyes found her face, suddenly clear and present. His mouth moved as if he wanted to say something. No sound came out but I saw something in his eyes. There was shock, and something else—understanding. He grabbed Matryona's hand. He held it with surprising strength. Then his eyelids closed and his body slackened, all at once, with his breath leaving his body.

Matryona stopped working.

Slowly, deliberately, she set the bag aside. She pulled Evgeny's head into her lap and held him there, her hand still clutching his, as if hoping to keep him from leaving. But nothing followed. Only the sound of leaves rustling in the wind.

She wept, holding her husband's head in her hands.

I felt my eyes tearing up. It was not my own pain that I felt. I had lost a friend, but we were *vory*, and there were times in IK-22 when we had faced death together. The pain I felt, the one that almost made me weep myself, was instead for Matryona.

She wailed loudly, as her body swayed and shivered. It felt incredibly cruel, how fate had reunited her with her husband, just to take him away forever.

We left the dacha four hours later.

Aslan and Misha carried large backpacks, heavy with supplies, while I had a smaller pack and a coiled rope hanging over my shoulder. I held a stretch of the rope in my hand; the other end was tied tightly around Artyom's body.

He stumbled as he walked forward. I had to kick and punch him at times to keep him moving.

We had made him watch, as Misha and I dug the grave for Evgeny. While we did, Matryona took time to disinfect and dress Aslan's flesh wound. Then those two went into the dacha together to prepare supplies for our trek through the taiga.

When we were ready, we gathered for our final farewells. Misha and I gently placed Evgeny's body, wrapped in a white sheet, into the grave and covered it with fresh forest soil. Matryona prayed as we worked, holding a chain with a cross in her hands. She didn't weep anymore. Not a single tear rolled down her cheeks during the burial.

Artyom, on the other hand, was shaking and crying. He kept saying he didn't mean to, that he just wanted to be back in Leningrad and would do anything to make it right. I had to kick him hard to make him stop.

When the burial was over, we grabbed our packs, and marched into the woods, westward. Before we left, Aslan asked Matryona whether he should dispose of Artyom, but she insisted we take him along. She seemed to have had a plan for him, and she clearly wanted to get deeper into the forest before she unleashed her vengeance.

We stopped after two hours in a small gully. There were mostly birch trees around and the ground was littered with their yellow and orange leaves. Heavy clouds hung over us, with a promise of unrelenting autumn rain.

Matryona told me to tie Artyom to one of the larger trees. The cook wasn't struggling anymore, he just mumbled incomprehensibly like a lost, hurt child, but I had no pity for him.

"You don't have to see this," Matryona said, taking out the kitchen knife Artyom had used to kill her husband. It still had some of his blood on the blade. "Go on ahead, I'll join you in a while."

We didn't move. Evgeny was our friend, and whatever the traitor had coming, we wanted to witness it. If it had been up to us, we would probably have just beaten him to death, but we left the punishment to Matryona.

In my lifetime, I witnessed a good deal of violence. I had seen men maddened by rage, fighting against each other, tearing each other apart like jackals in useless, bloody feuds. In prison, and on the streets men are quick to settle their disputes with force. We are used to violence and expected to be able to handle it. But I tell you, *droog*, don't ever cross a woman, because their vengeance can be the polar opposite of their normally caring nature. Cold, calculating, and absolutely ruthless.

Matryona walked to Artyom, who was looking at her, his eyes wide open with terror. He tried to plead, but Matryona put the knife to his crotch, stabbing at it gently but provocatively.

Artyom squealed, his lips stretching wide and Matryona's already raised hand shot out. She reached into his yawning mouth, and grabbed his tongue like a nimble fish. Artyom's eyes bulged, as Matryona pulled his tongue out, her fingernails pinching it so hard that I could see drops of blood rolling down her thumb.

"You betrayed all of us, and for that you will lose your tongue," Matryona explained, and pursed her lips tight, as she pressed the blade to the side of Artyom's stretched out tongue.

He begged with his eyes, moaning in a wordless plea, but the wise woman was unforgiving. She slid the knife up and down in rough sawing motions, and Artyom's moans turned to shrieks as the blood squirted, dripping down Matryona's wrist.

After a moment, she released Artyom's head. He shook it from side to side, gurgling and spitting blood. Matryona threw away the red lump of muscle without looking at it, as if she were getting rid of a vile insect.

"For taking the life of my husband..." She paused, taking a deep breath, as if steeling herself for what she was about to do. "Evgeny's love brought light into my life. For taking it away, I will make you spend your final days wandering in darkness."

With that, she placed her hand on Artyom's chin, pressing his head against the tree.

He tried to move his head, but she held it firm and with two quick strikes of the knife she stabbed at his eyes.

What had been a painful shriek before turned into insane howls of terror. Slime and blood ran down Artyom's cheeks, as he thrashed around with his head.

I was stunned.

I had seen brutality in prison, I had seen men tortured, and raped. But this was different.

To avoid feeling pity for Artyom at that moment, I reminded myself of what he'd done to the first person who showed me kindness in jail and became my friend. I thought about Evgeny – my brother, a *vor*, and a killer with a lover's heart.

And I thought about the effort Matryona put into being reunited with him. I couldn't imagine the pain she was going through, and I will not judge her for what she did.

Still, I must admit, there are moments when I regret not taking her advice to leave her alone to handle the traitor. His disfigured face joined the images that are the fabric of my nightmares to this very day.

She untied the rope and let Artyom loose.

He fell forward and began crawling, reaching out with his hands, and making heart-wrenching sounds.

Matryona told me to coil the rope, which I did with haste. I didn't want to look at Artyom any longer than necessary. When we left, he was creeping around the gully like a wounded snail dragging a bloody trail on the ground.

"For his sins, he will never see Christ's light again," Matryona said, her face tight with grief. Her eyes were hazed with the comprehension and acceptance of the sins she had just committed herself. She picked up a backpack and began walking to the west.

CHAPTER 15

NEVER BREAK YOUR FOCUS IN A TREACHEROUS CURRENT

We joined Matryona in silence and nobody spoke until the evening dusk made us stop and pitch camp. Even then we only exchanged words that were strictly necessary for functioning. No one was in the mood for chit-chat.

The rain started in the middle of the night and the temperature was just above zero. We had a single tarp that we spread between the trees. The four of us huddled together underneath it in bedrolls, to stay dry and keep each other warm.

The downpour continued throughout the next day, and we traversed the forest with water tapping on the waterproof rain ponchos we were given by Matryona.

So much preparation, so much work she had put into everything. There was no reason for her to continue. All her effort was for nothing, I thought, and I wondered why she didn't just abandon us. She could have taken the Lada and driven away alone, but she was the wife of a *vor*. She was the second cat in Evgeny's tattoo and she had her own code that she followed.

On the second night, we prepared to cross the Berd River.

There were settlements nearby and Matryona insisted we do it under the cover of darkness. We sat in the forest, close to the grassy embankment, and we waited for darkness to come. The rain subsided in the afternoon, and patches of clear sky showed up.

I had no appetite, but I forced myself to eat some crackers with lard. Painful anguish was burning in my stomach. Each time I closed my eyes, I would see Sidoy's mutilated body, or Evgeny's lifeless eyes. Waves of pain, anger, and doubt washed over me. I could see the same pain in others as we sat quietly, listening to the tapping of raindrops on our ponchos.

The sky turned purple-orange and I watched the colorful clouds, with the backdrop of a blue sky, as the sun was setting. For a moment, the beauty of nature brought my thoughts back to the present, but the pain remained deep inside.

Matryona kept quiet after explaining the plan of crossing the ford. Her face was like a burial mask, as if Evgeny's final grasp took a part of her to the other side. She showed no outward emotions, but I saw her lips moving in a silent prayer.

A few hours later the night came, dropping a cover of darkness over the open space by the river crossing.

We skulked through the meadow toward the ford. Further up along the river, I saw the lights of a village glimmering in the distance. I felt like a hunted animal, a wolf clinging to the wild and avoiding civilization and humans at all costs.

Soon, we reached the ford. The current was calm and the river shallow with white, sandy islands stretching along the middle.

We quickly took our boots and pants off. Despite the rain, they were not completely soaked and we wanted to keep them dry as much as possible.

The night sky, partly covered with clouds, gave enough light there in the open to see where we were going, but the water was dark, and we waited for Matryona to lead us as she knew this place.

The crossing was quick, with water reaching up to my thighs in the deepest place. We then continued into the forest, walking slowly through darkness, close to one another, until we felt safe setting up a camp.

For the next two days we continued westward through the thick taiga forest, where pines and birches grew over wavy terrain, with many ravines, hills, and small cliffs that we had to negotiate. Matryona gave me a compass, a map, and she explained the route in case anything happened to her. She was very cold and businesslike, and we all did our best to give her space. We put our focus on the matter of present survival. We navigated together, looking for features in the terrain that we could recognize from the map and double checked that our bearing was correct.

There were villages and industrial areas along the way west, and we wanted to make sure we didn't run into anyone, so we planned our route to keep us deep in the forest and far from human activity. There was still the risk of running into a hunter, and a few times we could hear the drum of a helicopter in the distance, so we refrained from making a campfire. This made life harder, as we couldn't warm up or dry our clothes beside the flames.

At least we had a gasoline-fueled *benzinovka* stove with enough fuel for a few weeks. We used it to boil water, while we ate military biscuits, lard, and cured meat that Matryona had made in the spring. It was salty and hard to chew, but it filled the stomach and kept us going.

We reached the river again at noon on the third day. The weather had taken a turn for the better. The rain that had bothered us since daybreak had turned to drizzle, then finally died down completely. Gray clouds covered the sky, and the forest was wet, dark, and submerged in a pervasive grayness.

We continued along the riverbank, looking for a good place to cross. The current looked strong; there were rocks, rapids, and frothy eddies. We walked for at least a kilometer before we found a calmer stretch and began considering how to cross it.

I had some insights from the military when it came to river rescue, since part of my duty I had been serving along the river Elbe, but it was Aslan who had most experience from crossing mountain streams and rivers of the Caucasus.

We discussed different options and after a while two main possibilities remained.

One was to cross the river holding each other in a wedge formation pointing against the current.

The other, to have someone swim across and secure a rope on the other side.

The current was strong enough to carry a person off and we didn't know how deep the water was. The uncertainty about the depth of the river and the possibility of all of us getting carried away by the current was too much of a risk. We had enough rope, so we took the second option.

We had to decide who would swim across, but Misha immediately volunteered. He said he was a good swimmer and had spent entire summers swimming in the Volga river. We agreed and rehearsed the plan twice to make sure everyone knew what to do, especially if something went wrong.

When everyone was ready, we put our plan into action.

Matryona cut two short pieces of rope to be used to attach the second and third person crossing to the main line. Misha and I gave Aslan our belts. He threaded the buckles on the remaining rope and looped the two shorter threads through them. He then prepared a harness at one end of the rope, while I attached the other end to a birch tree, close to the riverbank.

After Misha undressed, we placed his clothes in a large, water-resistant jute bag. The rest of the supplies we kept in our canvas backpacks. Misha then put on the harness made by Aslan so that the rope was hanging at his back, and he was securely attached.

The river was relatively calm in this section and around thirty meters wide.

Misha made a sign of the cross and grinned at us, presenting two gaps where the teeth knocked by the prison guards used to be. I thought then that if we made it out alive, I would get him new silver, or even gold teeth. The young brawler deserved it.

He waded into the river, and his muscles twitched as the cold water wrapped around his body. He turned to face the current, then lay back while gripping the rope with both hands. The current took him, and he used his legs to propel himself diagonally towards the other side.

Matryona, Aslan, and I held on to the rope, releasing it just quickly enough for him to move without hindrance, but also for us to be able to tighten it in case he got into any difficulty. He swam bravely on his back, grinning despite the cold and working with the current to get across. He was past the middle when suddenly, a rapid flow of water pulled him swiftly downriver. There were dangerous rocks down there, so he turned onto his belly, facing upstream, and began fiercely swimming.

This is when Misha's experience showed. He had saved his energy for that battle and with powerful strokes, he fought the river and began closing in on the shore. The current pushed him towards the rocks, over which the water frothed and roared, but he struggled with all his might.

Suddenly, his head disappeared underwater, and a pang of worry hit me. But then it popped back up again, and Boyets continued his fight, spitting out water and stroking vigorously with his arms.

After several minutes of struggle, he made it to the other side, where he crawled onto the mossy riverbank and lay there for a moment, catching his breath. He then got up and began moving. His skin was a pinkish-red after prolonged cold-water exposure, and he must have been freezing, but he swiftly got out of the harness and secured it around a rock on his side.

We pulled hard, making sure the rope was holding fast at his end, and then we tightened it at ours.

It was time for Aslan to go across.

Misha was sitting on his heels, with his hands under his armpits. It was crucial he got his clothes as soon as we could get them to him, so he could begin to warm up.

Aslan put his own clothes in the bag and sealed it. Matryona had checked the wound on his thigh earlier and pronounced it well enough to leave the bandage off. He was already attached to the rope stretched over the river, with the short cord tied around his waist and through the belt buckle that hung from the main rope. He looked at the sky and said a short prayer before entering the water.

The line was stretched over the river at an angle, with Misha's end downstream. As soon as Aslan got deep enough and allowed the current to take him, it dragged him down along the rope and towards the other side. He held on to the jute bag, which floated and bounced on the surface. It took him only a few minutes to cross, and with much less effort than young Misha had exerted.

When he was on the other side, he opened the bag and quickly helped Misha, whose hands were already numb, to get dressed.

Matryona was next. She undressed down to a shirt and used the second belt-buckle and a short thread to attach herself to the main rope. With a backpack in front, she entered the water and like Aslan, allowed the current to drag her diagonally across the river. She kept the backpack mostly out of the water and helped herself with one hand to move along the rope.

Soon, with Aslan's help, she was scrambling onto the other riverbank.

So far, everything had gone smoothly. The three of them were safely on the other side, and Misha, who had been exposed the most, was now fully dressed and wrapped in a blanket.

It was time for the last and most dangerous part of the plan.

I untied the rope from the birch tree and made a harness like the one Aslan had made for Misha. I could have used the rope to cross, but then we would have to leave it behind. We decided against it, as it could be useful again.

Aslan went upstream and attached the rope perpendicular from my position on his side. He was then joined by Matryona and Misha, and they tightened the rope and were ready to pull me in.

I went into the river with the last backpack on my chest. The water was icy, and my feet felt as if a thousand freezing needles were stabbing at them. I knew that sensation, and ignored it, moving one foot after another over the silt and rocks on the riverbed until I reached the waist-deep water. I then turned upstream and pushed myself backwards, allowing the current to take me.

The river was doing most of the work, pulling me across, while the rope, held tightly by the others, kept me from being dragged downstream. I moved through the water in an arc towards the far shore.

When earlier, I had watched my friends going through the rifts and eddies of the chilly waters, it had seemed easy. Now being there myself – the backpack dragging me down, the current pulling in one direction, the rope in the other, waves hitting my face, and struggling to breathe – the challenge was far harder than I had imagined.

I wanted to be out of the water. I wanted to be on the shore. To lie down, put on dry clothes, and warm up. Seeing the shrubs and roots along the shore closing in, I became impatient. Even though I knew better, I started reaching down for the bottom with my feet. I ignored Aslan's warning that I should not stand until I reached the shallow water and could grab on to something. I found a foothold and tried to stand up.

The water was up to my belly, and while holding on to the rope I managed to get on my feet. I remember waving at the others, who had moved along the rope and were not far away from me.

Aslan shouted something, but I couldn't hear him over the noise of the river churning around me. I took a step towards the shore, then the current suddenly swept me to the side. I fell, with the backpack dragged by the stream and pulling me under.

Everything went whirling, and in the sudden confusion, the water closed in around me. I splashed and fought with the current, but I lost all sense of direction. I began to panic.

My lungs burned and I tried to raise my head to catch a breath, but only water filled my mouth. I remembered hitting something with my shoulder, and then everything went dark.

I lie on board a boat, the sky above a deep blue, framed by wooden gunwales. The boat rocks smoothly; it is pleasant, and I just want to stay there and not be bothered by anything ever again.

I feel no pain, no fear. The gentle sound of waves lapping at the wooden hull is hypnotizing.

The sky then starts to darken in front of me, There are black clouds billowing on the horizon.

I sit up, taking in the landscape around me. The boat is floating down a wide, calm river.

The two riverbanks look quite different. To my right are golden fields of grain, rich and bright in the sun. Someone is among the stalks – a woman strolling along the river. She is wearing a white dress embroidered with red flower motifs. A round flower wreath adorns her head. She is young, but I recognize her immediately. It is my mother.

I yell at her and wave my hands, but the sound that comes out is muffled, as if I were underwater.

Mam looks with yearning towards the other bank and I follow her gaze.

An ancient forest of tall oak trees stretches out there. I see the figure of a man in the shadows; he carries a spear and a shield. He looks like my father. He walks out of the woods and into the sunlight. His brow is furrowed, his blue eyes are not cold but rather bright as the sky above him.

I yell again, but neither of them can hear me. They follow along the banks as my boat floats down the river.

Then I see the source of the darkening skies in front of me.

It is smoke.

A bridge ahead is burning, and oily, black smoke rises from the conflagration.

There are no oars on the boat. I try to use my hands to paddle, to stop it or change its course, but the boat moves inexorably towards the burning bridge.

I see my mother and father reaching the sides of the bridge before walking into the flames. I scream at the top of my lungs, but again to no avail. I lose sight of them as the boat gets closer.

I can feel the heat of the fire on my face, and as the boat floats down to the bridge, the heat becomes unbearable.

My voice breaks in agony. The bridge collapses, bringing charred beams and red embers down on me.

Darkness again... then a bright light and the smell of wet forest.

I coughed and opened my eyes.

Someone was holding my head. I blinked to remove a watery haze from my eyes, and I saw Matryona's face leaning over me, her concerned look turned into relief as our eyes met. I was laying sideways on the riverbank, with the others all around me.

Aslan explained to me that I almost drowned as the current toppled me over when I tried to walk towards the shore. I had a bruise and a cut on my shoulder, and a lump on the side of my head that must have come from hitting a rock.

I had been unconscious when they dragged me out of the river. They kept me laying with my head down and my airways open, to remove the water from my lungs and bring me back until I woke.

It had been too close.

For the first time in my life, I felt the icy cold touch of death on my skin. It is one thing to see someone else dying, and another to feel the Other Side and come back.

Something changed in me then; a new sense overcame me of how fleeting our time is. I thought about the people that I had lost, how quick and unexpected it always seemed. I could have joined them and finished my journey to freedom with one stupid, hasty move.

I pondered on it later as my head throbbed and we continued our march westwards.

The forest became thick around us, with many shrubs and short trees blocking our path occasionally. Here at the edge of the river, the underbrush was dense. Sometimes we tried to find a way around, but often we just pressed on, with branches and bushes slowing us down, sapping our energy at a fast rate. I don't think we managed more than two kilometers that afternoon, but at least we crossed the dense thicket and made our way into an older forest, with tall pine trees and little undergrowth.

Misha was the last one to emerge from the bushes. He staggered and almost collapsed when he freed himself from the last branches that were blocking his way.

Aslan, who was close by, moved in and helped him stand, but we could see something was wrong. Misha's face was waxy and pale, and his eyes unfocused. Matryona walked over to him and put her hand on his forehead.

"He has a fever. We need to let him rest," she said. "You stay with him, Aslan, and prepare the camp. Andrej, you come with me. We'll look for ingredients for a tea that will help with the fever."

We had been taking Matryona's elixir, the same that we produced in the penal colony, but Misha was exposed to the cold for a long time, and he was already fighting with hypothermia when he crossed the river but then he still had to wait for some clothing. The shock must have been too much for his already tired and malnourished body, and the wet, and cold conditions in the forest didn't help.

I followed Matryona, who gave me a small pouch and instructed me to find and collect fresh pine needles.

We walked in silence as I was focused on the trees, looking for bright-green tips on the branches, while Matryona scanned the area for other plants that she wanted to collect. From time to time, she would bend down and gather leaves from small bushes or some berries. We moved southwards, along the thicket, and after about half an hour we reached open land. Pastures and meadows stretched southwards, and farm buildings loomed on the horizon.

I thought that we would turn back, but Matryona pointed to a willow tree growing on the edge of the forest. We waited, carefully observing the farmland, but with no one in sight we emerged from the concealment and quickly approached the lone willow.

Matryona cut several young branches while I stood lookout, and then we hastily returned to the now homely shade of the pine trees. Before going back to camp, she carefully peeled the still fresh bark from the branches and put it in a bag with the rest of ingredients she had gathered.

As we walked back, I told her about the vision I had when I lost consciousness in the river. She thought about it for a while, before answering.

"The world is divided right now with the Curtain of Iron, which goes not just across the land, but cuts through people's minds." She spoke slowly, her eyes darting, as if searching for answers between the trees. "You, Andrycha, have blood of the West and the East in you. It makes you restless, but it could make you into a good leader. The one that binds together that which was separated. It will be hard for you to find a place you could call home, and yet if you follow God's guidance, you might build it for yourself, and others."

Matryona stopped and turned to look directly at me.

"But beware," she said slowly. "If you allow fear into your soul, you might lose it all."

I stood there and listened carefully, as I was beginning to learn to trust her wisdom, but the words about finding home brought a sensitive question to my mind.

"Why didn't you leave us?" I asked. "You could have just driven back home to Ukraine. No one would have stopped you."

She gave me a look so intense and angry that it made me shiver. But then her face became calm, as if she had reprimanded herself to not lash out at a child asking a foolish question.

"Evgeny wouldn't want that," she said after a long pause. "You are his friends, his brothers. It would be a dishonor to abandon you... even if he is no longer here to walk with us. God sees all, and Evgeny sees us too."

"I am sorry," I said, feeling foolish.

"It's alright, Andrycha." She looked away, smiling a sad smile. "God tests us in many ways. I will grieve; I will mourn my husband when the time is right. But for now, I will help you reach freedom."

I admired her faith. She was willing to sacrifice everything for the sake of her beliefs and convictions, for the sake of those she cared about.

Another question was bothering me, but I bit my tongue, not wanting to open another fresh wound in her soul. But she was wise, and she knew what I wanted to ask, without me saying a word.

"What I did to Artyom." She sighed deeply. "Perhaps I will have to pay for it. But I've seen worse. I was a child during the war, and the occupation. I've seen things no child should see. We all had to endure so much."

She stopped and pressed one hand to a tree, leaning on it for support.

"And Evgeny..."

Her voice broke and I thought she might not continue. She dug her fingers into the cracks in the bark, and her body stiffened.

"You know, I never fully embraced the part of him that was a *vor*," she said. "But he was so much beside that. They said he was a killer, but he was a good man. The man he killed was a local apparatchik. He was selling stolen farm equipment, leaving the kolkhoz without means to produce crops. He was scamming people, and we all struggled. Evgeny wanted to teach him a lesson, but it went too far and he ended up in the penal colony for what he did to the crook. He'd done time before, and I couldn't bear it. That is why I came here, wanting to have him back before we got old. Now, all I have is a memory."

Tears began to run down her face as she spoke, dropping from her chin.

I came closer and embraced her gently. I knew how she felt; I'd lost people too. My mother's life was cut short in front of my eyes, causing me to give up on life in the GDR and join Ziya.

Now, with the memory of Sidoy's gruesome death still fresh in my mind – I had lost another friend, without whom I wouldn't have survived in IK-22. I wouldn't have made it out, to be in that forest, cold and tired but free if it hadn't been for Evgeny. And now, he was gone for all of us.

Matryona hugged me and rested her head on my chest.

"Enough of grieving for now." She wiped her face with a handkerchief. "We need to get young Misha back on his feet."

With that, we hurried back to camp. When we reached it, we found the tarp had been set up and Misha, tucked in a bedroll, was sleeping underneath. Drops of sweat were glistening on his pale face.

Aslan was already simmering water on the stove and Matryona began brewing the tea.

First, she dropped the willow bark into the water and allowed it to cook for a while before she added green pine needles, leaves from a raspberry bush, and lingonberries. She explained that willow contained a substance like modern aspirin, and all the other ingredients were good for fighting fever and reducing inflammation.

A sharp, refreshing fragrance came from the steaming pot when Matryona took it off fire. The smell of pine resin was mixed with earthy aromas of the willow bark. She poured it into a cup, and asked Aslan to wake up Misha.

Boyets drank a cup of hot tea and went back to sleep while Matryona poured the rest into the thermos. We huddled together that night, with Misha in the middle, to give him the most warmth.

The next morning, he seemed to be a bit better, and after drinking another cup of tea with some honey, he said he could continue walking, but his voice could not hide the fact he was still unwell. It was a very foggy day, with thick, milk-like mist reducing visibility to a few meters. Matryona said we could probably start a real fire, then rest up for a bit, and we all agreed. The mist was too thick for either the flames or smoke of the campfire to be visible from a distance.

We had to look underneath the pine and fir trees for wood that was not completely soaked with rainwater. After about an hour, Aslan and I had a fire going and Misha moved with his bedroll to sleep beside it.

We made a clothesline by stretching the rope between the trees, then we hung our wet clothes on it while we squatted beside the crackling fire. After warming up, we gathered some berries and mushrooms.

The berries we quickly ate raw, while Matryona cooked the mushrooms. She first mixed in some lard, then once it was melted, added kasha. After days of eating dry, cured meat and biscuits, the warm meal, and a day of rest by a campfire raised our spirits.

When you spend some time in the wilderness, you begin to appreciate even the smallest comforts that contemporary life can offer.

Then, at the end of the day, before going to sleep, we took out stones that we had placed amongst the burning coals earlier. They were hot, but after some time their temperature dropped, so one could touch them without being burned. We placed these hot stones in our bedrolls for additional heat during the night.

I kept one between my thighs and another under my armpit, and as the pleasant warmth spread through my body, it lulled me to sleep. I thanked God for the fact that I was still alive. That I had friends who cared for me, and for whom I could care, but especially that I had a chance of freedom, despite all my wrongdoings.

People who know my entire story sometimes ask me, “Andrycha, you lost so much. Why didn’t it break you?”

I lost plenty, and I watched people close to me lose even more. Every time grief dragged me into the dark, it taught me the same lesson: you either carry misfortune, or it carries you away.

Here are my rules on how to deal with loss.

Number 1: Don’t fall apart in public. Easier said than done but keep your grief private. If you collapse in front of people, you invite predators, and you also weaken the ones who depend on you. Be their pillar to lean on. You’ll be surprised how much strength you get from holding others up.

Number 2: Accept that the world doesn't pause. The sun will rise tomorrow whether you are ready or not. Life continues, problems multiply, and your enemies move. So, you move too, even if your chest feels like it's full of stones.

Number 3: Don't romanticize the dead. They weren't saints. None of us are. Honor who they really were, the good and the ugly, because truth is the only respect that lasts.

Number 4: Use their memory as fuel, but don't live in the past. Remembrance is useful, it can push you forward. But if you crawl inside it and live there, then instead of honoring the dead you're hiding from life. Make memories into a tool to inspire you, not into a home to hide in.

Number 5: Carry on what you have shared. That is loyalty. Finish the mission you had together: family, work, a promise, even a simple way of living. When you complete what the two of you began, grief turns into duty, and you find peace in your soul.

Number 6: Don't stop moving. If you fell – rise and continue walking. One step at a time. Move forward, every fucking day.

CHAPTER 16

When You Can't Hide, Become Something They Ignore

The mist cleared the following day, and Misha was grinning again with his youthful enthusiasm.

Everyone felt better, as if a moment of rest and comfort dispelled the darkest thoughts from our minds. We were still escaped convicts who had to endure suffering and loss along the way, but at least we were still fighting and each day we survived and didn't get caught was a small victory.

We continued marching westwards, but the progress was slow. The forested area was getting thinner, with tall pines giving way to birch and aspen trees. We had to cross fields and roads several times. Each time we waited for the cover of darkness to do so, and it slowed our progress. We walked more at night and sometimes we slept during the day, living like a pack of wolves.

We bypassed a few more villages and after a week of this skulking, partisan trek, we found ourselves watching the train track running across the swaths of taiga and farmlands.

The rails were about five hundred meters away from the thick grove we hid in.

I felt like a reconnaissance soldier deep in enemy territory. Fields of dark-brown soil with short, grey-gold stubble remaining after harvest, stretched to our right. Beyond them we could see the gray housing blocks of southern Iskitim, like bones jutting out of the land.

To our left, a large industrial plant hummed with activity, its tall chimneys producing a steady stream of smoke and steam.

We had reached that grove the previous night, and since morning we had been on lookout, watching activity around the plant, and along the train tracks. We saw several freight trains stop in the fields, before continuing their journey south.

"Are you sure we'll be able to hop on the right train?" Aslan asked, cautiously. "What if it takes us in the wrong direction?"

"The tracks run south from here to Novoaltaysk, there is no other route, so don't worry," Matryona replied with confidence. "When the night comes, we will sneak close to the tracks and wait for the right opportunity. Since it is the only route at some point we should hit a cargo train going south. If we don't get on one today, then we will return here before morning. We can stay hidden in this grove for days."

"I don't like staying here." Misha's eyes darted between the buildings on the horizon. "Feels like we are sitting ducks in the reeds, just waiting for a dog to come and chase us out."

"Stop that," Matryona reprimanded him. "If God wanted you caught, you would be back in the camp already. We will make it, God willing. Now, get some rest, we will need to be alert and ready when the moment comes."

"Listen to Auntie," I said, using the familiar nickname we'd created for Matryona on our hard journey. "Just rest, I'll keep the first watch."

With that, Misha, Aslan, and Matryona retreated deeper into the small forest, where we had left our things between dense bushes. The grove was formed by several tall aspen trees with copper-red leaves shivering even without wind. Between them, smaller birches and various shrubs competed for space and sunlight. It was thick, and with the leaves still on there was no way anyone could spot us from a distance. Even if someone walked through the grove, they wouldn't notice our lair, unless they stepped on it.

I made sure I had the sun behind me before using binoculars to scan the area. I didn't want the reflective glare off the lenses to alert someone looking my way. It would be risky to walk through the open fields to reach the tracks, but we had to try it. All we had to do was to catch a train and after a few hours we would reach Novoaltaysk, where we would find refuge with Matryona's friend. I had my doubts about trusting a stranger, but she vouched for the man, who was supposedly some sort of a shaman back in Altai.

I kept my eyes peeled on the roads, the train tracks, and the coal processing plant in front of our position. It was a normal, drab, Soviet reality, sparsely colored with autumn leaves. No militsiya in sight, no unusual commotion.

I shared Misha's sentiment, I didn't want to sit in that grove for days, waiting for a better chance. On top of being in a vulnerable spot, we were running out of supplies, as our trek was longer than initially anticipated. It had taken us almost two weeks for what on a regular road could be accomplished in a day of hard marching, since concealment was more important for us than speed. Now we were about to abandon the safety of the woods and rejoin the civilized world.

The sound of Aslan's quiet footsteps snapped me out of my musing. He took over the watch and I went to rest myself. I fell asleep easily, since the previous night we barely got any shuteye, traversing pastures, and fields to get to the grove we occupied as our forward position.

When I woke up after a few hours, it was already getting dark. We used the twilight to gather our things and make our way to the edge of the field.

Night fell presently, covering the fields in black veil of darkness, my familiar friend that I carried on with me.

We went out from between the scrublands and trees and started to march rapidly across the grassy pastures and plowed fields. We were guided by the lights illuminating the coal-processing plant a few hundred meters to our left.

After twenty minutes we reached an unlit, asphalt country road, which we crossed and then found ourselves on a dike situated between the train tracks and the road. The train tracks ran across a raised embankment, so we climbed it and then slid down the other side. The shoulder of the embankment was covered in short weeds and small juniper bushes. We hid among them as they provided sufficient concealment, and we waited for a cargo train to hop on.

Time flew fast, with my heart beating loudly with anticipation. The lights from Iskitim were bright on the horizon, and the plant to the south hummed and rumbled as the nightshift workers kept the facility running.

The sound of a horn announced the train coming from up north. It was a passenger train and it clattered on the tracks at a steady pace without stopping.

I looked at the people in the carriage compartments, sitting in the yellow glow of the light bulbs. Some were gazing out of the windows, unaware that out there were a bunch of escaped criminals sitting in the bushes beside the tracks. The passengers resembled actors in some show that I had almost forgotten.

I was one of them once, I thought. Living as a cog in the machine, oblivious and afraid of that which lurked in the dark. Now, it was me that they feared when they gazed into the night.

The train passed us, leaving me with my thoughts. Two more trains came as we waited. Another passenger train going north to Novosibirsk and a freight train on its way south, but neither of them stopped.

A couple more hours went by, marked by our rising anxiety. We couldn't remain so exposed by the time dawn broke. There was civilization in all directions except where we had come from. We had to either get back to our grove or find a suitable hiding place near the tracks soon. Perhaps we could locate a drainage pipe underneath the embankment.

I wanted to talk to the others about it when another train horn sounded from the north.

The tracks vibrated as the train approached and began passing our position. It was a freight train, several hundred meters long, with dozens of open gondola cars. It passed us, rattling in a slowing down cadence, as the train came to a stop beside the plant. The brakes squeaked loudly, the cars jingled and hissed on the tracks before finally coming to a stop.

We were hoping for a train with boxcars we could hide in. With open gondolas, we could be spotted by anyone doing a check or simply looking from above.

"Boyets, go and see what's inside." I ordered Misha, who was sitting beside me.

He must have grinned, because I saw the white of his teeth interspersed with two black holes. He then ran towards the closest car and used the metal ladder on its side to climb to the top. He went inside and picked up something. Without saying anything he threw a black lump on the grass in front of us. I leaned in to touch it.

"It's coal," I whispered to Aslan and Matryona.

"Can't hide on top of a pile of coal," she said.

"So, we wait for a different train?" Aslan asked.

"No," I said firmly. I didn't want to wait. It was just a few hours' ride down to Novoaltaysk. We could make it. "I have a plan, let's see if it works. Come!"

I grabbed one of the backpacks and climbed into the gondola. It was filled with lumps of coal which formed a small mound in the middle of the car that sloped towards the edges. There was about half a meter of space between the bottom of the mound and the brim of the car, enough to conceal us from the side.

Aslan and Matryona got in after me. I explained my plan to them, and they agreed.

We took out blankets from our bedrolls and covered them thoroughly with coal dust, making them pitch black on one side. After that, Aslan, Misha, and Matryona positioned themselves with their backpacks in the three corners of the car. I covered each of them with a blanket, the black side of the rug facing upwards, and I dropped some lumps of coal on top for even more camouflage.

I took the last blanket and went to the fourth corner, where I began making more space by moving the coal to the middle.

A whistle came from the locomotive, followed by its horn.

I almost fell head first onto the coal when the train jerked and began rolling forward. With increasing speed, we were closing in on the plant and the lamplights illuminating its perimeter.

I rushed to dig a slightly deeper hole in my corner, before glueing myself to the wall, and covering my body with my coal-infused blanket. Around the edges, I could see shadows sliding over me as we passed beside the plant.

The train continued, and I breathed a sigh of relief. We had not been stopped, and we were on our way out of Siberia.

The boxcars rolled through the vast, dark taiga with a steady drum. From time to time, we peeked over the edge of the car to orient ourselves. The lights of villages and towns pierced the darkness, and whenever we approached train stations or lit-up junctions, we hid underneath the blankets to avoid detection.

We passed the town of Tal'menka while it was still dark, but soon the first bleak signs of morning appeared on the horizon to our left. We knew from the maps that the next bigger town would be Novoaltaysk, where we wanted to get off the train.

The sky was clear, and dawn was spreading across it, carrying hope for law-abiding citizens. And the threat of detection and capture for us. The temperature was around zero and I was getting shivers from leaning on the cold, metal wall of the car.

After about an hour, we entered a long stretch of a dark forest and Matryona said we should get ready. The train crossed the forest and then came to a halt at a junction on the north-eastern outskirts of Novoaltaysk.

It was already close to sunrise and we scrambled out of the car in a hurry. Our section of the long train stopped between meadows, a couple hundred meters from the tree line, and we began walking quickly in that direction.

There were houses nearby on the other side of the meadow and we could hear dogs barking in the yards as we hurried along the tracks and into the cover of the trees. A local road ran along the forest edge and as we reached it to cross, we saw a woman riding a bicycle.

It was too late to hide since she had seen us as well. She was maybe twenty meters away from us and she stopped, gaping at the sight of us.

We must have looked like a bunch of devils on a journey back from hell. Our clothes, faces and everything we carried were all covered in black coal dust. Every step felt heavy, our bodies cold and stiff after the ride.

"*Babushka*!" Misha stepped onto the path and yelled in a slurred voice, "Do you have any vodka? We are very dry here."

We followed his lead and shuffled onto the road, staggering, and groaning like heavily drunken bums. Matryona laughed hysterically, wrapping one of her arms around Aslan, who grunted and spat out some curses. I knew he never had a drink in his life, but he was making a good show of a boozer.

The woman stood by her bicycle with hands on the handles, looking like she didn't know what to make of us.

"If you don't have any vodka on you," I said, with my best imitation of a drunken voice, "can you point us to the nearest shop? We walk and walk, and there are no shops anywhere."

"The main road is that way," she said, pointing in the direction she was going. "Follow it and you will reach the milk factory. There is a shop on the other side of the road from it."

"*Spasiba, babushka*!" Aslan exclaimed, raising one hand in the air. "We need to rest first, right, comrades?" Saying that, Aslan sat in the ditch with Matryona hanging on his neck and giggling like a little girl. Misha and I joined them, and with growing tension, we watched and waited to see what the old woman was going to do.

She got back on her bicycle and rode onwards.

"What has become of our country," she muttered to herself, "Such a shame."

We waited until she disappeared along the road before entering the forest. We walked fast for a couple of hours until we felt safe enough to take a rest in a thicket and consult the map that Matryona pulled out of her poncho.

Her friend's dacha was five kilometers to the west on the bank of the River Chesnokovka. It took us almost a full day to reach it, as we again had to wait for night when we had to cross a major road and a couple of housing projects.

It was the morning of the following day when we hesitantly left the cover of the forest and stepped onto a dirt road leading to the dacha.

The four of us, still blackened with coal, unwashed and tired, entered the fenced-off piece of land through a squeaky, metal gate, and found ourselves on a neatly trimmed lawn outside of a two-story, wooden cottage. It was made of dark, impregnated wood, with intricate carvings on the beams and pillars supporting the structure.

We closed the gate behind us and shuffled towards the entrance. A gentle breeze awakened the wooden wind chimes scattered around the dacha, as if to announce our presence, and the door opened even before we reached the building.

Aslan, Misha, and I froze in sudden worry. I kept my fingers on the handle of the knife in my pocket, but Matryona walked on without fear.

A short man wearing glasses and a fur hat appeared in the doorway. He wore a light-blue tunic with silver embroidery that matched his bushy white beard. He moved slowly and deliberately as he raised his hand to greet us. He seemed completely unperturbed by the fact that four vagrants who looked like homeless coal miners stood on his lawn.

"Aykel-kam, so good to see you!" Matryona exclaimed, using an Altai honorific meant for the shamans, "I bring you guests."

"*Zdrastvuj*, Matryona-ene." The man stepped down and clasped both of his palms around Matryona's soot-covered hand. He then looked at us, standing behind her.

"Where is your husband?" he asked.

I couldn't see Matryona's face, but whatever Aykel saw in her expression, it made him embrace her tightly. She began to sob gently against his chest, her body trembling as he softly patted her on her back.

When I think about it now, I realize that there was more to why she was helping us. It seems to me that beside wanting to honor her man, she was simply afraid of grieving alone. So, she walked with us, a bunch of strangers, but also her late husband's final comrades. When we met Aykel, she could at last let go of her grief.

It took a while, and when they parted, the shaman's previously pristine tunic was covered in coal dust, but he didn't seem to care.

I took my hand out of my pocket, leaving my knife inside. I breathed in deeply, feeling the tension drain from my body. The air was filled with the smell of autumn leaves, fir, and pine needles, and freshly cut grass. A sound of a small river trickled nearby, adding to the peaceful atmosphere.

We were free, and we were safe, at least for the moment.

I felt something waking up in me – a hope that I had kept locked in a corner of my heart. Hope for a life out in the open, in the light, and away from the shadows and the depths of hell.

CHAPTER 17

Shock Can Cleanse The Mind, Humility Cleanses Soul

We washed ourselves in the nearby river. The gently flowing water carried away the sweat, dirt, and coal dust that covered my body. It felt almost as if I was getting rid of some of the darkness that had encased my soul in IK-22.

Aykel started a bonfire in front of the dacha and burned our blackened clothes on it. He gave us simple workmen's outfits, which didn't fit perfectly, but they were clean and felt good against my freshly washed skin.

Aslan, Misha, and I sat by the fire while Aykel and Matryona went into the dacha and prepared breakfast. We ate kasha with milk mixed with honey, assorted nuts, and some freshly gathered berries. I remember feeling like a king in clean clothes, heating my body as I ate a warm and savory meal.

We didn't waste much time, and at noon we climbed aboard a civilian version of the UAZ-469 off-road truck, painted in a faded, light-blue color which reminded me of the evening sky. We drove through Novoaltaysk and down south across the plains and fields of Altai Krai. The landscape was a refreshing change after seeing only forests and taiga for over three years. It reminded me of the fertile steppes in the west of Russia and Ukraine.

We were free, but still in unknown territory, and without an identity to hang on to.

As the kilometers passed, I looked at my hands, covered in tattoos, and I felt a pang of grief. I had just escaped from prison. I was free from the Zone, the barbed wire fences, the watchtowers and the prison guards with their rifles and batons. But was I really free? I still carried the darkness that I had to embrace to survive, and I could feel the pain that I inflicted on others.

Memories of lost friends, Sidoy and Evgeny, and images of their death were fresh in my mind. The bloody mess that Ivan's bullets had done to Sidoy's body. The snow-white face of Evgeny on the lap of his wife as he died. The memories came in images, covering the orange-gold line of trees at the side of the road as they passed.

I gritted my teeth, thinking about Ivan Rostovkin. I'd had him on the edge of my knife, but Sidoy hadn't wanted him dead back then. I wondered whether my mentor would have told me differently if he knew that Ivan would bring about his own end.

I touched my pocket, where I kept the folded letter Ziya had given me, and with that came a sting of anger toward my former associate. He'd used me from the start, and because of him I'd landed in that penal colony. He'd used me again inside, even after I'd cut my ties with him. Now he was using me once more, but at least this time I was getting something in return.

I realized I was holding my breath, and I exhaled, snapping back to reality.

Misha, sitting by my side, was napping with his head thrown back, and his mouth half open. Aslan was looking through the window on the other side.

The landscape slowly changed, from flat plains covered with fields, to a hillier terrain, and the road turned around knolls and through ramshackle villages. The foothills of the Altai mountains dominated the horizon. The mountaintops were already covered with snow, painted pink by the slowly setting sun. The beauty of the view was surreal, and it felt almost like a dream, too good to be true, and I half-expected militsiya to appear at any moment and bring us back to IK-22.

I noticed Aykel peering at me through the rear-view mirror and my *vor* instinct kicked in.

Could I trust this man? He was a *muzhyk,* not part of the brotherhood. What did he know about loyalty? Maybe he was fond of Matryona, but what ties did he have with the rest of us escaped convicts and career criminals? There was no ink on his body to tell the stories of what he stood for.

How could I know what he was made of and put my life in his hands?

A thought crossed my mind, that we should ditch him when we make a stop and use his car to get to Ukraine. I did have the names and numbers of a couple of Ziya's contacts there, we would have a fresh start with the information.

I snapped out of it, realizing it was my own inner darkness speaking to me. It sparked doubt and mistrust, and I was immediately ashamed of even considering going against the man who was helping us despite what we represented.

I turned my head and looked outside, as the road took us into a valley and deeper into the mountains of Gorno-Altai Autonomous Oblast.

The night was setting in when we passed the town of Chemul and turned onto a rural road. We drove through a forest with dark, pine-covered hills looming over the valley. Soon we stopped, the road ending in a courtyard surrounded by a handful of buildings. One of them had its lights on. A group of people walked out of it and into the courtyard to greet us.

Gravel crunched under our feet, as we got out of the UAZ. I stretched my body and deeply inhaled the crisp mountain air. It was fresh, cold, and pure, with a note of pine needles, and a mineral scent. The temperature must have been below zero as the air pinched at my cheeks and I saw silver frost on the birch leaves that carpeted the ground. The steady noise of a river flowing over rocks filled the space with a constant hum, and I could see white crests of waves frothing over rocks beyond a thin line of trees.

We shook hands with the three men that came from the large, wooden house. Two of them were Altaians, named Baidar and Talay. They were a bit shorter than me, slim, with young, smooth faces and narrow eyes. They wore brown winter coats, with fur on the rim of the hoods and sleeves.

The third one was a tall, bearded Russian, who introduced himself as Feodor. He wore a washed-up winter uniform of the Soviet army. His face darkened at the sight of tattoos on my hands, but he didn't say anything and helped with unloading our luggage from the car.

We each grabbed our things but as we moved towards the house intending to cross the threshold, I was stopped by Aykel.

"Forgive me Andrej-ini," Aykel said, calling me a 'younger brother' in Altai language. He raised one hand and blocked me from entering. "But I do not wish to have you under my roof tonight. There is trouble over your soul. A taint of Erlik. We will cleanse it tomorrow, but for now, would you mind staying in the guesthouse with your brothers?"

He glanced at Aslan and Misha, who had lined up behind me with their belongings.

"What happened to *'Gost v dom – Bog v dom' – 'Guest home – God home',* old man?" Misha sneered, using an old Russian proverb.

The two young Altai men stopped in their tracks, and Feodor's brow furrowed like a rocky outcrop as he dropped the bag he was carrying and clenched his fists.

I looked at Matryona who stood nearby, and she gave me a short nod.

"Shut it, *chort*!" I snapped harshly at the young Boyets, and I turned back to Aykel.

"If that is your wish. We are grateful for the help you have provided so far, Aykel Kam," I said with respect and using the same honorific as Matryona had to refer to the white-bearded shaman.

Aykel smiled broadly, as if nothing had happened, and then said something in Altai to Baidar who waved for us to follow him.

He led us to a large wooden building which we entered through a creaky wooden door. It was dark inside and it smelled of hay and animals. When Baidar turned on the rubber light switch by the door, I realized the place was horse stables, with eight stalls lined on two sides of a passage. Misha's face turned sour, but Aslan smiled and patted him on the shoulder.

"Smells better than Barrack 6 did, doesn't it Andrycha?" he winked at me.

"Indeed, *bratan*." I couldn't help but chuckle at his remark, which was true to be honest.

Baidar showed us to a ladder which led to a hayloft over the stalls. We climbed it and spread our bedrolls over the soft layer of hay. It was cold inside and we dug ourselves into the dried grass, then covered ourselves with the fresh blankets we had gotten from Aykel at his dacha.

Baidar from downstairs, asked if we were ready to go to sleep. When we said we were, he turned off the lights and left.

I lay with my eyes open for a while, adjusting them to darkness inside. I listened to the horses snorting below us, and the even hum of the river outside.

I didn't feel bad about Aykel not inviting us into his house that night. Somehow, I felt he was right, as I could still feel the sticky filth of the Zone deep under my skin. Aykel said we would cleanse it the next day, but I wondered whether I would ever really get rid of it.

I woke up to the sound of horses stomping and neighing in their stalls. I could see faint streaks of early-morning light piercing the cracks between the planks of the wooden wall of the hayloft. Misha was snoring gently, tightly wrapped in his blanket, but there was no sign of Aslan or his bedding.

I wiped the sleep from my eyes, stretched the stiffness out, then clambered down the ladder. I realized it had been the best night's sleep I could remember having since my incarceration. Baidar was there, tending to the horses in the twilight filtering through the open stable door. He looked at me over his shoulder and nodded.

Wishing him a good morning, I went outside. The young Altai lad reminded me of Talgat, the steady, brave driver who'd gotten us through the checkpoint in his truck. I wondered whether he'd gotten into trouble for being the victim of our escape, but then I chastised myself for my concern.

Why did I care about this *muzhyk*? Why did I care about anyone else other than my *vory* brothers?

At that time, the feeling became almost alien to me, but I couldn't deny it. Something from my past, the memory of Mam, of the last Easter I had with her, tugged at me, scratching at the surface of my hardened, tattooed skin.

I found Aslan by the river, kneeling on his blanket, facing southwards. His lips quietly repeated the words of Fajr, the morning prayer, and he bowed three times with his hands resting on his knees.

Dawn was slowly breaking over the mountains to the east, and I felt an urge to pray, myself. I made a sign of cross, closed my eyes, and began the Lord's Prayer:

"Our Father in heaven, hallowed be your name. Your kingdom come, your will be done, on earth as it is in heaven. Give us today our daily bread. Forgive us our sins..." I paused and I stood still, feeling the cool mountain breeze on my face. "...as we forgive those who sin against us. Lead us not into temptation, but deliver us from evil. For yours is the kingdom, and the power, and the glory, for ever and ever. Amen."

I said it three times and with each repetition, a sense of peace grew in my troubled mind.

When I finished, I walked to the courtyard to find Matryona standing there looking at the horizon.

"Aykel says a storm is coming," she said as I approached.

The air was warmer than the day before and I noticed here and there, water dripping from the roof of the house. The sky was reddish and clear to the east, while over us a heavy front of clouds gathered into a dark-gray, billowing mass.

"Do you trust the old man?" I asked softly, standing close to her, so that no one could eavesdrop on our conversation.

"With my life." She gave me a stern look.

My next words took longer to speak.

"Do you also think that I am tainted somehow?"

"You're not tainted Andrycha." Matryona smiled. "But your mind is still in prison."

I thought about that for a moment.

"He said that I have a taint of Erlik, who's that?"

"It is their God of the Underworld. The one who plagues the world through evil spirits." Her body shivered once as she spoke the words. "Aykel sees and knows more than I do." She put one hand on my arm. "Please, trust him, he means well."

"Trust..." I mused. "It's no longer in my nature to trust strangers, but I'll see what he has to offer."

"Andrej-ini," Aykel's voice came from the dacha's threshold. I had not heard him come out. "Gather your men, we'll be starting the ritual soon."

I wanted to protest and say that Aslan and Misha were not my men, that they were my brothers under the law, but I bit my tongue and walked towards the stable. Aslan was done with his praying and he was already on his way to the courtyard, so I climbed the ladder to wake Misha.

I wondered what kind of ritual the old shaman had in mind, but despite my misgivings I decided to follow Matryona's advice and give him the benefit of the doubt.

Aslan, Misha, and I met with Aykel, Baidar and Feodor at the back of the house, facing the river, the emerald waters of which churned excitedly about fifty meters away.

There was a small, round, wooden hut out there with a metal chimney producing a snaking stream of white smoke. The door to the hut opened and the second young Altaian, Talay, walked out, his half-naked body glistening with sweat. He shouted something to Aykel in their guttural language.

"The *banya* is ready," the shaman said to us.

He was dressed up in an embroidered green coat, with geometrical patterns running along the flaps and the collar. He had a fur hat on his head and held a leather hand drum in his left hand.

"Before the heat, you must wash yourself in the holy Katun River."

The sound of thunder echoed through the valley and I looked up at the sky. Autumn was about to finally give in to the coming winter as a mass of heavy clouds billowed to the west like dark, foreboding titans looming over the hilltops. The sun was still shining behind our backs, but the steadily progressing stormfront cast shadows down on us all. As if to remind us how small and insignificant we were facing nature and its power.

"Go, now!" Aykel commanded.

I cursed softly but obeyed. With Aslan and Misha by my side, we joined Feodor and Baidar, who were already walking down to the river. When we reached the embankment, Aykel's two men were undressing in a hurry, as if eager to enter the emerald waters. The wind picked up then, carrying with it a thin cold drizzle. We started taking off our own clothes. Feodor and Baidar had already stripped down completely and were waiting for us to do the same.

It dawned on me that we three almost looked like a different species, with our bodies pale, wiry, and covered in blue tattoos. Aslan had ink on his torso from during our imprisonment, with a lion on the side of his chest and a mosque with a crescent moon with three towers on his belly.

Misha looked the least haggard of our group, but even he wore the fresh tattoo of a knight with a lance that he got after his initiation.

This contrasted greatly with the healthy, athletic bodies of Feodor and Baidar, and their unblemished, suntanned skin. I looked the burly Russian in the eye, and for the first time, I saw something like a smile on his bearded, serious face.

"Come on, thieves," Feodor bellowed over the noise of the river and the wind. "Let's see who can stay the longest."

The embankment at that spot was rocky, with a narrow sandy beach leading into a shallow basin of relatively calm water. Large boulders and rocks shielded the basin from the main current, which raged beyond.

Feodor and Baidar waded in and squatted, submerging their entire bodies in the icy water. It wasn't my first time in the cold, so I moved without hesitation to join them.

The water was colder than I expected, chilling like the initiation barrel, but it also drained all the heat from my body as it flowed around me. The Katun River must have been fed by the freshly melted snow which blanketed the hilltops surrounding us.

I focused on my breathing, feeling the familiar, icy daggers stabbing at my bones. The drizzle became thicker, and it began to sting my scalp. I then realized it was hail, pea-sized and dense. It fell from the sky like a thousand icy wasps piercing the water surface and biting at our skin. As if the cold of the water was not enough.

The pain increased, the hail hitting my face broke my focus, and for a moment I felt an urge to get out, but then I heard a drum. Its steady rhythm calmed my heartbeat as I returned to focusing on my breathing.

Aykel was standing on the shore, beating the drum, unaffected by the hail popping off his coat and the unprotected skin of his hands. He began a song using his throat to produce a deep, guttural, bass sound, which carried through the noise of the storm.

It was the first time I had heard this kind of singing, and even though I didn't understand the words, I felt a surge of energy as the shaman's voice resonated with something in my very core.

The time passed, and my body began to feel numb. I could see Misha's face tight with concentration. He was struggling, we all were. Aslan kept his composure in the cold water, smiling faintly when I looked his way.

Feodor and Baidar were looking away, seemingly lost in a kind of meditation. The young Altaian's lips were moving, as if he was reciting a mantra, or a prayer. It reminded me of my own mantra, The Jesus Prayer, that used to help me through the pain. I began repeating its words in my mind.

Misha shifted in the water beside me and I saw a plea on his face. He wanted to get out.

"Hold on, *bratany*," I yelled, and moved closer, putting my arms on Misha's and Aslan's shoulders. We formed a little circle, with our heads bowed together.

"Breathe," I said, "Let's show these *muzhyki*, who we are!"

And so, we remained in the icy cold water and I began to feel the pain dissipating, as if taken away by the flow of the river and the energy we shared with each other. I breathed in deeply, and I could hear my brothers breathing beside me. We gave each other strength, and I suspect that without it, we might not have lasted against the fit, and trained locals.

I don't know how long we stayed there. I began to get dizzy, and could feel my body trembling involuntarily. It was too much, but then Aykel's song stopped. He kept drumming, but finally shouted for us to get out.

Feodor seemed unsatisfied with the challenge ending and he eyed me angrily. He muttered some curses about thieves and rascals as we all waded back to the shore.

We scrambled on land, shaking and the hail kept lashing our bodies, which were now red from the exposure to the unbearable cold. We grabbed our wet clothes and marched stiffly towards the steaming *banya* to the constant rhythm of Aykel's drum.

Tayal was waiting for us outside in a bathrobe and with a felt hat on his head. He handed each of us a similar hat, and we put them on before he opened the wooden door. A wave of hot steam felt good to my freezing body and I entered the *banya* eagerly.

There was an antechamber with fresh bathrobes and towels, and a metal stove encased in the wall. Feodor walked past me and opened a small door in the wall, releasing a churning, steamy mist into the room.

"*Davay, davay* – Move, move," he urged us and we hurried into the *parilka* – the steam room.

My body welcomed the heat as I sat on one of the wooden benches placed in two tiers along the walls. Against the opposite wall stood a metal frame filled with rocks. The stove pipe ran from the antechamber between the stones, heating them up. Nearby stood a water-filled barrel and a stool with a *venik* – a bundle of fresh oak twigs with the leaves still on.

Tayal was the last to enter, and he closed the door tight behind him.

The heat was intense. I'd never been to a *banya* like that before and I felt sweat almost immediately running down my back. I had to wipe it from my eyes from time to time, as it dripped from my forehead. I was grateful for the hat Tayal gave me – it protected my head from overheating. Slowly, the cold that had been gripping my insides began to fade, replaced by exhilarating warmth.

At first, everyone's faces were contorted, as if we were focused on hard work. Each time Tayal used the ladle to pour water on the hot stones, I had to close my eyes. I struggled to breathe the steam-filled air, which had a sharp, yet invigorating smell of pine resin mixed with the sweet aroma of oak leaves.

At some point, Tayal took the twigs, dipped them in the barrel, and after letting them sit on the hot stones for a while, began thrashing each of our backs with them.

I hesitated at first, recalling how I used to lie in the dirt with a guard's boot on my neck and truncheons beating me to a pulp. Seeing Feodor accept the process, I chose the path of least resistance and took my own turn.

It was a strange sensation, as the heated twigs delivered sharp snaps of pain, yet the twigs were soft, and the burning heat on my skin made my muscles relax. By the next round, I was the first to line up for Tayal to thrash at my body with the *venik.*

Aykel joined us after a while, naked and soaked from Katun's turquoise waters. The atmosphere began to become more relaxed and despite us all suffering from the heat, we started to smile and laugh.

We took a few more trips to the river's frigid waters to cool down, and then to repeat the cycle of heat and the *venik*. Each time we walked tall with excitement to the welcoming embrace of the holy Altai river. Never before had I seen grown men so joyful, almost intoxicated, without taking any drugs or alcohol.

I felt my life force surging in me, and as we put on bathrobes to walk back to the house for a well-deserved meal, I realized that I couldn't stop smiling. Something new appeared in my soul on that day, and whatever intention Aykel had in performing his ritual and giving us this experience, I think it worked.

We crossed the threshold of his house, and he welcomed us like guests to a proper feast prepared by Matryona, and a few women whom I hadn't seen before. We ate, we talked, and we laughed.

The dark thoughts that had bothered me since my escape were gone. I didn't forget Sidoy, Evgeny, or their deaths, but in some way, the burden became less painful, and I was able to let parts of that pain flow down the river with the wild current.

On that evening I felt truly free, not only from the barbed wire fencing of the prison, but also from something that had been growing inside me since my mother's death. A kind of resentment, a bitterness brought by the sense of injustice. It would take me more years to identify it and understand it completely, but that journey of self-discovery started with Aykel's sauna ritual, as the shadow that gnawed at my soul was dispelled, at least for a while.

After the feast, we were led to a large room. Sleeping mats had been laid out on the floor, and our bundles of belongings were already waiting for us. We stayed in Aykel's house, sharing a common space with Feodor, Baidar, and Tayal. The wooden room was cozy, clean, and warm, and it felt homely to me.

Everyone was exhausted after hours spent in the heat of the banya and the icy waters of the river, followed by a hearty meal. We lay down on our mats to rest. Some quickly drifted off, and I could hear Feodor snoring loudly, like a truck with no exhaust.

I felt drained too, but I couldn't bring myself to sleep as my mind was already racing with thoughts about the future. As I lay there and looked at the wooden rafters above, Aykel came over and nudged me to come with him.

Aslan gave me a questioning look as if asking whether he should join, but I gestured for him to stay and went with the shaman.

"Put on a jacket, Andrej-ini," Aykel said. "We'll go for a walk."

Outside, the storm was over and patches of clear blue sky were peeking through the fluffy white clouds. The old shaman led us into the forest, then up the surrounding hills. The hike up was steep, but Aykel kept a steady pace which made me think he must have been in great shape, despite his age.

We didn't talk much as we walked, and I appreciated the nature around us in silence. After a couple of hours, we reached a clearing on top of a hill and we sat down on a fallen tree trunk overlooking the valley. The Katun River looked like a turquoise ribbon from this vantage point and I could still hear its distant hum.

"What do you think?" Aykel asked with hands on his knees, leaning forward and peering into the valley.

"It is beautiful. Thank you for bringing me here."

"Altai is beautiful, that is true." His voice was weathered, yet full of energy. "But I am asking, what do you think about your future? What will you and your men do now?"

"They are not my men," I said with a shake of my head. "We are brothers."

"One does not exclude another," Aykel said calmly. "I see how they listen to you Andrej-ini. They might be your brothers, but they also see you as their leader. There is no point in pretending it is otherwise."

"We are all *vory*," I said calmly, "we are equals."

"There is no equality in the universe, except for the fact that we are all going to die. But you seem to know that yourself." He raised an eyebrow, looking at my hands.

The Grim Reaper, with the phrase 'I am here, and I am waiting', was a reminder of what he just said.

"I am not telling you this to flatter you," he continued. "The point is for you to accept this as a responsibility. These men look up to you. Others might join you along your path and you should make your choices carefully, taking into account that your leadership is guiding others."

I looked at the sky, and I thought about his question.

"We want to travel to Ukraine, with Matryona," I finally said, "but we need new papers for that."

"I can help you with the papers." He nodded. "My nephew works in the party office in Barnaul. He has his ways."

I was surprised by how well connected this unassuming old man was.

"What's the price?" I asked.

This time he looked away and took a longer pause. It reminded me of Sidoy, and the way I learned to listen to him on our walks along the fence in IK-22.

"This Brotherhood of yours..." Instead of answering my question, he stated. "It is based on a false premise."

"What do you know about it?" I snapped, angered that the old man spoke ill of the *vory*. In lockup this would be enough to deserve a beating.

"I know the world, Andrej," he raised one arm, gesturing at the view we had from the hilltop. "I have met many people in my life. They come to me searching for healing. Men with healthy bodies, with money, and power."

He lowered his hand and looked me in the eye. Not with challenge, but with compassion.

"When you have a sick soul, no amount of wealth can fill it. Some lose the fight and become puppets of the sickness that eats them from the inside. But others look for a way to rescue the light in themselves." He paused, then after a moment continued. "I have met *vory* before. I know about your Bratva, your rituals, and your code. Those serve only you, and that is the way of a predator. Among your brothers, you might be honorable, you might feel you're doing right, but for everyone outside, you're a menace."

He made another pause, letting the words soak in, painfully.

"In the end, what you give away will come back to you. You remember that and keep watch over your soul. One day, you will come back here." He finished.

Part of me wanted to curse at him, to tell him he didn't know anything. I got a hold of myself, taking a deep breath before answering.

"You don't know how it is in prison. What man must do to survive." I countered. "Without the code, there would be chaos, everyone fighting for scraps thrown by the guards, snitching, and making deals to keep themselves safe. It is the same outside, with the corrupt governments ruling over us and exploiting us at every step. Thank you for your advice, but I am a *vor*, and I will remain one."

"You're right to oppose the corrupt, the cowards, and the snitches. Just make sure not to become one of them in the process. Now, the price for the papers..." He clapped his hands on his thighs and smiled at me as if ready to tell a joke. "My other nephew needs help with felling trees this winter. Matryona-ana told me you've got plenty of experience at that."

I wasn't expecting this, and it brought with it another jolt of indignation. After three years of hard labor in the camp, he was asking us to do the same kind of work for him now that we were free.

But, looking into his eyes, corners of which wrinkled deeply as he smiled at me, I saw disarming playfulness. It was as if he knew that he was provoking a reaction in me, but at the same time, he wasn't afraid of my potential outburst.

Old Aykel certainly knew how to trigger a man's ego, how to make them doubt themselves, and their convictions. By doing that, he was able to make us learn. He was not the kind of teacher who lays down a complex theory and orders you to memorize his doctrine. Instead, he knew how to help us find the correct path on our own by asking questions, exposing us to hardships, and nudging us in the right direction.

"Fine," I said, unable to keep myself from chuckling. His positive demeanor was contagious. I felt the inner peace instilled in me by the *banya* ritual return. I scratched my head, already thinking about how I'd have to tell Aslan and Misha about our new job.

“We could use some fresh air and exercise.”

CHAPTER 18

Don't Let Old Hatreds Choose New Wars

I spoke with my *vory* brothers that evening, and I explained to them what the plan was.

Misha muttered something about doing *muzhyki* a favor, but he went silent when I gave him a scornful look. Aslan had no objections; he laughed hard at the irony of doing the same as we did in the camp.

"Let's hope the old man won't beat us with his cane if we don't fulfill our daily quota," he joked.

We still had some days of rest before the harvest. Aykel said we needed to wait for the full moon to pass, as the best wood was collected when the trees were cut down in the winter months, and during the waning moon phase. He explained that the sap was leaving the tree during that period. The best time to cut was at night and the wood obtained like that was drier, stronger, and free from insects.

I mused on this folklore method, and how none of these rules were adhered to in the forestry work carried out by the camp authorities. I took Aykel's words with a grain of salt at the time, my mind still infused with the modern scientific disdain for all traditional knowledge. But, over the years, I have found people in other parts of the world following the same principles and with great results.

Sometimes I think that it takes contemporary science a lot of time to catch up with what has been common knowledge over the ages.

We waited for a week, recovering, eating well, and doing work around the farm that Aykel ran with the help of Baidar, Tayal, and Feodor. The snow came after a few days, covering the valley in a white coat, while the frost began working its way to locking the river in an icy confine.

It was the end of November, and I recall those days with fondness, especially as the sense of freedom was chasing away the fear of being locked up again. Out in that valley, in the Altai mountains, life seemed to flow at a different pace than in the rest of the Soviet Union that I came to know.

I never saw any militsiya, even though a steady stream of people visited the farm. Some came to Aykel asking for advice, others to barter. He was not only a shaman, but also a silversmith, and a ring maker. During that week, when we waited for his nephew to come and take us to the forest, I watched people from all over the place coming to order or to pick up rings he made.

It was mostly Altaians who believed that the rings made by Aykel on the shore of the holy Katun river were infused with some sort of power, and that they held spiritual significance. Some travelled from as far away as Barnaul to spend some time with him, and purchase a ring to honor their ancestry, or to protect them from evil spirits.

There was something about both Aykel and that place. I could feel it myself, but my mind wasn't open enough at that time to fully grasp it then.

Before our departure to the forest, a photographer came in, and took our photos for the papers. By that time we all grew beards. To keep our appearance on the photos as different from our prison mugshots as possible, Misha and I trimmed our facial hair to make it look good for the pictures, while Aslan shaved clean. He wasn't happy about it, and for a while I couldn't keep myself from grinning whenever I saw his smooth, beardless face.

Two days after the full moon, a plump Altaian with full cheeks and eyes like narrow slits came to take us into the logging area. His name was Orman, and he drove a UAZ-452 van, otherwise known as a *Bukhanka* – a Loaf, since it looked like a loaf of bread on wheels.

The van reminded me of the Barkas B1000 that Ziya and I drove over the roads of the Eastern Block back in 1985, which felt almost like a different lifetime. *Bukhanka* had a bigger engine and was much more rugged and suitable for the tricky forest roads in the hills of Altai Republic.

I like cars, and sometimes I think about them in terms of personality. When it comes to the Barkas and Bukhanka, I saw a parallel between them and my own story. In the days when I drove the B1000 with Ziya, I was a milksop, a city boy, who liked to speed on the main roads, just like the Barkas. When I first drove the Bukhanka on the rural roads of Altai, I was a different man, and I got used to life outdoors. I was now resilient and capable, just like that off-road UAZ van.

We got in the van together with Feodor, who kept measuring me up like an angry wolf. He seemed to have had some problem or another with me from the moment I arrived at Aykel's farm. Every now and then he would throw a comment about thieves, and criminals. Other times he would just work quietly giving us silent, angry looks.

I did my best to ignore him, to respect our host's hospitality, but now that we were being driven by Orman to a remote forest I suspected things might get out of control with the Russian ex-soldier, and I was mentally preparing for the eventual confrontation.

During our more peaceful days, I asked Aykel about Feodor, and he told me that he was a relative of a friend from Barnaul. He had returned from Afghanistan with a mind full of horrible stories, and a habit for heroin, which helped him keep away his own darkness that was consuming him after his time in the bloody war.

When Aykel took him in, Feodor was a dope-fiend and a petty criminal, on his way to the Zone or into an early grave. A year later, the man had recovered and was as fit and strong as a bull. He held a strong grudge against the Soviet government which sent him off to war, and against the criminal underground which he blamed for his dope addiction.

It seemed odd that Aykel, an otherwise clever man, would send him with three *vory* escapees to work together in an isolated forest. But as I understood it later, it was just another method of testing both us and Feodor that the old shaman employed.

Orman drove us to a cabin up in the hills where we would find shelter during our forestry gig. He showed us the area we were supposed to work in and explained our tasks.

We were supposed to fell the trees from midnight till dawn and spend the rest of the workday debranching and debarking the trunks. I asked him about extraction, but he said we don't have to worry about that, and that the trees would be taken out of the forest sometime in the new year.

The trees we were targeting were Siberian larches, marked by Orman in the previous months. He said we had ample supplies and food in the cabin, including working clothes, and tools, and wished us good luck, as he got into the van.

"I'll come to pick you up in two weeks," he said through the open window. "Good luck."

"Wait," I said, surprised we were being left in the middle of nowhere without any supervision.

He looked at me expectantly, with his left hand hanging outside of the driver's window and a smoldering cigarette stuck between his thick fingers.

"What if we have any problems?" I asked.

"The village is an hour walk along the road. There is a phone there, they know my number." He took a drag of the cigarette and again allowed his hand to hang outside the van.

"What is the norm?" I asked, "How many trees do we need to cut down?"

"You do what you can. This is not a Kolkhoz or a penal colony. I trust you." He squinted at me and started the engine. "Anything else?"

I shook my head, and raised my hand, waving him goodbye as he drove off along the bumpy forest road.

Aslan started a fire, and we prepared a meal made of kasha and canned beef. Feodor kept to himself, squatting by the side, and seemed in a gloomy mood, while Aslan, Misha, and I enjoyed the food and told jokes about the Zone. We went to sleep early, ready to wake up past midnight to begin our assignment.

We woke up to the ringing sound of the mechanical clock we had found in the cabin when we got settled. It was half past two, and I thought that even in IK-22 we got more sleep. The three of us moved groggily, and we took our time eating a simple breakfast and filling our thermoses with hot tea.

Feodor, on the other hand, was quick to eat and waited for us impatiently by the cabin door, dressed and ready to go. He didn't say anything, but I could feel his eyes on my back as I sipped on my tea and talked to the others.

We walked out carrying axes and flashlights and we made our way into the woods to find the marked trees. It felt strange to be left to our own devices, with no barbed wire to limit our movements and no guards or foremen to yell at us and tell us what to do.

Aslan suggested we split into teams of two, to keep each other safe, and divide the work. He said we should have a little challenge in who managed to fell more trees before dawn. I liked the idea, and I said I'd team up with Feodor. I knew he had a problem with us, and I wanted to deal with it early on as we were supposed to live and work together for two weeks.

Without wasting time, and wanting to keep himself warm, Aslan began chopping down a tall, but slender Siberian larch, while Misha stood by with a flashlight.

I asked Feodor to come with me, and I walked through the shallow snow to find a marked tree a safe distance away from the others.

"You want to start?" I asked, holding up a flashlight, to illuminate the tree.

Feodor grimaced at me; his bearded face took on a haunted, angry look.

"I know your kind," he uttered. "You thieves would make use of me so you can get your pay from Aykel without lifting a finger."

The rhythmic thudding of Aslan chopping down a tree could be heard in the dark distance.

"Does that sound like we wouldn't work?" I asked him, trying to remain calm. "I can start if you want, and we can switch later."

"What were you in for?" He ignored my comment.

"What is your problem, *blyat*?" I felt myself losing the grip on my temper.

"Bunch of tattooed thieves," he spat in disgust. "You are up to no good!"

"And you? A fucking saint? How many people did you kill in Afghanistan, dog?"

My words were sharp and targeted, feeling the pent-up emotions from the past week finally working their way to the surface.

He must have had some shit bottled up as well, and my last comment made him explode. He threw the axe at my feet, which distracted me momentarily, and went for me with his fists.

I dropped the flashlight in the snow and raised my own hands just in time to block a powerful right hook.

Feodor immediately followed with his left hand, hitting me in the gut. It didn't land well but it was enough to make me partially drop my guard, and I barely managed to dodge his right hand again.

Back in IK-22 I had been regularly sparring with Aslan, and a few other *vory*. I had some good reflexes, decent technique, and I was fit, which helped me with the few scuffles I had been involved in in lockup.

But Feodor was well trained as well, and he was taller and stronger than me. Some of his punches landed, but high on adrenaline as I was at the moment, I didn't feel the pain. He was throwing his fists at me in a steady succession, and all I could do was to keep myself from getting obliterated.

Seeing an opening, I ducked under his arms and grabbed at his legs, while jamming my shoulder into his stomach. I managed to topple him, and I landed on his chest, immediately beginning to pound his face.

He covered himself at first but then pushed with his hips, dragged me by my jacket, and managed to toss me off to the side.

I stood up, and leaned on a tree, catching my breath for the next round.

Feodor got up too, and I noticed that some of my punches had landed well, as his lower lip was split and one of his eyes was swelling up.

We were both panting, and I realized I had blood trickling down from my nose. We eyed each other in the dim light of the flashlight reflecting off the snow at our feet. The axe was lying between us.

Another thud resounded in the distance, after which the familiar cracking sound was followed by the swoosh of a collapsing tree.

"They've already done one," I said, still panting.

Feodor looked away over my shoulder, as if trying to confirm that Aslan and Misha had been outworking us.

I turned my head, keeping Feodor in my peripheral vision. The flickering light of their flashlight was moving between the trees a hundred meters away.

"If we don't get our act together, they'll be way ahead of us before the day is over," I said, and it must have struck something in the *afganets'* mind. The rage that filled his eyes just a minute ago was fading away.

"Enough?" I asked, extending my hand.

Feodor spat blood out of his mouth, but after some hesitation, took a step closer, grabbing my hand in his powerful palm.

"Enough, *blyat*," he said, and picked up the axe.

We worked without much talking, focused on finding marked trees, and cutting them down as efficiently as possible. When dawn struck, we returned to the cabin to rest and have something warm to eat.

Aslan and Misha looked with bemusement at our beaten-up faces, but when Misha asked what happened, Feodor and I just shrugged and said almost at the same time:

"Nothing."

The atmosphere relaxed after that, and we all sat together eating and talking about the job we've done so far. They had managed to fell fifteen trees, while Feodor and I finished the night at thirteen.

After an hour's break, we returned to the forest, bright with sunlight reflecting off the snowy cover, and we proceeded with debranching fallen trees. When we were done with that, we returned to the cabin, and once more sat together for a warm hearty meal.

We had enough supplies to last us for a couple months, and we didn't spare food. It felt good to be able to satisfy one's hunger after a grueling day of labor, and it made a huge difference on how we did our work compared to how we had done it under the camp's regime.

The two weeks passed with the steady pace of hard yet satisfying labor, and it struck me that not one of us slacked off in the process. I must admit that I was quite eager to show Orman and Aykel what my brothers and I could accomplish, and I trusted that Aykel would hold on to his side of the bargain.

On the last evening, before the end of two weeks, we brewed *chifir* from half of our remaining tea. We drank it and smoked rolled-up cigarettes while sitting by the stove, dressed down to our fatigues and relaxing in the warmth.

At some point Feodor picked up a guitar that he found in a case under one of the beds. He had played with it before, but this time, high on *chifir* and the excitement of completing our assignment, he gave us a real concert of nostalgic songs from the war in Afghanistan.

One was called 'A Regular Bus', and it told a heartbreaking story of a World War II veteran scolding a young man who wouldn't give up his seat, only to find out the youngster himself was a veteran broken by the Afghan war. As much as I despised the military at that time, it stirred something in me, and made me think with more compassion towards men sent out to fight in the wars they didn't choose.

An idea came to my mind. A vision of something different, a brotherhood bound by honor, of fighting for the sake of each other and not the tyrants. Of not stealing from the innocent and helpless, but the ones who take from us all. When Feodor finished, I cleared my throat, getting the others' attention.

"We did a good job here, *bratany*," I said, embracing Feodor in my words as well, and feeling proud of what we had all accomplished. "But this is just a small step on the path we can take."

Misha and Aslan nodded with understanding, while Feodor looked at me attentively.

"Soon we will get new papers," I continued, "and we will be able to travel freely. We could split up, and try to return to our former lives, but we could also stick together and work, as we have worked here."

"Sounds good to me!" Misha immediately exclaimed.

"I want to return home, but perhaps it is not the right time. That's where they would look for me first," Aslan said.

"What kind of work do you have in mind?" Feodor asked, after a few moments. I hadn't really considered him in my plans, but ever since our scuffle, he had proven to be a reliable and honest man.

"I have contacts with potential business partners, and Matryona said she can help us settle in her village, close to Kiev." I leaned closer to the ex-soldier. "I won't lie to you, Fedya. We are *vory*, and we will steal again. But in this rotten land there are plenty of rotten people we can steal from.

Think about taking back what the state took from you by dragging you to Afghanistan. Think about what you've lost in that fucking Suki war."

Feodor's face darkened, and he fixed me in a hard stare.

"Enough," he snapped. "I'm not trading one war for another."

He stood up abruptly, knocking the chair back.

"The war is waged on us, whether we like it or not." I locked my eyes with his. "Better to have people you can trust by your side. A lone wolf is easily devoured by jackals. I learned it the hard way."

"I had enough of this shit in Afghanistan." He grabbed his jacket and stormed out into the frosty night, slamming the door behind him.

Misha and Aslan looked at me, but I just shrugged. None of us stood to follow Feodor. We knew him by now. If he wanted to be alone, it was better to leave him to it.

We sat in silence, listening to the crackling of the stove and drinking bitter remains of *chifir* from our cups.

It must have been half an hour since the brawny ex-soldier left.

"What if he is freezing out there?" Aslan said, hands wrapped behind his head, eyes on the ceiling.

"Maybe he went to the village?" Misha mused in turn.

Suddenly, we all straightened and shared a look, as if the same thought had hit us.

"The phone." Misha muttered.

"He wouldn't do that," Aslan said, but there was a note of hesitation in his voice.

"Let's find out," I said and quickly got my boots and jacket on.

We hurried outside with the flashlight, and quickly found Feodor's tracks leading down to the village. Following his footsteps as fast as we could, we marched down the valley through fresh snow. Despite the cold, I felt my head heating up with anger and anxiety. Was he going to call the militsiya on us?

The village lights welcomed us, brightening the white, winter night. We found the crossroads, where a grocery store and local barrelhouse were located. The store was closed already, but the sound of music and loud voices came from the bar.

It was late, and upon entering the faces of the few patrons turned in our direction. Red cheeks and hazy eyes over unkempt beards gave off a vibe of heavy drinking and sour moods. The place was far from welcoming, with metal chairs, and plastic table cloth on the tables. A few propaganda posters urged us to action from the walls, and behind the bar old, cheap decorations hung from a large set of deer antlers

Feodor was sitting in the corner, his eyes fixed on a glass of beer half-empty in front of him. A couple of locals were sitting beside him. One of them was waving his finger in front of Feodor's face, and must have been talking to him when we entered.

As we moved in their direction, the guy sitting closest to Feodor squinted at us.

"More outsiders? What the fuck are you all looking for here?" his voice slurred with too much vodka.

"Enjoying the nature," I replied, my eyes fixed on Feodor, who now looked up and held my gaze.

I could see he was furious, on the edge of bursting into a fight. The two guys must have been bothering him.

"Your friend here is very rude. Doesn't talk at all." The guy spoke again, grabbing Feodor by the arm of his jacket.

I walked over, while Misha and Aslan had my back, giving hard stares to the rest of the locals.

"*Droog*, you don't want to fight this bear, trust me," I said, putting my hand on his, firmly squeezing. He released his grip on Feodor's jacket, and stood up abruptly. The other guy followed and they were now facing me with drunken courage firing up in their eyes.

It was about to go down, and I took a step back, getting ready for a fight, but then Feodor finally lost it.

He rose from his chair, lifting the table with both arms, and hurling it forward with a wild scream. The table flew a couple of meters before crashing into the row of chairs and smaller tables, toppling some down. The beer spilled all over, and the glass shattered on the opposite wall.

"Why can't I just drink my beer in peace?" Feodor yelled as he grabbed the guy by the neck of his jacket, and lifted him up from the ground.

The other one reached into his pocket. I didn't wait to see what he would pull out. I threw a straight punch followed by a hook at his chin, dropping him instantly.

Behind me I heard metal chairs scraping the floor but I focused on Feodor who was squeezing the first guy by the neck.

"Let it be, Fedya. No need to get blood on your hands." I spoke calmly, putting my hand gently on Feodor's shoulder.

"Fucking ingrates," Feodor heaved. "Don't know what I sacrificed for this country."

"Relax, droog. They can't know. It's not their fault." I said. "Just let it go."

Feodor released his grip and shoved the guy backwards so that he slid on the beer stained floor and landed where the overturned table was.

I turned to the rest of the locals, who now stood in a semi circle with Aslan and Misha between us. There were eight of them. Silent, menacing, and suddenly very sober. A big bar fight was the last thing we needed right now.

"Sorry for the mess," I said, "But such things happen when you bother strangers."

Misha and Aslan backed up, and the four of us were facing the group of locals. Angry eyes measured us, and I saw one guy's gaze stopping on my hands.

"You're not welcome here, thieves," he spat.

"We'll be on our way," I said, putting an arm around Feodor and leading him out of the building with Misha and Aslan guarding the back.

We walked quickly into the frozen forest, and as I looked back, I saw the group spilled out of the bar, leading us away with hateful stares. We returned to the cabin in silence, and fell on our beds, exhausted.

Feodor came over by my bed the next morning, quieter than before. He stood by the window for a while, then looked at me.

"Why did you help me?" he asked.

"We work together, we bleed together." I stood up from my bed to face him. "Why did you go to that village?"

"I needed space to think."

"Not the best place you chose." I smiled briefly and fixed my eyes on him. "Did you call anyone?"

His eyes widened with a sudden realization. "You think I would call the militsiya on you? I am not a fucking rat."

I kept my eyes locked on him. There was no sign of deception. He seemed genuinely offended.

"I had to ask." I finally said.

He nodded, then looked at Aslan and Misha, before turning again to me.

"Is your offer still standing? Would you still have me?" he asked with a strain in his voice.

"You're a solid man, Fedya, and solid men should stick together."

"I'll join you. But under one condition. No drugs," he said, more firmly now.

The events of the previous night, and the long walk must have given him time and space to consider my proposal. He was like that, big Feodor. He needed time to make up his mind, but when it was done, he was moving forward like a locomotive.

"That you can be sure of, *bratan*!" I smiled and extended my palm.

We clasped hands, and I realized that my little gang just gained a new and worthy member.

When I think about it now, I see that both Feodor and I were broken men, doing our best to mend what was fractured. Despite our differences it brought us closer.

Years after that time in Altai, an old man from Kyoto told me about kintsugi, the art of repairing broken pottery. When it cracks, they do not hide the damage but seal it with golden glue, and the fracture becomes part of the design.

This is how you grow:

Number 1: Accept that breaking is part of becoming. Boys do not become men without something dying. An old identity must crack before a stronger one forms. If you fight the break, you stay small.

Number 2: Pain calls for meaning. I saw this in prison and in freedom. Pain plus meaning equals depth. Pain minus meaning is nothing more than bitterness.

If you ask, "Why did this happen to me?" you shrink.

If you ask, "What is this teaching me?" you grow.

Number 3: Own your transformation and the pain that comes with it. Boys become men through rites of passage, and those are always painful.

Those who say, "I am who I am," or "Let the world change; I won't change," will not grow from pain, because growth requires you to accept new identities without losing yourself.

I went from a soldier to a vor, from a vor to an entrepreneur, and from a prisoner to a free man. Identity is not a prison unless you refuse to outgrow it.

Number 4: Pride will stunt your growth. In the camp, I saw this clearly. The men who were strong, who grew, were not alone. They spoke about their pain without drowning in it, and they allowed support.

The ones who said, "I need no one," who saw vulnerability only as weakness, who refused a helping hand—they broke even more, year by year. They either turned inward, becoming subdued and depressed, or lashed out, hurting anyone who crossed their path.

Pride lies, telling you that you are stronger than you really are. Growth begins when pride cracks.

Number 5: Do not hide your scars, especially from yourself. Kintsugi does not conceal the fracture. It highlights it. Your scars are not shame. They are proof of survival and a rebirth.

Face your shadows. Inside you there is anger, fear, envy, weakness. If you pretend it is not there, it controls you. Look at it. Name it. Discipline it.

After all that I lived through, I realized that I did not chose what happened to me. But I choose who I would become.

CHAPTER 19

Each Sin Makes The Next One Easier

Orman came later that day, and raised his eyebrows with incredulity when I told him how many trees we had ready for transportation out of the forest. I asked him again how he was going to do that, but he just said that it was not my concern.

I later learned that he was running a '*nezakonnaya vyrubka*' – an illegal logging operation in a state-claimed forest. I had no problem with that, and it felt fitting that the labor we did for Aykel was a criminal act in the eyes of the system I detested.

Unfortunately, our visit to the village brought unwanted attention, and rumors were spreading in the area of a group of tattooed thieves beating up people and wreaking havoc. We couldn't stay longer on Aykel's farm, as the local militsiya could soon be on our scent. It was time to leave and take our chances elsewhere.

As promised, Aslan, Misha, and I received new internal and external Soviet passports with a good set of papers to take us to Ukraine, even Warsaw Pact if needed. In the Soviet Union, a citizen carried two kinds of documents: internal papers for life inside the country, and foreign ones for travel beyond its borders – if one was so lucky.

We embraced each other and we yelled and laughed in triumph. We were no longer *zeki*, we were free men, we were *vory* outside of the Zone, and we were ready to get on with business.

The young blood flowing through our veins demanded adventure. It craved success, wealth, and power. We had few belongings when Aykel drove us to the bus stop, where we waited for a bus to Barnaul. There we were supposed to catch a train north to Novosibirsk, and then west to Moscow and Kiev.

Before departure, Aykel came up to each of us to say his farewells.

I watched as he hugged Matryona, comforting her, and giving her words of strength for a life without Evgeny.

He then approached me, and his face wrinkled with a careless smile.

"Andrej-baatyr," he said. "I am glad you're taking Feodor with you. He is ready to embark on a new journey. But remember about your responsibility for the men who decide to follow you."

I nodded, accepting his veiled warning and we embraced and patted each other on the back.

"Why *baatyr*?" I asked, confused with the new honorific.

"It means a hero. You've proven yourself to be a capable leader and now you're embarking on a new journey with your tribe."

"Do you have any advice for the unlikely hero?" I chuckled, but I felt honored by his words.

"You have an uncertain future ahead of you, but there is light that will guide you. If you allow it... Whatever you do, remember to keep faith. Tengri watches over all of us," he said, referring to the God of The Eternal Blue Sky that many Altaians believed in.

He then fished out something from his pocket; it was a silver ring. It bore a symbol which looked like a cross of St. Andrew, with each of four arms split in three. Aykel took my hand and placed the ring in my palm.

"It is a symbol of your Slavic goddess, Marena. She takes care of death, but also rebirth. She will be a good partner for the Grim Reaper you have tattooed on your left hand. Remember that we are all mortal, and everything that we do has meaning because of this."

I took the ring and placed it on my left ring finger. It fit perfectly. Goose bumps spread all over my body. It felt as if Aykel had just married me to the Goddess of Change, and his words were etched into my soul in the process.

I waited for others to enter the bus, and I turned to nod at Aykel, before embarking myself.

He raised his hand and said over the roar of the Katun river flowing near the bus stop:

"Be on your way, follow your path, and be honorable!"

We traveled by bus to Barnaul, where we went straight to the train station, and joined a long queue at the ticket counters. My hands were sweating inside the gloves. I had gotten them from Aykel, along with a thin woolen scarf to hide the tattoos on my hands and neck. I didn't dare take them off.

The documents we got from Aykel's nephew were pristine, with fresh stamps and photographs showing our gaunt, post-prison faces. They were good papers. I trusted Aykel with that. But now was the moment to test them, and our lives depended on it.

When my turn came, I stepped up to the counter and handed my internal passport to the clerk asking for a ticket to Moscow via Novosibirsk.

He examined the document while my heart hammered, pumping blood into my head, sharpening every sound and movement. I watched his face the way a poker player studies his opponent. He had a large red nose, full cheeks, and eyebrows so thick they looked like a mustache laid across his brow. Strange details stick in the mind when adrenaline takes over.

"What is your business in Moscow, comrade?" he asked, eyeing me through the smudgy plexiglass.

"Visiting relatives," I replied, working hard to keep my voice and my face steady.

He handed the passport back and slid the ticket across the counter.

It worked? It felt almost too easy, and I kept looking around, waiting for an alarm bell to start ringing, and militsiya men to pour into the station to arrest me. But nothing happened.

I waited while the others bought their tickets, but my pulse was slowing down. A new world of opportunity was opening in front of us.

We boarded the train without issue and found a corner of the carriage where the five of us could sit together. It was a train from a bygone era, with a black engine and a red star emblazoned on the front. The carriages were simple, open spaces with wooden benches that grew more uncomfortable with every passing hour. As the engine jolted forward, it belched thick, black smoke into the frigid air before beginning its rhythmic clatter over the tracks. Shortly afterward, a strange sense of relaxation settled over me.

The train took us north to Novosibirsk, along the same tracks we had crossed not long ago while hidden under coal in a freight train during our escape. Now, with fresh passports, we were new men, Soviet citizens. As the white, frozen landscapes of Siberia rolled past the windows, I felt tension leaving my neck and shoulders. I leaned to the side and rested my forehead briefly on the cold glass of the window while an overwhelming sense of gratitude came over me. We were free, *droog*. We were free!

I basked in the feeling, and the five hours on the train passed quickly.

In Novosibirsk, we had to change trains before travelling west. We disembarked and split into two groups. Matryona went with Misha and Aslan, while Feodor joined me.

As we crossed the platform, heading for the main station building, I noticed a group of uniformed men standing by the main entrance. I changed direction and averted my eyes, turning my face away. In an instant, the exhilaration of freedom was gone, replaced by the cold blade of angst stabbing at my gut.

I recognized the uniforms, even the manner in which they stood forming a loose circle, hands near their belts, where rubber batons hung. The way convoy guards waited when a prisoner's transport was due. I even recognized some faces. These were not militsiya men, or the railway security. It was a detachment of IK-22 guards, led by none other than Captain Svietlov.

I didn't dare to look again until we mixed with the crowd. I drifted to the board with train schedules, and pretended to be focused on it while stealing glances at Svietlov and his Dogs.

What were they doing there? Looking for us? It had been weeks since our escape. Could it be that the news about us reached the colony all the way from Altai? 'It must be just a regular prison transport,' I reassured myself.

"What are we doing?" Feodor asked, leaning to my ear.

"Did you see Matryona and the others?"

"Yes, they turned around and followed the platform away from the main entrance."

I looked around, feeling like a wolf caught in the open. I kept glancing to the sides, watching for militsiya and for possible escape routes.

Then, someone caught my eye. A tall, bulky figure in a winter uniform. A hint of a square jaw and thick skull on broad shoulders. A slight limp, as if from an old injury, and a hasty confidence that forced civilians out of his way.

Ivan. It must have been him.

He passed through the gate and disappeared in the train station hall.

"Walk to the main entrance. I'll follow you," I whispered. "Go!"

Feodor turned and began pressing through the crowd. I joined his side with my head lowered. I had a beard and an ushanka hat covering my forehead, and the sides of my face. I hoped it was enough. When Feodor was passing the guards, I walked close to him, keeping myself obscured by his large frame.

I was terrified, *droog*, but something else was driving me. Bloodlust and vengeance.

We entered the hall and I scanned the grey crowd. It was easy to spot him. Tall and wide, like a gorilla. He was heading to the restrooms.

My vision focused, and I felt a rush. Memories of the nights stalking the Zone bled into the present, sharpening every shadow. I motioned to Feodor to follow me now, and we quickly closed in on Ivan, who now entered the men's room.

"I have to deal with something," I said. "Stay here, and make sure no one enters. If something happens – rejoin the others and tell them I met Ivan Rostovkin and that they should continue without me."

I was about to enter the restroom, when Feodor grabbed me by the arm, forcing me to turn and look at him. There was care written on his face, but mine must have been determined, or mad perhaps, as he let go, and simply asked: "Why?"

"It's a matter of honor. A debt for the blood of a friend."

His jaw tightened and his eyes narrowed with understanding. He nodded.

I entered the men's room.

Ivan must have been in one of the stalls. I entered one myself, and I fumbled to get the shank out of the hiding spot beneath my belt. I put it in my coat pocket, ready to use it. The vision of Sidoy's death filled my mind, covering the sickly green tiles on the wall, and the painted white plywood of the stall.

I heard the flush and door slamming open. Then the sound of water flowing from a tap.

I left the stall with the fingers of my right hand curled tightly around the knife's grip. His back was turned to me, as he washed his hands. An easy job. I was ready. This time it would not end with just an injury.

I moved behind him.

He leaned down, took a sip from the tap, splashed water on his face, and straightened.

For a moment, our eyes met in the mirror in front of him. His square jaw tightened, and his eyes measured me coldly. There was a nasty scar running from his cheek to his left eye, which was covered in a white web.

It was not Ivan. Just a soldier who looked like him.

His brow lowered and the side of his mouth twitched. "What the fuck are you looking at?"

"Sorry, comrade. Thought you were someone else." I mumbled, releasing the knife and pulling my hand from my pocket. "I lost someone out there..." I trailed off.

"I am sorry for your loss," he said, turning. His face slackened back into a mask of indifference, worn by those who had lost too much to care. "But don't skulk staring at people like that. You might get in trouble."

"Of course. Goodbye," I said, and hurried outside.

Feodor was there, squared up with a man who wanted to get past him. When he saw me, I gave him a sign that it was ok, and we left together.

"You look like you saw death," his voice was worried.

"I almost did, but it was a mistake," I replied. "Come, let's find the others and figure out what is going on with the prison guards at the station."

We went to the waiting room but there was no sign of our gang. We wandered outside and found them in a steamy milk bar, eating *pirozhki* and drinking tea.

Our train was leaving in two hours, and we had to decide what to do next. Matryona offered to ask around. She was always good with people, and she knew how to open their hearts and their mouths. We sat in the milk bar, watching the crude, black arms of a white clock crawl towards our departure.

Matryona returned with the news. A new consignment of prisoners was arriving at the penal colony. The convoy guards were there to pack them into trucks and bring them to the forests east of Iskitim. Not so long ago, it had been me arriving like that after a hellish ride in an overcrowded box car.

We kept our heads down until the train to Moscow pulled in at the platform. By then, there was no sign of Captain Svietlov or his convoy guards.

The conductor checked our tickets and glanced at our passports before allowing us on board. This was a more modern train, and we managed to secure a sleeping compartment for our group. It had four beds with surprisingly clean blankets. For three days, we lived on that train, passing the time reading, playing cards, sharing food, and mingling with other passengers in the corridors.

I remember the first day, sitting by the window staring out at the endless stretches of snow and frozen tundra-like landscape.

The future was a great unknown, and the past felt heavy with the weight of loss. Three years lost in the penal colony. People lost to unforgiving circumstances: Mam, Sidoy, Evgeny. But so much was gained as well.

I looked at my companions.

Matryona sat with her head bowed, her shoulders slightly rounded inward, as if guarding something fragile inside her. She was clutching a small icon of the Virgin Mary, her thumb rubbing the worn edge of the metal frame in slow, unconscious circles. Her lips moved silently in prayer. Without her sacrifice, we would have never left IK-22. We would not have been free.

Aslan was looking out the window with unfocused, distant eyes. As if he was trying to pierce the landscape with his gaze, and see his family back in the Caucasus. My dear friend. We had each other's backs. We have bled and suffered for one another. I knew I could count on him no matter what.

I turned to look at Misha who was leaning out the compartment, talking to a young lady in the corridor. He grinned, unfazed by his missing teeth. Boyets was quick to act and sometimes slow to think. He was eager, and he proved himself many times in the few months we got to spend together.

Beside him, Feodor was sleeping with his arms crossed, and head leaning down over his massive chest. He was snoring gently through his curly beard. I barely knew him, but he had proven to be an honorable man. Even if he was prone to dark thoughts.

Together we were about to begin a new path. It made me think of Ziya, and the journey I did with him in the opposite direction. I reflexively touched the pocket where I kept the letter he gave me, and the list of his contacts. It was a long way to Berlin, but he was right. Being free, I did feel a pull to my old homeland. I was also curious about the woman who made Ziya act so desperate and I wondered how my father was doing. How would he react if he saw me again?

Then there was Ivan Rostovkin. The incident in the Novosibirsk train station made me realize I had a debt of blood to settle for Sidoy's death. When would I get the chance?

The answers waited for me; I just had to reach out. Despite all the scars and the ink on my body, I still had a lot to learn about myself and about others. My life of crime was just getting properly started and it would take me towards riches, into war, and in its cracks, surprisingly towards God. Everything was to be gained, and lost all the same.

But first I had to figure out a way to start a new life with my brothers. A life outside of the barbed wire fence of the Zone, but within a greater prison of the Soviet state. Aykel's words resonated with me, and a new responsibility of leadership added to the weight I carried. I looked at my hand. The ring of Marena. The Grim Reaper.

A reminder, that when Death greets you, all you have is who you have become.

Gratitude

Stories change people. Movements change the world. Be part of both.

You've reached the end of this chapter, and we thank you for walking this path with us. Your time, focus, and emotional investment mean more than you know.

We hope this story stirred something in you: an insight, a memory, a sense of deeper purpose. If it did, then it has done its job.

None of this would be possible without your support. You are part of this movement now, and we're honored to have you with us.

To continue the journey, sign up at **thegrimseries.com** for exclusive content, insights, and updates on future releases.

The journey is just beginning. Honor will come.

www.ingramcontent.com/pod-product-compliance
Lightning Source LLC
LaVergne TN
LVHW091124080826
845145LV00008B/2032

* 9 7 8 8 2 6 9 4 1 3 2 4 3 *